always bayou

ERIN NICHOLAS

ISBN: 978-1-952280-58-0

Editor: Lindsey Faber

Cover design: Nail Qamber, Qamber Designs

Cover photography: Wander Aguiar

about the book

A friends-to-lovers, second chance, small town rom com!

They grew up next door to one another.
Not exactly friends.
Not really enemies.
But definitely not crushes or lovers.

Until...they were.

A scorching three-month affair, an amicable breakup, a year-and-a-half of what-the-hell-are-we-now, and suddenly they're both back living next door to each other, and now their entire hometown is trying to play matchmaker.

Yeah, there's an actual contest going on.
There's even a trophy up for grabs.

A little fake dating, a little road trip with only one bed left in the charming bed and breakfast (of course), a not-so-little waking up together in Vegas with a vague recollection of a wedding chapel, and Beau and Becca are going to need to figure out just what *they* want this thing to be.

Are they best friends forever?
Or are they each other's actual forever?

prologue
INCONVENIENTLY BAYOU

*quick note: you may have previously read the prologue,
Inconveniently Bayou, in my newsletter or as a free gift somewhere
else. I didn't want to leave it out in case a few readers missed it, but
if you've already read it, you can just skip to chapter one to read the
rest of Beau and Becca's full-length happily ever after!*

BEAU HEBERT REALIZED ALMOST IMMEDIATELY upon stepping into the Bollier family's kitchen that glitter was going to be his ultimate downfall.

Yes, glitter. The sparkly, seemingly innocent substance that people used to decorate things like arts and crafts projects, homemade Christmas and Valentine's Day cards, and, apparently, New Year's Eve decorations.

He'd spent the past two months believing it was pumpkin spice lattes that were going to be his undoing.

But no, it was definitely going to be glitter.

Glitter. And his next-door neighbor, Becca Bollier.

The girl who had moved into the house just to the east of

his childhood home when they'd been ten. And who had been the first person to tell him he was an asshole. And the first— and only—girl to punch him.

Both of those things had happened when they'd been ten too. Well, the first time.

Ironically, if there really was such a thing as having a devil and an angel sitting on his shoulders, giving him bad and good advice, Becca would have been the angel. She'd smoothed out his rough spots and kept him from becoming, mostly, an even bigger asshole.

Thank God Becca hadn't gotten gorgeous until she'd been eighteen and on her way out of town to college.

She'd gotten pretty at about age fifteen. She'd gotten beautiful around sixteen-and-a-half. Not that he'd been keeping track. But *gorgeous* hadn't happened until the summer they were eighteen.

And she hadn't turned into a woman who he couldn't be within ten feet of without wanting to run his hand through her hair and over the sweet curve of her ass until... well, about October twenty-seventh of this year.

Okay, *exactly* October twenty-seventh of this year.

When she'd been—ironically—dressed in a satiny red devil's costume that hugged her breasts and barely covered that sweet ass and had matching thigh-high red leather boots.

She'd walked into the kitchen in that thing, and he'd swallowed the bite of pumpkin muffin down the wrong pipe, shoved back from the table to try to keep from choking to death, and then spilled his pumpkin spice latte down the front of him and into his lap. And onto his sudden and extremely inconvenient erection.

He'd never drank a pumpkin spice latte before that day.
Or since.

But now, the smell of cinnamon, or pumpkin, or the sight of whipped cream, made him hard.

Which had also been *very* inconvenient considering that had happened five days before Halloween, and between October twenty-seventh and today, December twenty-seventh, there had been *a lot* of pumpkin, cinnamon, and whipped cream around.

But now, seven seconds after walking into Becca's mother's kitchen on December twenty-seventh, he realized it was glitter that was going to finally take him down. He didn't know how, exactly. He didn't know what he'd done to deserve this, either. But he had the sense he was in huge trouble. That was certain.

Everything was exactly as it had been two months ago. But bigger. And sparklier.

So much sparklier.

"Hi, Beau!"

"Beau! You came!"

"Happy holidays, Beau!"

Becca's three friends from college—Savannah, Toby, and Daniel—were sitting at the huge, oak kitchen table. The table that Beau had made with his own two hands. Exactly where they'd been sitting when he'd walked in to fix the garbage disposal they'd broken by putting pumpkin rinds into it back in October.

The table had been covered in pumpkins, pumpkin guts, and pumpkin gutting tools. The pumpkins were partway to becoming jack-o-lanterns and there were pumpkin muffins, pumpkin cookies, pumpkin cheesecake, toasted pumpkin seeds, and the fucking pumpkin spice lattes *everywhere*.

The whole place had smelled like he'd walked into a pumpkin pie.

And he'd been okay with that. He'd actually been happy. Hungry. He'd *grinned*.

3

After he'd fixed the disposal and told them to keep all the pumpkin rinds far from it, he'd taken a seat at the table, sampled all the treats—the pumpkin cheesecake had been fucking amazing—and even been willing to try a pumpkin spice latte for the first time.

He wasn't really the latte type. In any flavor. Certainly not *that* flavor.

But her friends had been so *nice*. And Becca had been dressed in blue jeans and a light flannel with her hair in a high ponytail and her glasses on and...she'd looked like regular Becca. Beautiful sure, but just Becca. Sweet, smiley, and a little nerdy—they were twenty years old and carving jack-o-laterns at her mom's kitchen table and talking about the Halloween party they were throwing when they got back to LSU, for fuck's sake. She was just the girl he'd lived next to for ten years. And seriously, that pumpkin cheesecake had made him groan out loud.

Strangely, right after that groan, Becca and her friends had all looked at one another and Savannah had said, "Ask *him*."

October...twenty-seventh to be exact...

TOBY NODDED. "DEFINITELY ASK HIM."

Becca shook her head. "No. That's okay."

Daniel agreed. "You should. He'd definitely know."

"Yes, he's the best one," Toby insisted.

Becca looked at Beau. And sighed. "I know."

Beau paused with a bite of cheesecake halfway to his mouth. "Best one for what?"

"I just need an opinion on something," she said.

Beau took the bite, chewed, swallowed, and shrugged. "Okay."

Something he and Becca had done since they'd been twelve had been give each other pure, honest, no bullshit opinions about things. Even if those opinions were unsolicited.

It had started when his dad had died when they'd been twelve. The night after the funeral she'd brought him brownies.

Heartbroken and angry at the world, he'd taken a bite of one and said, "These are the worst things I've ever tasted."

They had been. They'd been awful.

She'd punched him in the jaw and said, "Just because you're sad doesn't mean you have to make other people feel bad."

She'd also gotten grounded for a week for being mean to the kid next door whose dad had just dropped dead from a heart attack.

But she'd been right. So, he'd taken her a peace offering two days later. He'd climbed the tree outside her window, knocked, and handed her a chicken and broccoli casserole.

She'd looked at it. And started laughing. "What am I supposed to do with this?"

"It will be a hundred times better than the brownies," he'd told her. "But I didn't make it. It's from all the food people have been bringing us. Because I'd rather bring someone something good. And I know that I can't make anything good."

She'd shaken her head. "You're kind of an asshole, you know that?"

He hadn't. For the whole twelve years he'd been alive he'd been pretty sure he was awesome. That's what people had always insinuated. And told him. "You think so?"

"I do," she'd said with a nod.

"Why?"

"Because you know that I brought you those brownies to say I was sorry about your dad and to let you know that I cared. You *know* that you should have just said thank you and pretended they were delicious."

"I did say thank you," he reminded her. When he'd first taken the plate from her, he'd mumbled a *thanks*.

"And you should have just left it at that."

"You should know that your brownies are terrible though," he said. "Seriously," he added when she rolled her eyes and started to shut her window. "Wouldn't you rather give people *good* brownies? I mean sure, the idea is nice even if they suck. But having *good* brownies to eat in my room later that night would have been even better."

She'd just looked at him for a long moment. He'd looked back.

"Fine. Yes. I'd rather make good brownies."

He'd nodded. Of course she would. That just made sense.

"And wouldn't you like to not be an asshole to people who are just trying to be nice to you?"

He'd thought about that. Yeah. He didn't want people to think he was a jerk. "Yeah. I guess so."

"If I make more brownies, would you try them and tell me if they're good?" she'd asked.

"Yes. And I'll be totally honest."

"Okay."

"And if I'm an asshole again, will you tell me?" he'd asked.

"Oh, definitely," she'd said. Emphatically.

And she had. Over the next eight years they hadn't been *friends* in the way of friends who hung out and texted all the time and told each other *everything*, but they always went to one another when they needed an unvarnished opinion about something. Or when they saw the other doing something that needed an intervention.

Like when they were fourteen and he'd started just ignoring the girl he wanted to break up with instead of having a conversation with her. Becca had stomped over to his house and let him have it right on the front porch.

Or like when they were fifteen and overnight she'd started wearing the same baggy black hoodie Every. Single. Day. And her hair in a ponytail. And the stupid black converse tennis shoes she'd had since they were twelve. He'd gone over after two *months* of her dressing the same way and told her she needed to knock off whatever crazy, emo shit she had going on.

He'd told her that wearing black made her look whiter than the inside of a potato—he had not been great at thinking on his feet at age fifteen—and that low ponytails in tangled hair made her face look too thin and kind of like a rat, and that her Converse were falling apart and they kind of smelled.

He'd actually had no idea if her shoes smelled. But she'd had them for three years and all of the shoes *he* owned for more than about six months definitely smelled, so he'd just assumed.

And her dad was the principal of the high school and her mom was a teacher over in Bad, the next town up the bayou, and so they had enough money to get her new shoes.

Dressing like that was stupid. He'd told her that too.

Then she'd told him that two months before, Remy Hodgin had tried to feel her up in the parking lot after school and told her she should consider his attention a favor.

So he'd also told her that listening to anything Remy Hodgin said was stupid. And letting his opinion take up space in her head when she didn't even like him being in her personal space was *really* stupid.

Of course, he'd also gone and beat the shit out of Remy right after that.

He wasn't sure which of all of the things he'd said had

gotten her out of that hoodie and those shoes, but he'd never seen them again.

In fact, she'd come to school the next day in a cute yellow top and denim capris with sandals on her feet and her hair loose and falling in long spiral curls and he'd felt like someone had punched *him* in the stomach.

He'd really enjoyed watching Remy walk up to her in the common room with all the lockers and apologize to her. Publicly. With his black eye and swollen lip. And he'd really loved the little look she'd given *him* across the room that said she knew he was responsible for Remy's eye and lip.

The smile and the *thank you* she'd mouthed to him had made his gut clench in a brand new way than it ever had for Becca before. But he'd liked it.

Now, sitting at her mom's kitchen table, surrounded by pumpkin spice *everything*, his gut had clenched again. Because of Becca.

He just wasn't sure if it was a good clench or a bad clench.

She just sat, studying him, chewing on her bottom lip.

He took the opportunity to finish off his cheesecake. Then he set his fork down and said, "Okay, come on, what do you need an opinion about?" He glanced around the table. "That I'm the best one to give you?"

"It's about a guy," Savannah offered.

Becca shot her a frown. "It's not really about a guy. It's about a Halloween costume."

"But you want to know what a guy thinks about that costume," Daniel said with a smirk. "Because of another guy."

Beau watched Becca. Her cheeks were a little pink now. "You're a guy. Why can't you give her the opinion?" he asked Daniel.

Maybe the costume she wanted to wear was super ugly. Or silly. For some reason other people in Becca's life had a hard time giving her their honest opinions. It was because she was sweet. He knew that. It was always hard to hurt the feelings of truly nice people. He supposed that for him and Becca it was different because she had no trouble telling him the honest truth as well. Even if it hurt his feelings. They'd established this relationship a long time ago and they both appreciated it. Telling the God's honest truth at age twelve was different than at age twenty, but because they had so much practice and because it had always turned out for the best, they both valued this particular role in the other's life.

"Yeah, but I'm not a guy like you," Daniel said.

Beau arched an eyebrow. "What's that mean?"

"It means that we need the opinion from a guy who has a lot of experience with girls trying to get his attention," Savannah said. She leaned over and squeezed Daniel's forearm. "Danny's awesome, but most girls haven't quite caught on to that yet."

"I was a total geek in high school." Daniel lifted a shoulder. "I'm growing out of it. Slowly. Late bloomer."

"Please don't grow out of it completely," Becca said. "Brainy guys are hot."

Beau slid her a look. Becca had hardly dated in high school. Actually, now that he thought about it, he wasn't sure she'd dated *at all* in high school. And now that he was wondering about it, he wondered if she dated in college at all. And if so, what was her type?

She hadn't always been cute—when he'd first met her, she'd had crooked teeth and never seemed to know what to do with her hair and had been downright gangly—but she'd always been sweet and kind. Even when she'd been telling him he was an ass. She'd meant it to make him a better person.

She had, however, become cute around the time guys started noticing that stuff. And she'd definitely been beautiful when she'd gotten older. But yeah, he could see why Becca and Daniel had become friends.

Becca had been a nerd in high school. She'd been the smartest one in their class by far, and had always preferred books to people. She'd never gone out for any sports, had never tried out for cheerleading or dance squad, had never been in any school plays or musicals. She wasn't even a band kid.

All he ever remembered seeing her do was read. Well, and study. Which also included books. He knew she'd tutored some kids, including a couple of the football players to keep them eligible for the team.

He knew she'd been on the speech team at least once, though, because she'd delivered an impassioned speech about the nineteenth amendment one year in their social studies class as practice for the big state speech meet that, if he remembered correctly, she'd gone on to win.

He also remembered that she'd spent a lot of time volunteering down in the elementary school. She was now planning to be a kindergarten teacher. And it was the most perfect fit of anything he'd ever seen anyone do.

She was sweet, patient, passionate about education, loved books, and was great with little kids. Becca seem to fit into teaching the same way he fit into woodworking. And she'd been the one that had talked him into finally telling his mother that he didn't want to go to college in spite of the football scholarship and that he wanted to do an apprenticeship with a woodworker instead. Beau was never more at ease and sure of himself than he was with a huge block of wood in hand and a set of tools on his hip.

"And obviously *I* can't help her with what men like in the women who are seducing them," Toby said.

"Obviously?" Beau asked the other guy. "Why is that obvious?"

Toby laughed. "You're adorable. I *obviously* like boys, not girls. I can tell her when she looks stunning, but I don't know what's going to get a straight, pussy-loving man's engine running."

Wow. Toby had just said pussy-loving out loud. Okay, then. Beau focused entirely on Becca. "You're trying to get a straight, pussy-loving man's motor running?"

Now, her cheeks were not just faintly pink, they were bright pink. She was not someone he would have imagined saying *pussy* to before now. He kind of liked it.

"There's a guy. We have class together. I'm just trying to get his attention."

Savannah laughed. "She's got his attention. They're partners in their science lab. It's completely cute and cliché. But our shy little flower has established the fact that she's sweet and smart and a very good *friend*. Now she needs to let him know that she can be more than that."

Beau identified the kind of clench he was feeling in his gut now. Bad. If he didn't know better, he would've called it jealousy. But he did know better. This was Becca. He wasn't jealous of this other guy. He was...concerned.

If he rejected her, he could make her feel bad. But worse, if he was a player, he could actually hurt her. Either break her heart or literally hurt her. Yeah, the clench in his gut was definitely a bad one.

"What's the guy like?" Beau asked. He was aware his tone was brusque now and he was scowling.

He knew because Becca scowled back.

"He's nice," Becca said.

"He's a lot like you," Savannah added. "Big. Lots of muscles. Hot. Probably has lots of female attention."

Beau realized Savannah probably meant all of that as a compliment, but he wasn't taking any of it that way. Becca didn't need a guy like him. She needed a nice guy. A nerd. A guy like Daniel.

"Why don't the two of you date?" he asked, gesturing between Becca and Daniel.

They looked at one another and laughed.

"Because we're friends," Becca said, as if it was obvious.

"I love her. She's awesome. We just don't feel that way about each other," Daniel added.

"What way? She's beautiful, right?"

Daniel eyes widened, and he glanced at Becca. "Well, yeah. Of course."

"And you said you really like her. Like spending time with her. You know she's a great person."

Daniel nodded slowly. "Yes. To all of that."

"So what's the problem? You should take her to the Halloween party."

"It doesn't work that way," Becca said. "Danny and I are friends. We feel... friendly toward one another. We like each other. We enjoy hanging out. And yes, I think he's handsome. But that doesn't mean we have any chemistry."

"Yeah, the idea of kissing her just..." Daniel shrugged again. "Doesn't do anything for me."

Becca laughed. "Same." She gave Daniel an affectionate grin.

But Beau felt another clench in his gut. Because *fuck*.

He and Becca were friends, based on all of those same things. In fact, they were not even as close as she and Daniel. They didn't hang out. He didn't go visit her at college. She had been home on fall break for two days and this was the first he'd seen her. Clearly she and Daniel spent more time together and had more in common. But Beau had known her for ten years. She really did know things about him no one else did. She felt comfortable saying things to him in a way no one else did. And yet, the idea of kissing her *absolutely* did things for him. Not welcome, but very obvious yeah-I-want-that things.

In fact, now he was thinking about it, he was having a very hard time not thinking about it.

Her lips would be soft. For one thing, she didn't spend time outside in the wind and sun getting them chapped and dry. For another, she was always using lotions and lip balms and body sprays. For a nerd, she'd always been really into girlie things like that. Things that smelled good. And that were creamy and would make her skin soft and very touchable.

He would guess that her lips would taste very sweet. Like sugar. No, something even more specific. Like brown sugar or cotton candy. Or the sparkly purple and yellow sugar that had decorated the vanilla cupcakes that she'd made for her graduation party. Wow, talk about specific. Why was he thinking of that now? And how much better she'd gotten at baking since those brownies? But yeah, she'd taste like something sweet, and fun, and colorful, and light. Something that would make him smile even as his entire body was hardening and tightening and heating...

"Beau?" Becca snapped her fingers in front of his face. "Are you okay?"

He was *not* okay. He'd been fucking staring at her mouth and thinking about purple sugar.

"Yeah." He frowned. "I'm fine. I'm not taking you to this stupid party though, so I don't know why you think I care about this costume."

He should *not* care about this costume. But he did. He wanted to see it. And he didn't want this other guy to see it. And he didn't even have the first clue what it looked like.

She gave him one of her I-have-totally-failed-in-making-you-a-nice-person looks. He hated when she was disappointed in him.

"Never mind," she said with an eye roll.

"Bec—" he started.

"No, come on, we need his opinion," Savannah said. "Beau is the best one to tell you if Luke will like it."

Beau hated Luke.

"But Beau is definitely not my type so why do I care what he thinks?"

He wasn't her type? Really? Why was that? Because he wasn't brainy? Because he had calluses and sweated somewhere other than the gym? Because he drove a truck out of necessity rather than because he needed to compensate for his tiny dick?

"Show me the damned costume," he said, trying to sound bored.

He didn't. He sounded pissed.

He didn't know what his growly response did to everyone else, but he liked the way it made Becca's cheeks flush and her eyes spark.

"No. I don't care what you think of it."

"But you want to know if you can get a guy who has a lot of women vying for his attention goin', right?" Beau asked. He leaned back and laced his fingers together on his stomach. Right above his belt buckle. Which was right above his fly.

Her eyes, predictably, followed.

"We don't do anything for each other, but if your costume can get *me* goin', then it'll work on Lance, right?"

He was lying. Completely. Becca did something for him. Suddenly.

Fucking fuck.

Becca swallowed and pulled her eyes back to his face. "Uh. I guess."

He smirked. She didn't even correct his using the wrong name for this guy she was so enamored with.

"So show me."

"She's got three costumes," Savannah jumped in. "A devil, a Greek goddess, and a woodworker."

"Woodworker?" he repeated, sitting up a little straighter.

"It's a *construction* worker," Becca said. "It's got a hard hat." She wouldn't meet his eyes.

"It's got a sexy little tool belt," Savannah said. "But you can't pick that one just because of that," she told Beau with a grin. "We can't decide which one is best. You need to see her in each one of them and help us decide which she should wear to show Luke she can be more than his study partner."

Beau draped an arm over the back of his chair, determined to look completely nonchalant about this. The one time Becca had come over to his house when he'd been working on a project and offered to help him sand some edges, she'd almost taken her skin off. She should *not* be a construction worker.

But could he give her an opinion on which costume would catch the eye of a straight, red-blooded man? Absolutely. Easiest favor she'd never asked. "Start with the devil. That seems most appropriate."

Becca narrowed her eyes. Then she pushed back from the table and headed upstairs for her bedroom.

"Do you want to help us carve jack-o'-lanterns?" Toby asked.

Stabbing a knife into something? Sounded great. But he shouldn't feel that way. He should not be worked up, worried, or wondering about Becca and this guy.

"Nah. I'm good. How about another latte?" See? He was totally cool. Just a guy having a pumpkin spice latte ...and he reached for a pumpkin muffin now...with some new friends.

Toby, who was a part-time barista at the coffee shop on campus, got up with a smile and fixed him another mug. He set it down and Beau took one sip before Becca walked into the room.

Dressed as a sexy as fuck, if-that's-hell-I-can't-wait-to-go she-devil.

The dress dipped low in the front, clung...everywhere, barely covered her butt, included a pointed-at-the-end tail, horns, black fishnet stockings, and thigh-high red leather boots.

She stopped right in front of his chair, propped a hand on her hip, which pulled the skirt up just a bit more to show a flash of matching red panties, and said, "Well?"

That was when he ended up with pumpkin spice latte in his lap.

He shot back from the table, exclaiming, ironically, "Jesus Christ!".

Which caused him to start choking on the bite of pumpkin muffin in his mouth.

After he'd gotten the muffin crumbs out of his lungs and Toby and the fistful of napkins away from his crotch, Beau braced his hands on the back of his chair and met Becca's eyes. She still stood there, hand on her hip, watching him.

"No," Beau said simply. "Definitely not."

She glared at him. "Why not?"

"Because you want a boyfriend, right? Just one? And not just a one-night stand?"

"Just because the skirt is short and the outfit sexy, doesn't mean that I'm looking to get laid, Beau," Becca said, her eyes flashing. "I think this costume is funny and it makes me feel confident and if I want to wear it, I should be able to without anyone taking any other messages from it."

He nodded. "Sure. But does it make you feel confident? Are you wearing it just for fun? Or are you wearing it to get his attention? Because I'm pretty sure that's what y'all have been tellin' me this whole time." He was aware he was gripping the back of the chair tightly and hoped no one else could tell.

Becca frowned and moved her hands from her hips to cross her arms. "That is what we said, yes," she admitted.

"I think that you're thinking about this one guy. Who's probably been really nice to you. When he's seen you in t-shirts and jeans. But Bec, I'm not sayin' he should *do* anything about it or expect anything, but when he looks at you in that, he's not gonna be thinkin' about *studying* with you. Does that make you feel sexy and hot and confident and excited?" He paused. "Or does that make you feel nervous?"

He studied her face. He knew this girl. She was not a vixen. She wasn't even much of a flirt. She didn't have a lot of experience with guys. She didn't party. She'd never had a serious boyfriend. If that costume made her feel sexy, great. She should wear the hell out of it. Pun intended. But he wasn't so sure it would. Not when it came to a big party full of people she didn't know all that well, who may or may not be drinking, and throwing caution to the wind.

Was he worried about her? Yes. But more, did he want her to go in there and actually feel confident and have fun? Yeah.

"And how about the other guys in the room?" he asked, as she thought about what he'd said. "They're *all* gonna notice you, honey. Again, not that they should do anything about it, or even say a fuckin' word." He scowled thinking about a roomful of college guys ogling Becca as she walked through dressed like this. "But think about how it will feel when they're all lookin'. If that makes you feel sexy and confident and empowered, go for it. You definitely know how to take a man down with your words...and your fists... if needed." He rubbed his jaw with one hand and gave her a half smile.

She returned it and his chest felt a little less tight.

"But, I'll bet you're gonna be uncomfortable and constantly

pulling that skirt down to try to cover more of your ass—" His gaze dropped to the aforementioned skirt. And ass. "Or you're gonna be fiddling with that top to make sure your tits are covered."

He focused on those. And damn, they looked good. He'd been aware when Becca's breasts had come in, but he hadn't really *appreciated* them. Until now. "Or you're gonna wobble on those heels." He eyed the boots. And she would wobble on those. Even after she'd gotten rid of her ratty Converse, she'd still been a tennis shoes, flip flops, and flats kind of girl. And when the hell had this girl's thighs gotten that toned and smooth and lickable?

Lickable? Shit. This was bad.

He made his eyes focus on hers again. "If you're gonna look awkward and weird and like you've never had a sexy costume on before..." He trailed off because he knew everyone in the room knew she hadn't. "Then you're better off choosing something else because all the fidgeting and clumsiness will *not* be attractive."

She frowned. But then she blew out a breath.

This is what Beau and Becca did for one another. The pure, honest, no-holds-barred truth.

"Fine. God, you're such a jerk." But her response lacked any heat.

He knew she appreciated him being straight with her.

And he knew that she knew he was right.

She turned on her heel and headed back upstairs.

Beau blew out a breath. Why was his heart racing?

Toby cleared his throat. Beau looked at Becca's friends.

Daniel's eyes were wide. Toby looked amused. Savannah had a knowing look on her face.

What did she think she knew?

"Do you need to...change your pants?" Savannah asked, her

eyes dropping to the front of his jeans where they were still wet with pumpkin spice latte.

"I'm fine." He jerked his chair back and sat. He needed to get this over with.

"More latte?" Toby asked.

Beau could have sworn the other man was trying not to laugh.

"I think I'm gonna stick with water, thanks." Or beer. Or whiskey. A whiskey sounded really good right now.

"You were right. On all of that," Savannah said as they all settled in around the table and got back to making jack-o-lanterns. Or pretending to as they all waited for Becca to come back down in her next costume.

Beau didn't even pretend. He just sat and scowled. "All of what?" he asked.

"How she'd feel in that costume. She was focused on making Luke's mouth drop open, but not the bigger picture. That costume wasn't her. She would have felt uncomfortable for sure."

He studied Savannah. She was leaning in, seemingly concentrating on cutting a mouth into the pumpkin in front of her. "I'm gonna think she looks weird in any costume," he finally said.

Savannah looked up. "Yeah?"

"She's the most straightforward person I know. Costumes, pretending to be something she isn't, even for fun, don't really fit."

Savannah looked at him for several beats. "You sure that's the whole reason you didn't like that one?"

"She was practically falling out of it. Like I said, she would've been fiddling with it all night and actin' like a damned virgin who's never put on so much as a lace bra."

"Well she *is* a virgin, so I guess that makes sense," Toby

said, absently as he painted something on the front of his pumpkin.

Beau's attention snapped to the other man. He felt his brows slam together. "*What?*"

Savannah shook her head. "You shouldn't have said that."

Toby looked up. "How does he not know that?" He looked at Beau. "How do you not know that?"

"Becca and I don't talk about sex," Beau said flatly.

Fucking *hell*, she was a *virgin*?

But the next second he realized that *of course* she was a virgin. Who would she have become not-a-virgin with? He would have known about it if it had happened in Autre. Guys from Autre were generally good guys, with a few exceptions—like Remy Hodgin—but they were still guys. They talked. And if someone had gotten in Becca's pants, he would have heard, even if he wouldn't have wanted to. He probably would've bloodied another guy's lip too. That one might have been harder to explain.

He supposed he'd assumed she'd taken that step in the two years since she'd been at LSU. But he hadn't given it a lot of thought. Now that he was, he realized why he hadn't thought about it much.

He hated the idea. No guy would be good enough for her. Certainly not some college prick named Luke who was probably studying finance or some fucking thing.

"Well, you know Becca," Toby said, with a shrug. "She *seems* pretty virginal, doesn't she?"

He had no idea. He wasn't sure he knew too many virgins actually.

"The problem is, Becca is the type to only sleep with a guy she's really serious about," Savannah said. "And that hasn't happened yet."

Yep, she was totally that type. Becca was a forever girl.

"So she really does want to date this Luke guy? Not just hook up, right?" Beau asked.

Savannah nodded. "Yeah. She's not the one-night stand type. At all."

No, she wasn't. "That's not a problem," Beau muttered.

Her friends all looked over.

"It's not?" Daniel asked.

"Her waiting to be serious about someone before sleeping with him? Hell no, that's not a problem. You should all be encouraging that," Beau said. "What kind of friends are you?"

Their eyes all widened.

"We're *supportive* of whatever journey Becca wants and needs to go on," Savannah told him.

Beau rolled his eyes. "Fucking some guy because he's nice to her in science lab and she thinks she's too old to still have her V-card isn't a 'journey'," Beau told her, using air quotes around *journey*. Good God. "Journeys require a full tank of gas, a kickass playlist, and at least fifty bucks worth of junk food."

He saw Toby's mouth quirk up at the corner, but Savannah was looking huffy. "Look, Beau, I know you and Becca have this blunt-honesty thing going, but I don't find your rudeness as cute as she does."

He did not think Becca would describe his style as *cute*. "If you don't like it, you know where the door is."

She blinked at him. "You're telling me to leave?"

"This is how it is. Take it or leave it."

"*You* could leave."

"You're on my territory."

Savannah's eyes narrowed and she leaned in. "The house or Becca?"

"I think you know."

Toby gave a little gasp and Daniel cleared his throat.

Savannah held Beau's gaze for another few seconds, then she nodded. "Yeah, I think I do."

Beau felt his heart racing, but worked to not give away everything he was feeling. Protective and possessive were not typical feelings he had for Becca Bollier. But damn, they'd come on swiftly.

And it was clear that was exactly what he felt. He wasn't jealous of her time with these three. He didn't care if she spent time or shared secrets with them. It wasn't that. But if they weren't going to take care of her, then yeah, he would step in.

"Okay, how about this?"

He looked toward the doorway. And was really glad he didn't have anything in his mouth to choke on.

Holy. Shit.

This time she was dressed in short, *short* denim shorts that cupped her ass, a fitted white tank top that cupped her breasts, ankle-high brown boots that probably cupped her feet just as nicely, and, sure enough, a tool belt. Oh, and a hard hat. He didn't care about the hat. Or rather, he couldn't focus on it. The belt kept pulling his eyes to the flare of her hips, which emphasized her narrow waist, which emphasized the curves of her breasts. In the tank her arms and shoulders were bare, her smooth, fair skin looking very strokable. And her legs... they were bare too, of course. Those lickable thighs looking even more delicious now.

She spread her arms, meeting his gaze. "Better?"

Worse. So much worse. Because this was a much more normal outfit. In the devil costume he could chalk his reaction up to one of shock and no-way-that-doesn't-work-for-her-at-all. But these were...shorts and a tank top. Ninety-nine point nine percent of the girls he knew had worn that at some point in their lives. Okay, not that tight and short maybe, but still. These were normal clothes. Hell, he'd probably seen Becca in shorts and a tank before. And they were definitely working for her.

But now he had new things in his head. Thoughts of virgins and college guys just out to get laid and no one looking out for her and...okay, how hot she looked. Hey, he was still a guy too.

"No," he said.

Becca sighed. "Come on. I won't be wobbling on heels." She lifted one boot and wiggled her foot. "I won't be constantly pulling this down to be sure it covers my ass." She turned and wiggled her butt.

Beau barely kept from groaning. He cleared his throat. "That looks like a major wedgy waiting to happen."

She faced him, arms crossed. "Don't worry about my wedgies. What's wrong with this one other than that?"

Well, she looked like...Luke What's-His-Name's next girl-friend. That was what was wrong.

"You're gonna get a lot of attention in that," he said.

"Isn't that the idea?"

"Is it?" He met her eyes directly. Challenging her. Was that what she really wanted? If so, fine. "Let me put it this way," he said after several ticks. "You're gonna walk out of that party with a date. I don't know if it will be Larry or not, but some-one's gonna offer. Probably more than one. Be sure about what you want."

She held his gaze for a few more beats. Finally she swal-lowed. "Just look at the last costume."

"Fine."

Again, she hadn't corrected his misuse of Luke's name.

"How about carving a pumpkin now?" Daniel asked as Becca disappeared.

"Yep. That'd be great." Beau took a knife and an innocent

gourd and went to town. He was nearly done gutting the thing when she came back into the kitchen.

This time as a Greek goddess.

And dammit. She was definitely leaving that party with a date. With whoever the fuck she wanted one with.

She was stunning.

The costume was made up of a long white dress that brushed the floor. It was cinched at the waist with a gold belt that matched the gold leaves that circled her head and the two bracelets that wrapped around her wrists. The bodice of the dress tied behind her neck, leaving her arms and shoulders bare and did show off some very nice cleavage, but it sure as hell covered up more than either of the other two.

He still didn't want her wearing it. Or going to that party at all. Or going out with Luke. Or even smiling at Luke. Or anyone else.

He blew out a breath. He was in really big trouble here.

"You're not going to trip over that hem, are you?" he asked, eyeing the bottom of the dress.

He couldn't just suddenly start babbling about how fucking gorgeous she was. She'd think he had a brain tumor. Though they *had* always told each other the full, honest, you-can-count-on-me truth. And the truth was...she took his breath away.

She lifted a foot, showing him the gold strapped flat sandal she wore. "Nope."

"And be sure you wear a bra. That material is really thin. Don't need to give Lars a nip peek ahead of time."

Both of her eyebrows went up. Her cheeks got pink again at the mention of her nipple, but she asked, "Are you saying you approve of this one?"

"Unless you've got a clown suit up there with super baggy

pants this will have to do. Or maybe you could go as... a hippo or something."

"Wow. Okay, so since I have no other costumes, particularly ones that will make me look ridiculous or like a *huge animal*, I guess I'll go with this one."

Beau nodded. "Okay then."

"Okay."

He set the knife down, went to the sink, washed his hands, dried them on a towel, then turned to the group. "Well, the disposal works and you have a costume that works, so I guess I'll just get out of here."

He was very aware of why his gut was clenching now.

He grabbed his toolbox and headed for the front door.

"Beau!"

He stopped, silently cursing, as Becca came running after him.

He turned in the front foyer. "Yeah?"

"Thanks. I know you don't care about this and this seems stupid to you and it's not what you came over here for but..." She looked down at the goddess costume she wore.

Beau's hand tightened on the handle of his toolbox.

She lifted her head and met his eyes. "I know I can always count on you to be honest with me, even when it's to tell me something is stupid, and that means a lot."

Fuck, fuck, fuck.

It meant a lot to him too.

"The party isn't stupid," he said. "And that costume isn't stupid. In fact, you're a fucking knock-out in it and Luke isn't going to know what hit him."

Yes, he'd used the fucker's correct name. This mattered to her.

Her smile was sweet and genuine and even a little shy. "You really think so?"

"Definitely. You're gorgeous. And that costume is the only one that's even remotely fair to him."

"Fair to him?"

"The others would kill him."

She gave a surprised laugh, then said simply, "Thank you."

"Be safe."

"Of course."

"I hope you have fun."

Then he turned and left. Because he'd just said the least honest thing he'd ever said to Becca Bollier.

December...twenty-seventh...

AND NOW IT WAS GLITTER.

The table where the pumpkin...everything...had been two months ago was now covered with scissors, glue, thick poster-board, various other craft supplies and so, so much glitter.

"Hey guys," he greeted Savannah, Daniel, and Toby. "I, uh, got a text that Becca's mom needed me to fix something?"

Please let it be the disposal again. Something easy. Or a faucet. In another room. Being in another room would be great. Or a lamp. In another room. Even better, I could just take that with me and...

"Oh, I think Becca texted you," Savannah said.

"No. It was Maureen." He really wanted it to have been Maureen.

"I think Becca might have just used her mom's phone."

"Why would she do that?"

"To be sure you'd come over."

Beau just stared at Savannah. Had he been immediately aware that Becca was not in the kitchen? Of course. That was likely why the feeling of trepidation had been so strong. And immediate.

He was hoping she was just upstairs getting more...glitter.

No, he didn't hope that. They did *not* need more glitter.

"Is she okay?"

"She's...not sick or anything," Savannah said, casting a glance at Toby.

Toby nodded. "She's mostly, basically fine. But...she needs your opinion on something."

Beau sighed. "That didn't go so well last time."

"You have no idea," Toby muttered.

Beau frowned. "What do you mean?"

Had something happened at the Halloween party? He'd wanted to know how the party had gone for two months. He'd been telling himself almost every single day that it was none of his fucking business and he did *not* actually want to know. But he'd been clinging to the idea that if Becca had a new, serious boyfriend she'd been seeing for two months and was madly in love with, Maureen would have told Heather and his mom would have spilled the beans at some point, and since he hadn't heard that, it must mean Becca was not on her way to becoming Mrs. Luke What's-His-Face.

And the fact that he'd been *clinging* to anything and actually keeping his ear out for gossip told him everything he needed to know about how he felt about Becca.

Of course, the fact that he hadn't been out with another woman since October twenty-seventh spoke pretty loudly as well. He'd tried. He'd been to a couple of parties, more than a couple crawfish boils, had hung out down at Ellie's bar, and gone out with his buddies Owen, Mitch, Zeke, Zander, and Fletcher Landry. Going out with those guys always meant there would be women around.

But he hadn't been interested in anyone.

He'd thought about, wondered about Becca the whole time.

"What the hell happened at the party, Toby?" Beau asked. Okay, more or less growled.

"It...didn't go according to plan," Toby said. He gave Savannah and Daniel another one of those looks that said there was more to it.

"Meaning?" Beau pressed. Definitely with a growl this time.

"Luke didn't ask her out," Daniel said.

Oh, really. "Dumbass," Beau replied.

Daniel nodded.

"Is she okay about it?" he asked.

"Well, that's kind of why she texted you to come over," Savannah said.

He felt his damned gut clench. He did not want to hear about this from Becca. He didn't want to hear that she was disappointed or have her ask him what was wrong with her that Luke didn't notice her. He could not have this discussion with her. "What now?"

"She's upstairs."

"Is she...crying or something?" He'd never seen Becca cry. He wasn't sure he could handle that.

Savanna smiled. "No. She's not crying."

He blew out a breath. Thank God. "So what then?"

"She has a new plan. And she needs your input."

He already hated the plan. For one thing, he suspected it had to do with Luke. For another, he suspected it had to do with glitter. "Is that what this is all about?" He gestured at the table.

"We're having a New Year's Eve party," Toby said with a grin, holding up a glittery cut out of a 2.

"Another party, huh?"

28

"Yep."

"And is she inviting Luke?"

"Yep."

"And she wants my opinion about what to do with him once he's there, right?"

Toby and Savannah and Daniel all said, "Yep," at the same time.

Well, *hell*.

Fine. He could tell her what to do with Luke. Nothing. A big fat nothing. Because *he* wanted her. He was going to be there on New Year's Eve.

"Okay." He started toward the hallway, but looked back. "Any lattes today?"

"Peppermint!" Toby said perkily.

"Great. Let's do that." What the hell? His whole life was changing right? He was going to tell Becca Bollier he was crazy about her. He might as well embrace peppermint lattes on the same day.

"You've got it." Toby looked thrilled.

Beau climbed the steps to the second floor of the Bollier house. He'd been up here a few times to fix things for Maureen, but never with Becca. They just didn't have *that* kind of friendship. It felt strange coming up here and heading for her bedroom.

"Bec?"

"Hey," she called from the second door on the left.

"They said you wanted to talk to me."

"Yeah, come in."

He stopped in the doorway. He'd seen her room in passing. He'd rewired a ceiling fan up here and fixed the faucet on the tub and he'd glanced in.

The room was just like Becca. Light, sweet, straightforward. She had a queen-sized bed with a yellow and green duvet and three pillows. No extra throw pillows. No extra blankets. Just the basics. There was a dresser with jewelry and a few bottles, books, and framed photos on the top. There was a tall bookcase in one corner, filled to the brim, with books stacked on top of the books shelves and more on the floor in front of it. Her bedside table had a lamp with a shade that matched her bedspread, an alarm clock, more books, and a bottle of lotion and a bottle of water.

All pretty and feminine but also just...straightforward.

"Hey," he greeted, propping his shoulder against the doorjamb.

She gave him a smile. "Hey." Then she spread her arms. "What do you think?"

She was wearing a midnight blue dress with spaghetti straps. It was simple, silky, clinging to her curves seductively but not tight. It made the blue of her eyes even more intense and her skin look even creamier.

He tucked his hands into his pockets so he could move his fly away from his I-love-that-fucking-dress cock. "So much better than the devil costume."

She smiled. "This is for New Year's Eve."

He nodded. "You look absolutely amazing."

His response clearly surprised her. Maybe because he wasn't usually so nice.

"Thank you."

"Is that it?" He pushed away from the door.

"Uh, no, actually."

He stopped. "No?"

She wet her lips. "No."

"What else do you need?"

"You were wrong."

"About?"

"The costume."

He frowned. "How so?"

"He didn't go for it." She shrugged. "Luke didn't ask me out on Halloween. I think the costume was too sweet. He's still been friendly and everything. We still kind of flirt in class and stuff. I just don't think he got the message that I'm interested in more."

"If he didn't ask you out after seeing you in that costume, he's stupid." That was just a fact.

"I don't think he's stupid."

"Maybe he's just not into you."

Her eyes widened.

He shrugged. "It's possible, Bec. I mean, I can't imagine that's the case, but maybe he doesn't feel that way about you. Like Daniel." A guy could hope.

She frowned. "I don't...well, okay then. I want to know for sure."

"You should just be upfront. You should ask *him* out." He didn't want that. At all. But it was the truth. If she wanted to know how this guy felt, she should just fucking ask him.

She nodded. "I think you're right. I should be upfront with him. Find out how he feels once and for all."

"Okay, then. Great. Good luck with that." He started to turn away again.

"Which is why I need you."

There was that gut clench again. A bad one. "What do you mean?"

"I need you for something. And I can't ask anyone else."

"I... Okay." It wasn't like there was a chance in hell he'd say no to her. Especially when she put it like that. "But me calling him up and asking him how he feels about you is kind of third grade, don't you think?"

She laughed and came toward him, reaching for his hand

and tugging him further into the room. "Yes, I agree. Let's not do that."

"Then what?"

She stood directly in front of him and pressed her lips together. Then she took both of his hands in hers and said, "I need to practice kissing."

If Beau had been given a million dollars to guess the next five words out of Becca's mouth, those five would have never crossed his mind.

"Beau?" She looked up into his face with concern. "Did you hear me?"

He nodded stupidly.

"So, will you help me?"

"I—" He cleared his throat. "Define 'help'," he said.

Then he started praying. Though he wasn't sure if he was praying for her to say she wanted him to help her find someone else to practice with or if she wanted to practice with him.

Because both answers would kill him.

"I need you to let me kiss you," she said softly.

He blew out a breath.

Well, fuck.

His gaze dropped from her eyes to her mouth. Then to her cheek. His gaze traveled down her neck to her collarbone, then across her shoulder.

And he realized *this* was how glitter was going to be his demise.

Her skin was dusted with glitter. And that made him lift his hand and draw his thumb over her collarbone to attempt to wipe it away. And his touch made her suck in a little breath. Which made his gaze fly back to hers. And when their eyes met again, he realized that he was definitely going to kiss Rebecca Jean Bollier.

And that was going to change everything.

"And then what?" he asked, his voice gruff.

"Tell me how to be better at it."

A terrible thought occurred to him and his hand dropped away from her shoulder. "Did you kiss Luke?" Had that fucker told her she was a bad kisser?

"No."

He took a breath.

"Not yet."

Bad gut clench.

"I want to be sure I'm good at it before I do."

"That's a terrible plan," he told her.

She frowned.

"You showed up looking like a *literal* goddess, and he didn't ask you out. Now you're just gonna grab him and kiss him? Maybe you should ask him out for coffee or something first."

"I've been flirting with him for four months," she said, clearly exasperated. "New Year's Eve is the perfect chance. There's a good reason to just kiss him. And then I'll find out how he feels about that. If he kisses me back, then I'll know he's interested. If not, then he's not. And I can quit thinking about it."

"You know the difference?" Beau asked, suddenly feeling downright annoyed.

"The difference?"

"Between just kissing him and him kissing you back?"

"I...think so."

"You've been kissed before, right?"

Did he want to know this? No. Did he need to know? For some reason, yes.

To give her good advice. Sure. That was why. Or that sounded like a good reason anyway. If she'd never kissed a guy, then this was a different ballgame. It was one thing for her to have never had sex—and yes, he absolutely remembered that little piece of info from her friends in October—but to never have been kissed was entirely different.

"Yes, I've been kissed."

"And did you kiss that guy or did he kiss you?" Beau pressed.

"Um...he kissed me."

"Was it your birthday or mistletoe or another New Year's Eve thing or was it a kiss on a date or what?" Was he torturing himself with this? Yes, he was.

"Kind of in between," she said with a little frown. "It was the Fourth of July."

"Someone kissed you on the Fourth of July?"

She nodded.

"Just out of the blue?"

"We were outside Ellie's watching fireworks. He turned to me with a big grin and said that it was a little-known tradition to kiss a pretty girl whenever a really bright, beautiful firework went off. He said nothing would make the forefathers and all the soldiers who fought for our freedom happier." She gave Beau a little smile. "How could I say no to *that*? I mean, I'm a good American."

He rolled his eyes. "It was Zeke Landry, right?"

She laughed. "Yep."

Zeke Landry was a good time, there was no question. He was also a shameless flirt. And full of bullshit up to his eyeballs.

"Who else?" Beau asked.

"Mitch Landry kissed me one New Year's Eve a couple years ago."

"Anyone who *isn't* a Landry?" Beau asked dryly. He presumed that most girls in the parish had been kissed by at least one Landry boy at some point.

"Ben Watkins kissed me after the Homecoming dance our Junior year."

What? Ben was already married to their Prom Queen. Who he'd knocked up at the Prom where she'd been crowned, incidentally.

Beau shook his head. "Okay."

"And that's it." Becca lifted one shoulder, blushing.

"Well then, yeah, you probably need some practice."

Her moment of shyness vanished and she narrowed her eyes. "Maybe I should ask someone else." She started to pull away.

He gripped the hand he still held and tugged her even closer. "Who else you gonna ask?"

"You sayin' no other guys in Autre will kiss me if I ask them to?" She was clearly trying for haughty, but her voice was breathless.

"I'm sayin' no one else is gonna tell you the God's-honest truth about if you're any good at it or not. You'll walk away wondering. With me, you'll know for sure."

And it was going to be really, really good. He could feel it in his stupid gut that kept tightening whenever he was around her.

"And," he added, his voice dropping to a lower, huskier note. "I'm willing to work on it with you until you're good, so no worries."

Her lips parted and her tongue darted out to wet the bottom one.

He almost groaned.

"Okay," she said softly.

"But we need to cover the difference between kissing someone and that someone kissing you back," he said, his gaze focused on her mouth.

She swallowed and nodded.

"So, kiss me, Becs." His voice was gruff.

She hesitated, then leaned in, lifted her face, and pressed her mouth to his.

He felt the contact rock through him. It was a simple press of lip to lip, but *damn*. She tasted even sweeter than purple sugar. Her lips were soft and immediately everything in him itched to be against *all* of her. He wanted to bury his nose in her hair, run his hands all over her body, hear the soft whimperings and moans and gasps that he knew he could elicit.

Holy shit.

She pulled back a moment later. And stood, staring at him.

Yeah. He was pretty sure he was staring too. He made himself blink and nodded, hoping like hell he'd sound normal when he spoke. "Okay, so that was kissing someone."

"Right."

"Now do it again."

They both knew what was coming.

He could hardly wait. His palms tingled. His cock twitched. His gut clenched. A good clench.

She wet her lips again, then took a tiny step forward, drew in a little breath, and put her mouth against his.

He let her kiss him for about three seconds.

Then...he kissed her back.

He let the low growl at the back of his throat sound. One arm wrapped around her waist, tipping her back slightly while the other moved to cup the back of her head. He slid his fingers into her hair as he pressed her closer, belly to belly. He tilted her head, fitting their mouths together more fully, then he licked his tongue over her bottom lip.

She gasped softly and he tasted the tip of her tongue with his as he turned her and walked her back until she bumped into her bedroom door. He cupped her face with both hands then and her hands moved, sliding up his arms to link behind his neck.

He urged her mouth open and his tongue stroked along hers. She sighed as she went up on tiptoe to get closer. He changed the angle of his head, wanting to taste her more fully.

He felt her fingers in his hair, the way her tongue met his, the way she arched into him. He knew it was all instinct. None of this was any kind of seduction on her part. And it was all so damned sweet. And hot.

And...he didn't want any other guy to have any of this.

He pulled back, holding her face, and looked into her eyes, both of them breathing hard.

"*That* is a guy kissing you back," he told her gruffly.

She nodded, her eyes wide.

"I promise, you'll know when it happens."

After a long moment of just drinking her in, he let her go, stepping back and tucking his hands into his back pockets, sucking in a huge lungful of oxygen. He wanted to run his hands all over her. He wanted to lay her out on her bed and kiss every inch of her.

He wanted to do a hell of a lot more than that.

He needed to reign this in.

She smoothed her hands down the bodice of the dress, pressing them into her stomach. Finally, she blew out a breath. "Well, holy crap, Beau."

He gave a short laugh. "Yeah."

One corner of her mouth tipped up. "Yeah?"

"Yeah." He gave her a nod. "I did a lot of the work though."

She snorted softly. "Right." She ran a finger over her lower lip. "But...it means I have potential."

Fuck. So much potential. And he wanted to help her discover it all.

"I think you'll go far," he agreed. "But, I don't think you have time before New Year's Eve."

"You mean to get good enough to kiss Levi?"

"Y—" Wait, had she just used the wrong name for Luke? He narrowed his eyes. "Yeah."

"So, you're saying I definitely should *not* kiss him on New Year's Eve?"

Beau gave her a nod. Or ever. But they could start with New Year's Eve. "That is absolutely what I'm saying."

"But now that you've showed me how good it *could* be, I want to kiss *someone* on New Year's Eve."

He saw the look in her eyes. And his gut *definitely* clenched. In a very, very good way.

Becca didn't want to kiss Luke What's-His-Name anymore.

But this girl was definitely getting kissed on New Year's Eve. And as many other eves...and mornings and afternoons... that she'd possibly let him.

"I think a New Year's Eve kiss can be arranged. But," he added, stepping close again and pulling his hands from his pockets. "We should probably practice some more before that."

"I was hoping you'd say that."

She grinned and went up on tiptoe and he caught the sparkle from the glitter on her cheek just before his eyes slid shut and his lips met hers.

one

Three months later...

ORGASMS WERE GREAT, but Becca would really like to try sex.

She knew having a really sweet boyfriend who wanted everything to be perfect for her and who was determined to take his time and show her all kinds of delicious *other* things first was amazing. She knew lots of women wished their men took more time with foreplay and would spend more time on things like oral sex.

But...come *on* already.

She and Beau had been dating for three months now and it had been a lot of fun. They saw each other every other weekend at a minimum despite the five-hour drive between them and in between those visits he'd introduced her to sexting and phone sex.

It had only taken about two weeks for her to convince him that she was *all in* on *everything* and she was more than ready to take their friendship not just to a romantic place but very much to a physical place. He'd been pretty easy to persuade.

But they still hadn't done *it*. He was holding back from that, insisting that when it happened it had to be perfect. Romantic. Sweet. Memorable.

Becca blew out a breath and took another sip of the *very* strong punch her friend Lexi had made for the party tonight.

That perfect romantically sweet, memorable night was supposed to be tonight.

And he was late.

Really late.

He'd texted. She knew he was okay. She knew he was on his way. But he was running *three* hours behind because he'd gotten swamped at work and he was really sorry and everything.

She believed him.

Kind of.

At the same time, she couldn't help but wonder if he was *really* sorry.

Their night was all off track now and while *she* didn't care —he could throw her in the bed of his truck and strip her naked there and she'd shout *alleluia!*—*he* would care. He'd already "rescheduled" this romantic night of lovemaking twice.

Once because her roommate, Savannah, had had a fight with her boyfriend and had thus lost the place she'd been planning to spend the night while Beau rocked Becca's world. Savannah had had other options—which she and Becca had both told him—but Beau had insisted that Savannah stay in her own room with her best friend and that he and Becca could reschedule.

Becca had asked why they couldn't go to a hotel. He'd said he didn't want to stain the hotel sheets with the chocolate covered strawberries he was going to bring.

She'd rolled her eyes about *allllll* of that.

The second time he'd cancelled had been because she'd *stupidly* mentioned that she'd had a stomachache the day before. The. Day. *Before.*

Becca was absolutely convinced at this point that he was just trying to get out of it. And that made *no* sense.

He very much enjoyed all the other stuff they did. *Very* much. It was obvious.

And he was sweet and romantic and dirty and sexy during *all* of that. He'd taught her things like how to give the perfect blow job and that when a guy said, "sit on my face" he meant, "*sit* on my face". All the way. No hovering. No bracing yourself with your legs or with your hands on the headboard.

He'd taught her about toys. He'd taught her about lube. He'd taught her the difference between orgasms with fingers, tongues, and toys.

But he hadn't *fucked* her.

And she was so ready.

And now he was three damned hours late for the Big Night.

"He's still not here?" Savannah asked, sliding in next to where Becca was leaning against the living room wall. Here she could be out of the way of everyone dancing and playing beer pong, but could still see the door where Beau would enter.

"Nope." She took another drink. Then handed the glass to Savannah. "Here, take this away from me. I'm sure if he thinks I'm 'too drunk' he'll just use that as an excuse not to do it tonight."

Savannah, of course, knew everything. She was *that* kind of best friend. The kind you told everything. Even the I-don't-think-my-boyfriend-wants-to-have-sex-with-me embarrassing stuff.

"He better not," Savannah said with a frown. "This is crazy. That guy has to have a raw hand from all the jerking off."

"I don't know. Maybe not." Becca lifted a shoulder.

Savannah laughed. "You think he's *not* getting himself off?"

"Why would he? If he wants it, it's right here!" Becca gestured at her groin with an open hand. And a voice that was definitely too loud judging by the people who turned to look.

"Yeah, and he takes good care of that when he's around," Savannah said, grabbing Becca's hand and pressing it against her stomach.

"But not as good as he *could*," Becca said.

Savannah frowned. "Yeah. Okay. That's fair."

"And now he's late. This is never going to happen."

"Well...maybe you need to move on." Savannah took a big sip from the glass Becca had just surrendered, watching her over the rim.

"What?"

"I'm just saying, maybe Beau's given you all he can. Or all he's willing to, anyway. You know a lot more now than you did before. He's taught you a lot. He's given you more confidence for sure. Maybe you need to find someone else to *complete the mission*."

Becca's eyes widened. "But...we're *dating*."

"I'm not saying *cheat* on him. Break up with him first."

"What? But...I love him."

Savannah shrugged. "I know. But honey, he's not taking care of you. And you deserve to have a guy who will give you *everything* you need. Find someone else to fuck and fall in love with."

The fuck, *then* fall in love was the order Savannah preferred. And sometimes she did the first without doing the second at all. Savannah loved sex. She hadn't been a virgin when they'd come to college. She had a lot more laid-back attitude about relationships in general and sex in particular than Becca did.

But she had a really good time and was very happy with her life.

Becca swallowed. This was *Beau*. They'd been friends forever. She knew him so well. He knew *her* so well. And now they knew each other even better. The things they'd done were *so* intimate, even though they hadn't had sex. She almost couldn't imagine being with another guy in that way. Being completely naked, letting someone see, touch, *taste* her body the way Beau had made her also feel so vulnerable. She couldn't imagine another man's tongue in some of those places.

"Tell him it's not working. Tell him to fuck or get out of the bed." Savannah drank again.

Becca narrowed her eyes. "How much have you had to drink?"

"A bit," Savannah admitted.

Okay, so she needed to take this advice with a grain of salt. "I just need to tell him how much I want it. That I'm ready. That it has to be *tonight*. No more excuses."

"You *have* told him that."

"And I've fallen for the *I've never been in love before, Becca. Let me do this the right way* stuff he always gives me." She smiled and felt warmer just thinking about that. "And he said he's never been with a virgin. He's admitted that he's a little worried about making my first time good."

Savannah rolled her eyes. "He fucking worships you. It's so annoying."

Becca grinned. "Being the center of Beau Hebert's attention is pretty intense," she said. "And awesome."

Okay, so she wasn't getting laid. But she was adored. He texted and called. He randomly sent her flowers and pizza. He drove five hours one way to go to college basketball games and parties with her when she knew he hated them.

They were living totally different lives. He was running his business in their hometown, hanging out with other people who worked real jobs and paid bills and had responsibilities other than studying for exams and...yeah, that was about the extent of her true *responsibilities.*

And then, when he had free time, he came to Baton Rouge to see her.

And, clearly, he thought about her a lot even in the midst of his day. She knew he was busy. He was the best woodworker and custom furniture maker in southern Louisiana. In her opinion, he was the best in the state, but the internet said southern Louisiana. For now anyway.

Beau claimed to be head over heels for her and that he'd never felt this way before. She believed him. She'd known him forever. She'd never seen him act romantic for another girl. She'd never known him to buy flowers or chocolate-covered strawberries.

So yes, she believed his feelings were real.

She just didn't know why she couldn't get rid of her v-card for real.

"I'm just saying, you don't *have* to sleep with Beau Hebert. There are lots of other options," Savannah said, nodding in the direction of Luke Swanson.

Luke had been her lab partner last semester and she'd hoped back then that he'd ask her out for months. He never had. He's always been very nice and friendly, but he'd never made a move.

Now that she was with Beau, Luke had asked her out twice and had almost kissed her at a party last month. One Beau had *not* been at, of course.

Luke no longer gave her even one tingle.

Which was a little...concerning.

She didn't want to go out with Luke. She didn't have any

intention of doing anything with Luke. But she didn't find him attractive anymore? All of a sudden?

Had Beau ruined her for other men?

Without even officially sleeping with her?

She might be in really big trouble if that was the case.

Unless Beau was going to marry her.

And that thought *did* give her tingles.

Luke noticed them looking in his direction and grinned. Then started toward them.

"Well, crap," Becca muttered.

"Just talk to him. You deserve to have *someone* here appreciating how hot you look if your boyfriend is going to hang out in Autre playing with his wood by himself."

Becca snorted. Savannah often teased about Beau's "wood" and his "tools" and how much "nailing", "pounding", and "screwing" he did. Even in front of him. Beau wasn't amused by it. But Savannah amused herself enough for both of them.

"Hi, Becca," Luke greeted.

"Hey, Luke."

"You look great. How are you? We haven't talked in a while."

A while meant about two weeks. She'd seen him crossing campus between two of her classes not that long ago. "Good. Really good." *Still very virginal, but other than that good.* "How about you?"

"Good." He looked around. "Are you here alone tonight?"

Savannah cleared her throat. "Uh, hi."

He gave her a grin. "I meant, I don't see Becca's very big, very protective boyfriend anywhere."

Becca didn't either. "He's on his way."

"Too bad."

"Is it?" Becca tipped her head and studied Luke. She wasn't

sure why she'd asked the question. Though she *was* curious what he meant.

"Sure. I was kind of hoping you'd broken up. No offense."

"Why?" she asked. Maybe it was the really strong punch. "You could have asked me out before Beau and I started dating. I *wanted* you to. But you never did. Why are you acting interested now? Because nothing can actually happen since I'm with him? This is just dumb flirting?"

Luke looked taken aback. "No. I mean...I guess...I just didn't think about you like that at first. We were friends."

"Friends," she scoffed. Maybe a bit loudly, considering a number of people again glanced in their direction. "Right. Friends have to just be friends. There can't be any flirting or... or...*fondling*...if you're friends. And you can't think of someone some other way. *That* would be terrible. That would just shake the whole world up!" She swept her arms wide.

Yeah, her voice was definitely louder now. More people looked. Luke's eyes were wide and he took a step back. Savannah snorted.

"I mean, everything has to be so specifically defined, right?" Becca asked Luke. Though she was really asking everyone—or anyone who had an answer—or maybe the universe in general. "Why can't people just *do what feels good?* Why do we have to be so worried about labels like *friends*, and *romance*, and *virginity?*"

Luke took a step back.

Savannah snorted.

"Why can't everyone just *fucking relax?*" Becca asked. Or shouted. Yeah, it kind of seemed like she was shouting now. "And just...*fuck?* Why do there always have to be so many *feelings* about everything?"

She narrowed her eyes and pointed at Luke, who had taken another step back. "I would have just fucked you, you know.

You wouldn't have had to fall in love with me. I mean, I might have thought so then, but turns out, that makes it complicated. So, yeah, you should have just done that. But nooooo," she went on when he opened his mouth. She drew out the O, shutting him up. "You thought we were just friends. So no fucking for you. And you missed it. Because as soon as Beau Hebert kissed me, it was all over. And now I'm here, and I'm still a virgin and—"

"Okay, that's enough."

A big arm wrapped around her waist and she felt her feet leave the floor. Suddenly she was being carried through Lexi's house, through the kitchen, and out the back door.

She'd known after about two seconds who was holding her. The feel of him, his scent, his voice, just the *way* he touched her and the way she responded, she would have known him anywhere.

She didn't even struggle.

She was probably in trouble.

Beau shoved the French doors leading to the back patio open with the hand not holding Becca's, then kicked them shut after he'd stepped out into the darkness.

He took five long strides before stopping and putting her down.

She turned, finding him towering over her.

"What the *hell* was that?"

"How much did you hear?"

"You telling an entire roomful of people, including fucking Luke Swanson, that you're still a virgin."

"Well, that's like telling a roomful of people, including fucking Luke Swason, that the ocean is salty."

His eyes narrowed and he leaned in. "You unhappy about something, Becca?"

"Um, *yes*. Being. A. Virgin."

She watched the muscle tick along his jaw, but he simply asked, "Are you drunk?"

She shook her head. "I knew you would use that as an excuse tonight. So no."

He reached up and gathered her hair in one hand. He tugged on it, tipping her head back, and leaned in. He studied her eyes.

It was dark out here, but there were soft lights around the edge of the patio and the moon gave some illumination.

"Let me taste." He covered her mouth with his, deepening the kiss immediately. His tongue stroked along hers, tasting and taunting.

There was no slow sweetness here, just heat and an edge of frustration and possessiveness that she responded to in a way she didn't entirely understand. But she sank into it fully and without question. She grasped the front of his shirt, rising onto tiptoe, opening and letting him lead the way.

He lifted his head nearly a minute later. "I think you need a reminder of just how much you've enjoyed these last few months."

"I know I have. I just want more."

He ran his hand down her arm, wrapped his hand around her wrist, and tugged her forward. He walked backward, leading her to the side of the house. It was more shadowed here, but they weren't far from the back door. "More? So greedy. Do you know how many men couldn't find a G-spot with a map and a flashlight? And who wouldn't know what to do once they got there?"

"I just —"

His hands landed on her hips and he turned her before she could finish speaking.

"Hands up."

His big body was right behind hers, his front against her

back. She could feel his hard cock pressing against her lower back and she felt hot and achy. She put her hands up, palms flat on the bricks of the house without thinking.

"Good girl. Now don't move them."

"Beau—"

"Shhh." His mouth was right next to her ear and goosebumps danced down her neck and over her shoulder tightening her nipples. "I'm here now. You've been waiting for me, right?"

"Yes," she said, her voice breathless.

"And tonight's a big night."

She caught her bottom lip between her teeth and nodded. Even though it was dark. She wanted him so much. Yes, she'd just been complaining about how he wouldn't listen and do things her way but now that he was here, she wanted him to take over. Yes, she wanted him to follow *all* the way through, but she was so happy to let him lead the way every step. She loved him, she trusted him, and she couldn't imagine anyone else making her feel like this. Ever.

"Good," he said. His hand dropped to her left thigh. "But I think before anything else happens, I need to remind you that I *have* been taking care of you." He started gathering her skirt up in one hand.

She'd worn the dress with boots, knowing how much he liked her in skirts. It was March and it wasn't quite warm enough to wear dresses with thin straps like this one, so she'd had a jacket on top when she'd arrived at the party. It was somewhere inside.

She definitely didn't need the jacket keeping her warm right now. Even as the night air rushed over her bare thighs and she shivered, it was definitely not from cold. Fire was licking through her limbs and everything was tingling.

"I don't like hearing that you think I haven't been taking

care of you." He moved his other hand to the strap on her right shoulder. She felt the tug on the bow that was holding the strap in place and then the material give as he untied it. He pulled the front of the dress away from her right breast. She wasn't wearing a bra with the dress and her nipple immediately beaded.

"Beau, I—"

"No more talking. You said enough inside."

His voice was gruff and firm and it sent a shaft of heat through her. Beau was always sweet, gentle, and romantic with her. Well, since they'd started officially dating, anyway. This was none of that. This was exciting. Hot. She sensed a frustration in him and an almost angry edge.

She wasn't afraid of him. She could never be afraid of Beau. He would *never* hurt her. But this was reminiscent of the growly guy she'd known before they started dating. She loved his sweet, romantic side too. Especially the fact that it only seemed to come out for her. But this gruffer, demanding side of him was appealing, and she didn't feel bad if she'd poked him a little bit tonight.

In fact, suddenly, she wanted to know just how far she could push him.

She arched her back, pressing her ass against the front of his jeans.

That got a little growl from him.

The hand holding her skirt squeezed her thigh. "Oh, you think you know what you want, but I'm in charge here, Bec."

Yeah, gruff and growly voice, but the short, affectionate form of her name, was a powerful combination.

She pressed again, but his fingers curled into her thigh. "No moving. Unless I tell you to."

Oh yes, she liked this very much.

She waited for him to reach up and cup her breast, but he

didn't. He brushed his knuckles across her nipple, but that was all. She sucked in a quick breath. Then his hands were at her waist.

"Hold your skirt up," he told her.

She didn't respond right away.

He squeezed her waist. "Becca, hold your skirt out of my way."

Out here? She was just going to hike up her skirt for him?

Well yeah... of course she was.

Her hands dropped away from the wall and she gathered the material from the bottom of her skirt up to where his hands rested on her waist.

"That's it. Keep it there."

His hands coasted from her waist down to the front of her panties, over the silk and then down to the front of her thighs, where he rested his hot palms against her.

"Spread your feet, baby."

She did, positioning her feet a little further apart.

He stroked his big hands up the insides of her thighs, coming closer to her center, but not touching her. He stroked a few more times and she gave a little whimper.

"So you think this sweet pussy needs to be filled with cock tonight, but it's been just fine with my fingers until now."

His mouth was right against her ear, and that rough voice, and the words themselves, combined to make her hot and wet and merely panting.

"In fact, you've been pretty loud about your appreciation of my fingers." He moved one hand, stroking it over the front of her panties and then down between her legs. She was sure he could feel how hot and wet the silk was.

He gave a little groan. "Oh yes, I think you do remember."

She moaned.

"You're going to have to be a little louder about it than that."

He ran his finger over her center again, pressing a little more firmly against her clit.

"Someone might hear." Her answer was barely audible.

"Oh, I fucking hope they do. I hope someone comes looking for you. I hope it's Luke. I hope he thinks he's going to be some big hero, checking on you, being sure you're okay. Then he'll hear you come apart for me, calling *my* name as I make your pussy clench around my fingers. *Just* my fingers, Bec. Because even that is enough to make your pussy happy. You're not going to forget that." He stroked over her clit again with the silk still between them.

She whimpered and let her head fall back against his shoulder.

"Say, please," he said, circling over her clit. "If I can hear you, I'll give you what you need."

"Please Beau," she said a little louder than a whisper.

He slid his hand into her panties, finally, skin against skin. "That's my girl. Now as I make you come, you're gonna tell me how you feel. You're gonna say *please*, and *Beau*, and *yes*, and all of the other things I love to hear. Loudly."

She whimpered again, but nodded. "Yes, *please*."

"Very good." He pressed the pad of his middle finger against her clit and circled deliciously.

He lifted his other hand to her breast and took her nipple between his thumb and finger, rolling it gently.

"Everyone sees you as so pretty and sweet and kind, and no one has any idea how greedy this pussy is and how hot you burn," he told her, tugging harder on her nipple.

"*Beau*," she begged. "More, please."

He must have thought that was loud enough because he

circled faster as he pinched her nipple and she felt her inner muscles squeeze.

"I love knowing that I'm the only one who knows that you can take three of my fingers, but you need to work up to it because you're so tight," he said, his voice deep as he finally moved to slide one finger into her.

She moaned. "Yes. *Yes.*" She wanted to drop her skirt and grip his arms to hold herself up but she was afraid he'd stop. He was *into* this bossy thing tonight and she was loving it.

He pumped that finger deep, slowly, then faster, curling it just right and finding that G-spot that, apparently, other men had difficulty with. "You have no fucking idea how hard it's been to keep only loving you with my fingers and mouth, Bec. No—" He thrust deep then pulled out. "Fucking." He thrust again. "Idea." Then he added a second finger. "But you have been *very* well taken care of."

"Beau," she gasped, her head falling forward. "Yes."

"Tell me how many orgasms I've given you, Miss Bollier," he said.

She'd told him how the young students in the classrooms where she'd done some work for one of her classes had called her Miss Bollier. He'd loved how sweet that sounded and now used it as a term of endearment at times.

At the moment, it sounded incredibly dirty.

"I—" She gasped as he put his thumb against her clit while still pumping with his two fingers. "Don't. Know. So many."

"So fucking many," he agreed on a near growl. He circled her clit faster, squeezing and rolling her nipple.

She needed to move, but had no idea what to do. She was at his mercy. She circled her hips, trying to press closer even as his fingers were as deep as they could go.

He stopped moving his fingers, put his mouth against her

ear, and pinched her nipple. "Stay still. This is all me. *I'm* going to make you come, Miss Bollier. Hard."

"*Beau*," she gasped. "Please." Her fingers curled into the fabric of her skirt. She would walk back into the party with a very wrinkled dress and everyone would surely know why. That also turned her on. "*Please.*"

Suddenly, he pulled his hand away, but before she could protest, she felt his hands at the top of her panties. He stripped them down her legs, moving so fast she wobbled from the lack of support behind her.

"Give them to me," he ordered brusquely when he got them to the tops of her boots.

She lifted one foot, then the other as he yanked her panties off.

Then he was back, one hand possessively covering her breast, teasing the nipple with the perfect pressure that he'd figured out she loved. The other dove between her legs, sliding into her wet heat easily with two fingers deep and that thick, callused thumb on her clit.

"If you want to move these hips, I'll let you ride my face later. You can swivel and buck all you want then," he told her, suddenly thrusting his fingers deep and fast. "You can grind this pussy against my mouth and coat my tongue. *Later*. But right now, I'm going to finger fuck you to orgasm, no help needed."

She felt that orgasm bearing down, and she willed herself to stay still. God, she needed it. She let her head tip back onto his shoulder again, pressing her lips together, squeezing her eyes shut, and concentrating on *not* moving while Beau worked his fingers in and out.

He moved to add his third finger but growled. "I guess I have to spread you out wide on your bed to get three inside you, Miss Bollier. You're too tight, like this." Suddenly he dropped his hand from her breast to her thigh, wrapping a big, hot palm around it and lifting.

She gasped as he opened her thighs.

"Ah, there we go," he said, sliding his third finger inside. Barely.

It was still a tight fit and had been the last time he'd done it too. Becca immediately felt her climax coiling deep and low.

"Oh, *God*," she moaned. "Beau."

"That's right. Let me hear it. Let everyone hear it."

She had no idea if anyone else had stepped outside, but the idea that someone possibly would overhear what Beau was doing to hear made heat arc through her like a bolt of electricity.

"Yes, *yes*," she said, even louder.

His fingers moved faster, and deeper, and her orgasm was coiling, hot and intense.

"Coat my fingers, Becca. I need to taste you, and until I can get you back to your room and bury my face between your legs, this is how it's gonna have to be."

That was enough. She shot over the pinnacle, coming with a hard clench around his fingers, heat rolling through her, calling his name out. Anyone on the patio or even the front yard would definitely have heard that. And there would have been no mistaking that for anything other than a shout of pleasure.

"That's right," he praised, continuing to thrust his fingers deep but slower as the waves of her climax washed over her. "That's my girl. That's what I want to feel. Give me all that sweetness."

Her body sagged against his as the waves began to fade and he finally pulled his hand away. The tingles remained, however, even without his touch.

"Turn around," he ordered softly.

She did, letting her skirt drop. She started to pull the front of her dress up to cover her breasts.

"Don't."

She stopped. Then watched as he lifted his hand to his mouth and put his fingers in his mouth, sucking her from them, slowly, his eyes on hers.

His hand then went to the back of her head, and he pulled her in, also slowly, as if to make a point, before kissing her. Deep, slow, stroking his tongue along hers, making sure she could taste what he'd just tasted.

She was melting. God, this was hot. Things had been hot between them for sure. He was right. He'd given her *lots* of orgasms before this. But this was different. If things had been a six or seven out of ten on the heat scale, this was easily an eight or nine.

But she wanted ten.

Finally, he lifted his head, then *he* pulled her dress up, and retied it.

"Let's go." He took her hand and tugged her around the corner toward the back door.

"You want to leave?"

"I definitely want to leave," he said without looking at her.

Yeah, these parties weren't his thing anyway, and she'd clearly unleashed something here. No way was he staying at a college party with a bunch of people he didn't know.

"We can just go around to the front from here. Savannah will know I'm with you. If we leave, she won't worry."

He glanced at her now. "Oh, we're walking back through that party."

She lifted her brows. "Why?"

"Because you look like you just came very hard and I want to be sure *everyone* sees you like this."

Becca felt her cheeks heat. "You mean Luke."

"Luke," Beau agreed. "And *everyone*."

"You want to rub it in his face."

"Yes." He didn't even bother to try to deny or downplay it. "But if you think he's the only guy in that house who wants to fuck you, you're crazy. Hell, there's probably some girls too. And they *all* need to know who just made you look like *that*."

Her free hand flew to one hot cheek. "It's that obvious?"

He gave her a very smug grin. "Yeah."

She was also very aware that she was *not* wearing underwear. "Do you have my panties?"

"I do." And that was all he said as he pulled the back door open and ushered her inside with a hand at her lower back.

two

BEAU KNEW that he was acting like a caveman.

He often had that urge when it came to Becca. But he suppressed it. Usually.

Becca had been his friend since childhood. She was everything that everyone inside this party thought she was. Kind, generous, funny, and self-deprecating, innocent.

Well, she had been innocent before they'd started dating. She was definitely less so now. Virginal still applied though. At least technically.

But she'd pushed him tonight. She'd tried before, but he'd been able to hold her off. Tonight he was feeling far less in control.

He'd been late getting up here. He'd had a shitty last two weeks. He was getting by on very little sleep, a lot of stress, and feeling like he was pretty much failing everyone. He wasn't doing his best work when it came to his woodworking business, he'd put off several small jobs for his mother that she depended on him for in her bed and breakfast, he hadn't seen his friends in days, cancelling on them because he was working such late hours trying to get everything done. And he was definitely failing when it came to being a good boyfriend.

The five-hour drive between him and Becca was a bitch. But they were making it work. At least they were trying. He was up in Baton Rouge as often as he could be, and she'd come home several times. But it wasn't the same as being able to see each other every day or having her right next door as he had most of his life. He missed her so damned much when they weren't together.

He liked to think that without the distance between them, he'd be a much better boyfriend. If he could just stop by after work, take her some dinner, maybe pop by in the middle of the day and just see her, even for a few minutes, all this would be so much easier.

And then there were these fucking parties. He was the same age as these people, but he felt like he had nothing in common with them. The last time he had studied for an algebra exam or written an essay about something was...never. Even in high school. He hadn't spent a lot of time with his books.

He'd planned to go to college on a football scholarship. Until Becca had finally convinced him to be honest with his mother about not wanting to play football. He'd ended up opening his business, getting to work with his hands and create for a living, and staying in Autre where he'd always wanted to be. But it was tough getting a new business going.

People knew he was a good carpenter and would hire him for jobs like making new cabinets, and redoing staircases, and things like that. But what he really loved to do was make furniture. It took time to build a reputation for that. It took care to turn out high-quality, unique, gorgeous furniture that people would show off and talk about and keep in their families, handing it down to generation after generation.

He was definitely still in the building process.

But he'd gotten a huge contract three weeks ago. A guy who knew his mother because of her bed and breakfast had hired Beau to make new dining tables and chairs for his four bed and breakfasts.

It was a huge deal. Not only was it the largest order he'd had so far, but it was a chance for Beau to get his furniture into places where lots of people would see it, use it, and possibly ask about it. If guests at the bed and breakfasts liked his work, his name could spread from that alone.

He had to put his all into this project. But it was definitely cutting into his time for other things. Socialization, helping his mom, seeing Becca, sleep. Not necessarily in that order.

So he'd showed up to this party, late, frustrated at himself, to find her announcing to the party that he had not been giving her everything she wanted.

And he'd kind of snapped.

He didn't want to be here. Not at this party. Not with these other people he didn't know. He wanted to be with *Becca*.

And that crap about her not getting what she wanted? He was here specifically to give her all of that. To be here *for her*. Becca had enjoyed every fucking minute they'd been together, and he resented the fact that she believed otherwise. And that she would fucking tell anyone else that. Especially Luke Swanson. The guy she'd initially asked Beau for advice about. The guy who had been looking at her a few minutes ago with a lot of oh-I'll-take-care-of-you-baby.

She hadn't been trying to make Beau jealous. He knew that. She hadn't even known he was there. But his lack of sleep, his already wound-up energy, and then walking into that had culminated in a need to not only publicly claim her, to make damn sure that Becca herself knew he was the guy to deliver anything and everything she needed.

Tonight was supposed to be the big night anyway. It was mostly why he was pissed he was running late. Showing up late to a stupid college party was one thing, but tonight was supposed to be *the* special night. She was ready to lose her virginity. There were many people who would not consider her an innocent virgin, even now. He'd very thoroughly schooled her in just about everything else. But tonight was going to be The Night. Was he putting a lot of pressure on this? Yes. This was Becca. He'd never been with another virgin anyway, but the fact that it was Becca meant everything. She was his friend. She was the first girl he'd ever been in love with. She could have her pick of men. The idea that she was going to let him be the first one she let do these things to her meant a lot to him.

But there were no flowers, no chocolate-covered strawberries, no whipped cream, he hadn't even changed his shirt before getting in his truck and speeding all the way to Baton Rouge.

He was definitely not at his best right now.

Still, as he tugged her through the house, with her wrinkled dress, her flushed cheeks, and her panties shoved in his front pocket with just a bit of lace hanging out to make sure everyone got the point, he didn't feel bad about it.

He was being dirtier with her than usual, but she was with him. He could tell. He would never push Becca beyond her boundaries unless she wanted him to. So far, every time he'd nudged her beyond where she'd been previously, she'd been wholeheartedly into it. He'd made sure. Outside on the patio had been no different.

People were definitely looking. Luke Swanson was definitely looking. Beau met his eyes. Luke looked away.

Perfect.

"Find Savannah. Tell her goodbye," he said to Becca.

"She knows I'm with you."

He squeezed her hand, and she met his gaze. "I want you to make a point of saying goodbye."

She pressed her lips together. Then nodded.

Becca had been telling him off their entire lives. She was the only girl to ever punch him, even if she wasn't the only one to ever *want* to. She called him an asshole on more than one occasion. Of everyone in his life, he could depend on Becca to give him true input about how he was acting.

That was why when she got a little submissive for him, his dick got harder than any other time.

They trusted each other.

Things had changed between them since they'd started dating. Things had softened. *He'd* definitely softened.

He couldn't help it. He couldn't help but be sweet and romantic with her. He wanted to take care of her. He wanted to make her smile. He really did think about her all day and when he sent off a text in the middle of his workday that said *miss you*, he meant it.

But they still knew the other one would tell them the fully unvarnished truth. Which meant when he pushed her, and she went with it, he could trust that she was okay.

He knew she was not afraid of him. He knew that she trusted him as well. He was going to deliver on absolutely everything Becca wanted and needed.

It'd been harder than hell holding back this long. They'd been interrupted for the big night twice because he'd wanted it to be perfect. But he was done with that. She was done too. Obviously.

Tonight was not perfect and she could change her mind at any point, of course, but barring a *no* from her, he wasn't going to be able to hold back anymore.

"Okay," she said. She looked around.

"Over by the window."

He'd spotted Savannah right away. The fact that Savannah hadn't come over to them told him a lot as well. Savannah also trusted him. And that was definitely saying something. Savannah was a ball buster. She also loved Becca fully and unconditionally. If she thought Beau was bad for her friend, she would definitely let him know.

Becca started in that direction.

A moment later he felt a hand on his shoulder. He turned. Luke Swanson stood there.

"You better treat her right. There's a line waiting for when you fuck it up. And I'm at the front."

Yeah, Beau knew that. He almost admired the guy's balls for saying so, however.

"You'll never measure up after me, Swanson. I promise you that."

Luke cocked a brow. "Aren't you supposed to say something like *I'm not going to fuck it up?* Or *I'm the last guy Becca will ever be with?*"

Probably. But hell, Beau had known, even before he'd kissed Becca in her childhood bedroom when they'd started this crazy dating thing, that this wasn't going to last.

He was going to enjoy the hell out of it while it did, though.

"You had your chance, and you were too stupid to take it," Beau told Luke. Which was true. Becca had wanted Luke to ask her out for the entire semester they'd been lab partners or whatever. "You're too late."

"We'll see," Luke said.

Sure. Swanson could think that. But Beau was going to make *damned sure* that Becca knew how a boyfriend should treat her. And that she had *very* high standards for sex when she and Beau called it quits. That was not going to work in Luke Swanson's favor.

Beau was also going to make sure that he and Becca would

always be friends. So when she said something about Luke asking her out in the future, Beau would make sure to dissuade her.

He wouldn't be an asshole about their breakup, though. He wouldn't make her cry. He wouldn't beg her to reconsider. He would say he understood—because he would—and he would tell her that he'd always be there for her and that he'd miss the hell out of her and that if any other guy ever treated her as less than a princess, she'd better let him know.

And then he'd say goodbye.

And get rip-roaring drunk. At least three nights in a row.

Becca rejoined them just then. He put his hand on the back of her neck and they started toward the door.

"I don't even get a goodbye?" Luke called after them.

Beau kept Becca moving toward the door, but he looked back. "Oh, you'll get a goodbye from her eventually. One that will really matter."

They made it all the way out to his truck before Becca asked, "What was that?"

"Just me and Luke coming to an understanding."

"Fighting over me?"

That made Beau's heart squeeze. He wouldn't fight Luke over her. If Becca wanted someone else, he'd let her go. He would always give Becca whatever she wanted.

"We just had a talk," he told her. He reached for the passenger side door and pulled it open.

"I didn't say those things to flirt with him. And you're right, I shouldn't have said those things to anyone at all."

Beau turned her and leaned in, resting his forehead against hers. "I'm not upset with you. I'm pissed at myself. I'm sorry I was late tonight."

"Did you have a good reason?"

He swallowed. Was it a good reason? His business felt like a good reason. But when he was standing here like this, breathing her in, her warm breath against his mouth, knowing he let her down, it didn't feel that good. "It was work."

She nodded. "I figured."

He wasn't sure if it was good or bad that she knew what had kept him away.

"And I didn't get flowers, and I was too late to pick up the chocolate-covered strawberries I ordered, and I totally forgot about the whipped cream—"

Her hands came up to grip his wrists, and she squeezed. "I don't need flowers or whipped cream, Beau. I want you to take me back to my room and I want you to fuck me. I mean it. I want you. Tonight. No more excuses. I want this. *You.*"

He sucked in a breath. Hearing her tell him she wanted him was hot enough. Heat and desire unlike anything he'd ever felt before stabbed him low in the gut. But yeah, hearing Becca Bollier ask him to fuck her was something he was never going to be able say no to. She'd never said it like that before. Which was probably the only reason he'd been able to hold back.

"I'm just trying to make it perfect." His voice was scratchy.

"Well, your idea and my idea of perfect are different," she said. "You think we need all this other stuff. But I don't. I just need *you.*"

God, he wanted that to be true. Forever.

He knew she loved him, but he was just the first. Her first lover, her first boyfriend, the first time she'd fallen in love. Could he convince her this was it? That she should move back to Autre after graduation, marry him, make a life with him in Autre? Yes, he knew he could.

But he shouldn't.

He'd chosen Autre. He'd given up football scholarships to three different colleges to stay home, to be there for his mom,

65

to build a business from the ground up, with his own two hands—literally. To never leave.

And some days he wondered if he'd made the right choice.

A lot of days he wondered that.

Was he making a difference? Was he doing something important? Was he where he was supposed to be? Was Autre, Louisiana enough? Was it *right* for him?

He didn't want Becca to limit herself. She was going to be a teacher. She *was* going to make a difference and do something important. And she could go anywhere to do it. He could *not* talk her into coming home to Autre for him. He couldn't spend the rest of his life wondering if she was as happy as she could possibly be. Or if she wondered *what if?* Or if she resented him and the small, simple life he'd seduced her into.

But he had her for tonight. And he was sure as hell going to be her first, even if he wasn't going to be her last.

He grasped her waist, lifted her, and tossed her onto the front seat of his truck. He slammed the door, stalked around the front of the truck, and got in. "You have from here to your apartment to figure out if this is what you really want tonight. But know this," he looked over at her. "You're poking me. And there is a very thin thread of control holding me together tonight."

She studied him for a moment, then a very sly, unusual grin slid across her face. "That's very good to know."

A shot of lust crashed over him, along with a shiver of trepidation. He might not survive a seductive, sly Becca.

It was about fifteen minutes from the house party to her apartment.

Without strawberries and whipped cream, and with her pushing his control, he needed to be sure she was ready for what lay ahead.

They pulled up to a stop light, and without looking over at

her, he said, "I want your fingers in your pussy right now."

He heard her sharp intake of air, but refused to look over. He gripped the steering wheel, staring straight ahead.

She didn't move or say anything.

"Becca," he said, growling the warning. "Do it."

In his peripheral vision, he saw her gather the skirt of her dress up and then slide her right hand under the hem.

He clenched the steering wheel, forcing himself to pay attention to the traffic.

Just as the light turned green, he heard a little moan.

"I want you to move those fingers in and out until I tell you to stop," he told her.

He could see her hand moving under her skirt.

She kept at it until the next stoplight.

"Let me taste."

Again the little intake of air. Then she pulled her hand from under her skirt and leaned over. He grasped her wrist with his hand and met her eyes as he slid her fingers into his mouth. She'd been doing it. The sweet taste of her pussy was like a drug. A very familiar, very addictive drug.

"This is so hot," she told him.

The light turned green and she settled back into her seat and started to move her hand under her skirt again, but he stopped her with a hand on her thigh. "My turn. Spread your legs and lift your skirt.

She did. But when he glanced over, the skirt still covered everything but her thighs.

"Higher."

She looked out the window. It was four-lane traffic here, and at the next stoplight, anyone pulling up next to them would be able to see into the truck if they looked over.

"But —"

"Lift it up."

She took a deep breath. Then did.

His cock was so hard behind his zipper he felt actual discomfort. Beau shifted on the seat, trying to seek some relief. But there was none. He was thick and throbbing.

He cupped her, easing his middle finger into her pussy. She was hot and wet. She likely had been ever since the patio.

He teased her, not going too deep, making sure that he slid out and circled her clit as well.

She was panting by the time they pulled up to the next stoplight. Sure enough, there was a truck next to them. A man in his forties glanced over. Then looked again. Becca's head was thrown back against the seat. Her eyes were closed. Her skirt was up and Beau's hand was clearly underneath. The guy couldn't actually see any intimate body parts with Beau's hand there, but it was obvious what was going on.

Beau hoped that helped the man and his wife have some fun tonight when he got home.

Both trucks pulled away from the stoplight as it turned green and the man in the truck next to them seemed to be trying to keep pace. Beau smirked as he turned left at the next block, leaving the truck and a probably-horny stranger behind.

They pulled up in front of Becca's apartment building.

He stopped the truck, threw it in park, and turned to face her, his hand still moving inside her. "How close are you?"

"So close," came her breathless reply.

He worked her for another few seconds, feeling her pussy start to clench around his fingers. Then he pulled out.

Her eyes flew open. "*No.*"

"Upstairs. Now."

She scrambled out of the truck, and he met her on the sidewalk. They walked quickly to the door, and she fumbled with her keys.

He took them from her, calmly inserted the key, and

turned, pushing the door open and ushering her inside. They made their way to the elevator, and stepped on alone.

She turned to him as the doors closed. "Kiss me."

He tucked his hands in his front pockets and leaned back against the wall. He was miserable behind his zipper, but he *was* going to control this interaction. As much as possible anyway. "Nope."

Her mouth fell open. "Seriously?"

"Seriously."

"Please. I need you."

"I know."

"Now." She started to step forward.

"If you touch me now, I won't bend you over your couch and fuck you the second we walk in the door."

She froze. She stared at him. Clearly she was calculating which she wanted more—making out in the elevator or what he'd just promised.

"If you're good, the *second* you cross the threshold of your apartment, I will strip you, bend you over, and eat you until you come, then fuck you to your third orgasm of the night."

Her breath caught and her cheeks flushed.

And she didn't make any further move toward him.

He knew her.

"I had planned to give you flowers, drink some wine, kiss you for an hour, then spread you out on your bed, feed you chocolate and strawberries, trail them all over you, paint your body with whipped cream, and lick it all clean before making love to you slow and sweet," he told her, watching the numbers change above them. As if they were discussing the weather.

"I don't ne—"

"But you've made it very clear that what you want is a screaming orgasm and to be done with this whole virginity thing." His eyes found hers. "You've made it very clear how you're feeling tonight. Bad girls don't get strawberries and whipped cream."

He watched a little shiver go through her and fought a grin. She liked this dirty stuff. She liked when he was a little firm and bossy with her.

That was not brand-new information. He'd definitely had his rougher side come out a few times before, but he tried to hold back. She was a virgin, and all of this was new to her. He wanted to be gentle and go slow. He wanted to give her a chance to adjust and to ask for what she needed while not overwhelming her.

But maybe he'd underestimated her.

Or perhaps he'd created a monster.

Either way, he liked being able to let this side out. He could do chocolate-covered strawberries and flowers for this woman. But if she just wanted to be fucked well, he was absolutely the guy for that.

The elevator finally arrived on the tenth floor, and the door swished open. Without a word, they stepped out, and Becca turned left, leading him to her apartment door. She was walking very fast. He chuckled from behind her.

She looked back. "You realize you have my hopes really high, right?"

He crowded her close against the door as she worked to get the key into the lock.

He swept the hair back from her neck and leaned in, dragging his beard up and down her neck and shoulder. "You don't even know what you're hoping for." He bit down lightly on her neck. "Brace yourself."

The shiver that went through her this time was much more pronounced. She finally got the door unlocked and pushed it open.

He pushed her through it, less gently than he'd intended, and kicked it shut behind them.

She turned to face him. Her hand lifted to the tie holding the right strap of her dress up, but he was there, tugging it loose and pushing the dress to the floor before she could even say his name. The material pooled at her feet.

He ran his hands up and down, from her hips to her breasts and back. He loved everything about her body. The curves, the silkiness of her skin, the weight of her breasts, the hard points of her nipples, the dip at her waist, the curve of her ass. He appreciated all of it with his hands in long slow strokes, then he turned her, pulled her back against his chest, and moved to cup between her thighs. He pressed his middle finger deep where he knew she was still hot and wet.

She moaned. "I'm still right on the edge."

"Good. I need you hot and ready."

She was ready to lose her virginity tonight, and he was more than ready to help her. They'd done so many other things. He taught her about hand jobs and blow jobs. He'd jerked off watching her masturbate. They'd used toys. But he hadn't been inside this sweet pussy yet.

It was time. They both needed this. He wasn't intimidated about being her first. He *wanted* to be the first. He wanted her first time to be the best and he knew *he* could do that for her. But if she didn't want strawberries, then damn, he was done arguing.

He nudged her forward to the couch. He'd been eyeing this thing for a couple of weeks, ever since he'd realized the height of the back of couch would be perfect for this activity. When her thighs met the back of the couch he pressed a hand between her shoulder blades, bending her forward, and slipping his hand from between her thighs. She flattened her palms on the cushion as he ran his hands down her back and over her ass.

"You're so fucking gorgeous," he told her.

She moaned as he kneaded her ass cheeks, then knelt behind her.

"Oh God," she said breathlessly.

"That's Beau to you," he corrected. Then he gave her ass a little slap.

She moaned louder. "Beau," she said obediently.

"That's better." Then he leaned in and gave her a long firm lick.

She cried out. He knew this wouldn't take long. She was on edge, as planned, but his mouth had been watering since he'd gotten her off at the party. He licked her again, then circled her clit and felt her legs already shaking.

This, they'd done plenty of times, and he knew exactly what she needed and what she liked. He loved knowing her body this well. He loved that he'd helped *her* learn her body too. She needed to know what she needed and liked. She also needed to be vocal about it.

"Beg me," he said firmly.

"Yes, Beau, *please*."

"Be exact, Bec."

"Harder, faster." She pressed back against his mouth. "*There*," she told him when he flicked his tongue across her clit. "Yes, there," she said again. "Suck it. Harder."

So he did. And she came. The climax washed over her hot and fast, and she cried his name into the couch cushions as he made her come apart.

She slumped forward as he stood. He yanked off his shirt but couldn't help running a big hand up over the curve of her ass to her shoulder and back down before opening his fly. The relief of having that pressure off his throbbing cock was strong.

"You ready?"

"Yes. So ready."

He shoved his jeans and boxers to his knees and fisted his shaft. He squeezed and stroked, looking at the woman draped over the back of the couch, spent.

"You sure you don't want to move into the bedroom?"

"No," she said quickly. "Please. Right here. No more waiting."

He rolled a condom on. "This is not how I imagined this."

She looked up over her shoulder at him. "It's so hot, though." She wiggled her ass. "Please fuck me hard."

He couldn't deny her. Even if he wasn't hard as steel and on the verge of losing it, if this is what Becca wanted, this was what he'd give her. There was time for strawberries and whipped cream and silk sheets and romance later.

Hell, they'd done the romance. Thoroughly. He needed to get out of his head.

He stepped forward, letting her feel his cock against her ass.

"I've never wanted anyone like I want you," he told her gruffly.

"Show me."

She was taunting him, he knew that. But he wanted to show her. Gladly. She had no idea what he'd been like with other women. At least, he didn't think so. It was hard to know what talk she'd heard around Autre. He hadn't asked what she knew, and she hadn't volunteered any gossip. He'd always been a demanding lover, he liked dirty sex, he was a dirty talker by nature. Hell, it was the romantic side of him that was new. Because of Becca.

Thinking about strawberries was new. Fingering his date in the car was not.

He settled one hand on her hip, then positioned his cock at

her entrance. He ran the tip through her slickness, letting her feel him and mentally adjust, then pressed forward just slightly.

She moaned and spread her knees a bit. "Yes, Beau. Yes."

He eased in a little further. They'd played with fingers and dildos. The time romancing and playing with Becca had been heaven and hell combined. It'd been fun and intimate and had taught him things about the female body, and even his own, that he had never fully appreciated before. But damn, it felt like he'd been winding this spring tighter and tighter over the past three months. He'd never taken this long between realizing he wanted someone and taking them to bed.

She reached back and gripped his hip, pulling him forward. "Please, Beau."

"Gotta take it easy," he said through gritted teeth.

"No, you don't. I need you."

"Easy girl."

"More, Beau. *More*."

And he couldn't hold back anymore. Her words, her body, the three months of torturous foreplay, all combined and he took hold of both hips and thrust forward.

She cried out. "*Yes!*"

He held his breath for a count of three. Then he couldn't help but move. He pulled out and slid forward again. Then again.

The sounds she made definitely spurred him on—moans, and gasps, and sighs. She pressed back against him, clearly seeking more, and his body responded. He took her with long, deep strokes and his pace quickly picked up.

Her *yeses* and *Beaus* and *oh Gods*, convinced him that she was good, and with him every step, and soon he felt his climax bearing down on him.

"Becca," he gasped. "Babe, need you with me."

She shook her head, her hair brushing the cushions. "Don't stop. Don't slow down."

He wasn't sure he was capable of that. He'd like to think he had control at all moments, but buried deep inside this body, doing this with this woman, was the moment when his control completely shattered. He pounded into her, her body gripped him tightly, and he felt his orgasm rip through him.

He shouted her name as he came, the pleasure and relief so intense that it took him a few moments to even take a deep breath as it all rolled through him.

When he finally was able to suck in oxygen again, he scooped his arms underneath her, pulled her up against his body, and hugged her tightly from behind. He pulled out of her and swept her up into his arms, carrying her into the bedroom. He deposited her on the bed, then went into the bathroom to clean up.

He returned to find her exactly as he left her but with an arm thrown over her eyes.

"You okay?" he asked, joining her on the bed. He rested a hand on her lower belly possessively.

She uncovered her eyes and rolled her head toward him, giving him a sleepy smile. "Holy shit, I've never been better."

He chuckled. "Glad to hear it. I was afraid there for a minute I'd lost you."

"Definitely not. But what a way to go."

"Well, we're just getting started." He gave her a wicked grin. "By morning, you might feel differently."

She rolled toward him. "I'm going to be really sore tomorrow, aren't I?" She almost sounded excited about that.

"I'm going to try my best," he told her, stroking his hands up and down her back and then cupping her ass to bring her up against him.

She climbed on top of him, her legs straddling him as they

lay chest to chest. "Can I ride you next time?"

A surprised chuckle burst from him. "Girl, you can do anything to me you want."

"I've been reading a lot of erotic romance," she admitted. "I've got a lot of ideas of things I want to try."

He gave a happy groan as his hands settled on her ass and he felt his cock stirring. "I'm the one who's going to be sore tomorrow, I'm thinking."

She lifted her head and grinned. "Maybe."

He squeezed her. "Bring it on."

SHE DID. And the sight of Becca Bollier riding him cowgirl was the hottest thing he'd ever seen. Flipping her to her back and pounding into her good-old missionary style was pretty fucking great too.

And he was sure taking her on all fours would have been heaven.

But he fell asleep.

And then his phone rang before he could wake up and get her going for round four. Or five. Or whatever they were on.

He fumbled in the dark, feeling for his jeans on the floor next to the bed, and finally pulling his phone from a pocket. "What?"

He hadn't even looked to see who was calling.

"Beau. Oh my God. There's water everywhere."

"Mom?" He propped up on one elbow and blinked. The room was almost black except for slivers of light coming through the blinds. "What's going on?"

"A pipe burst on the second floor! There's water everywhere! I don't know what to do."

What? No. *No, no, no.*

He shoved himself up to sitting and scrubbed a hand over

his face. He pulled the phone away from his face. Two a.m.

Fuck, he hadn't even been asleep for an hour.

"Have you shut the water off?" he asked.

"I... no. One of the guests just woke me. I went out to your cabin but forgot you were gone. I don't—"

"Mom," Beau broke in firmly. "You need to shut the water off. Then you need to call Mitch and Zeke. I'm on my way."

Mitch and Zeke were cousins to his cousins. They were basically family. As was everyone else in Autre, especially those with the last name Landry. But more importantly, Mitch and Zeke did construction and knew their way around plumbing. They could at least provide emergency assistance. And calm Heather down until Beau could get there.

But *motherfucker*. Water damage. That was the worst. What the fuck had happened?

"I didn't know who else to call when you weren't here," Heather said.

He knew that. It was the middle of the night, for one thing. For another...he was always there. Or always had been. Until Becca.

Fuck.

"I know. It's okay. I'm heading back."

But it was five hours. He wouldn't be there before the sun came up. "Are the guest rooms okay?" he asked.

"The ones upstairs are. Three of them downstairs are not." Heather's voice was shaky.

"Okay, get them up to the motel," he said.

The B and B would have to pay for those rooms. The motel would work with them, of course. Thankfully in a town like Autre, the motel and Bed and Breakfast didn't consider one another competition. Which was probably strange, but it was true. There was enough business for all of them.

"But call Mitch and Zeke first."

"Okay..."

Oh, Jesus, she was crying.

"Mom," Beau said firmly, but gently. "Where's Crystal?"

"Here. She's right here." His mom's best friend ran the B and B with her and lived in one of the rooms on the main floor.

"Let me talk to her."

He felt the mattress shift and then Becca's hand on his back. "Beau?" she whispered.

He reached back and put a hand on the closest thing he could touch—her thigh, it turned out. He just squeezed.

"Beau?" Crystal asked a moment later.

"Hey, you okay?"

"Yeah." She paused. "No. I guess. I mean, we're physically okay."

"Yeah." He swallowed. Fuck. He hated not being there. It had just been him and his mom for so long. They had tons of family and friends. It never had been *just* them. But he was the one Heather always turned to first and he'd always taken that seriously.

He felt Becca shift behind him and he felt his chest tighten.

He wanted to be there for her too. He wanted her to turn to him first too. He wanted...her. Everything about and with her.

But his life, his responsibilities, the really big ones, were in Autre.

"Okay I'm going to go ahead and call Zeke and Mitch," he told Crystal. "And Hannah. She can come over and help with getting the guests resettled."

His aunt Hannah, his mom's sister, would help calm her down and would be great with the disgruntled guests.

"Thank you, Beau. We'll be okay," Crystal said.

"I'm on my way back." He felt Becca's thigh tense under his hand.

"Oh. You don't have..." Crystal sighed. "Your mom would

78

really like to have you here."

He knew that and he'd feel strange *not* going back. This was a big deal. This wasn't a clogged drain or a burned-out light bulb someone else could fix in his absence. Even that would bug him. Those things were his responsibility. But this was a *big* deal and Heather needed more than just someone who could deal with the water. She needed his emotional support and his help with the business side of things. They'd need to contact the insurance company, deal with the upset guests and refunds, figure out how long they'd be down three rooms, and more.

Heather had started the B and B, with his encouragement, when he'd been in high school and when he'd decided to stay in Autre and not go to college, she'd expanded the business because he'd promised to be there and help.

Heather and Crystal were the best when it came to creating a comfortable, gorgeous, welcoming environment with amazing food and décor and friendly, charming faces. They did well with inventory and some of the social media and marketing tasks, but they hated accounting and happily turned over anything involving the accountant and the attorney to Beau.

"I'm leaving as soon as I can but..." He blew out a breath. "It will take me some time to get there. I'll get people over to help."

"Of course. I'm sorry to interrupt your weekend."

His fingers curled into Becca's thigh. Yeah, he was sorry too. "See you soon."

They disconnected and he pulled in a deep breath.

"What happened?" Becca asked softly.

"Major water leak at the bed and breakfast," he said.

"Oh crap,"

"Yeah." He pivoted on the mattress to face her. "It's bad. I have to go."

She didn't cover her disappointment quickly enough. He saw it before she gave him a smile. "Of course. I understand. But it's the middle of the night. Are you going to be okay to drive? You hardly got any sleep."

He was going to have to be okay. He'd been tired even before he'd gotten on the road *to* Baton Rouge. He'd been putting in long hours over the past week to free up today and part of tomorrow to be here with Becca. It looked like he wasn't going to be catching up anytime soon. "That's what coffee was invented for, right?"

She still looked concerned. "Zeke and Mitch can't handle it?"

He swore. "I have to call them."

He wanted to comfort Becca and make sure she understood he was sorry to be leaving, but he really needed to get people over to help his mom. "Hang on." He quickly punched in Mitch's number.

He hated to wake his friend up in the middle of the night, but Mitch had been awakened by things like this before, and he would understand. In fact, both Zeke and Mitch were the type of guys who would be upset if Beau *hadn't* called them once they found out what happened.

"Beau? What's up?" Mitch asked seconds later, his voice scratchy.

"There's a water leak at the B and B. I'm in Baton Rouge. Can you—"

"On my way," Mitch said before Beau even finished the question.

Fuck he loved that guy. "Thanks. I owe you."

"Bullshit. We all owe each other so much at this point there's no reason to keep track."

Beau huffed out a laugh. "Good point."

"I'll grab Zeke."

"Was gonna call him next. But I need to get a hold of Hannah too."

"No problem. We'll be up there in a few."

"Thanks, man. I'm heading back but obviously it'll take me a bit. Call me when you get up there and see how bad it is."

"'Course."

They disconnected, and Beau immediately dialed his Aunt Hannah.

"Beau? What's wrong?"

Yeah, another thing about middle-of-the-night calls, people assumed it was something bad. Because it almost always was.

"Hey, sorry to call so late. There's a water leak up at the bed and breakfast. I'm out of town. Mom needs help with some of the guests."

"Of course. We'll go right up."

"We" included his Uncle Jerry. "Thank you. I'm on my way back, but it will be a few hours."

"Are you with Becca?"

"Yeah." He couldn't even look at her. He was disappointed, but he knew she was even more so. No doubt she had plans for them for tomorrow.

"I'm sorry," Hannah said. "Tell her hello from us."

Beau knew that his entire family—hell, the whole town— loved that he and Becca were together. They seemed like a match made in heaven to everyone in Autre. Two hometown kids who'd grown up as friends and then fallen in love. He supposed on paper, that made sense. Because he and Becca were like all of them. So of course everyone would assume they would want the same things everyone else in Autre wanted.

But this was hard. Being five hours apart, feeling like his life was pulling him in two very different directions, feeling like he wasn't doing a good job at any of it, was wearing on him.

Like the fact that they'd just made love for the first time and now he was leaving her in the middle of the night to go confront a major catastrophe back home.

"I will, I'm sure she says hello back."

He finally snuck a glance at Becca. She was watching him, chewing on her bottom lip. The combination of concern and disappointment still obvious on her face.

Dammit, he hated letting people down. Anyone really, but especially the people he loved.

Becca and his mom were the top of that list. And right now he was literally having to choose between the two of them.

Except it wasn't really a choice. Becca *wanted* him here and he wanted to be with her, but she didn't need him. Heather did. His life in Autre did.

"I'll see you when I get back," Beau finally said to Hannah.

"Drive safe."

Finally, Beau turned back to Becca. "I have to go."

She just nodded.

"Bec, please," he said, not even sure exactly what he was asking. To not make him feel bad? To understand? To not be disappointed in him?

She leaned over and turned on the bedside table lamp. "It's okay," she said. "Of course you have to go."

He took in the sight of her in the light. Her hair was mussed, she had the soft look of sleep about her, she'd pulled on a simple t-shirt, and he knew she had nothing on underneath. She had whisker burns from him along her neck and cheek.

She looked sexy as hell and suddenly the knowledge slammed into him that she was going to be waking up in the morning, her first true morning after, alone.

"This is not how I planned this to go," he said. He blew out a breath. "I feel like I say that to you a lot."

She frowned. "Maybe you need to quit making plans. Everything's okay."

"Last night..." He told off for a moment, not totally sure what he was going to say. "Last night, some things changed. It was amazing. But it was a little rough. You're probably gonna be sore."

Her cheeks got a little pink, but she smiled. "I thought that was the goal."

He lifted a hand and cupped her cheek. "Yeah, if I was here to take care of you. To tease about it. To maybe rub some sore muscles."

She laughed. "Rubbing those muscles is what made me sore, right?"

He shook his head. "Not what I meant."

She lifted her hand to cover the back of his. "I know. I'll be okay."

He really hated this. A moment ago, he'd realized that his mother needed him more than Becca. But after everything from last night, he wasn't so sure.

Heather definitely needed him. This was a big deal for the bed and breakfast—for their business—but physically, and even more so, emotionally, he felt very weird about leaving Becca suddenly. If they hadn't slept together it would be different. If this was like all the previous weekends it would be easier. But things had changed between them last night.

They'd definitely taken another huge step. He wanted to be with her the day after to see how she felt. Not just physically. Again, the lack of romance was bugging him. If things had gone according to his plan, if everything had been sweet and loving, he might feel better about this. Instead, he'd acted like a possessive caveman at a party in front of all of her friends, dabbled with exhibitionism on the way home in the truck, and then actually taken her virginity roughly over the back of the couch.

He frowned. Dammit.

She lifted her hand and rubbed her index finger between his eyebrows. "Stop. You need to go back to Autre."

He did fucking have to go back to Autre.

Right now, in the middle of the goddamn night.

He was going to have to climb out of the bed of the woman he loved, leave her after making love to her for the first time, and go back and deal with a bunch of bullshit-headache-adult-responsibility stuff.

This really sucked.

He leaned in and captured her lips in a kiss. He pulled back and looked directly into her eyes. "I love you."

She nodded. "I know. I love you too."

He knew she did. But everything really felt off.

Still, he forced himself to climb out of bed, get dressed, then grabbed his stuff and gave her one final kiss.

"I'll call you later."

She nodded. "Yes. And on your way back too if you start to get tired. I'm worried about you driving back."

He was less worried and more pissed off about driving back, but he nodded. "Okay. We'll talk soon."

She nodded.

He gave her one last kiss and then made himself leave.

His feeling of restlessness and frustration seem to grow with every mile that passed, and he was particularly pissed off when, after three hours on the road, he suddenly jerked himself upright and realized he'd fallen asleep at the wheel just in time to see the front of his truck dive into the roadside ditch.

three

A year and a half later...

"BECCA NEEDS YOU."

Those three words would never fail to stop Beau Hebert in his tracks.

He turned away from his mother's stove where he'd just swiped a cookie from the cooling rack. "What?"

"I sent her up to the attic to grab a tablecloth for me, but she's been up there longer than I expected," Heather told him. She didn't look at him. She just kept stirring whatever dough she had in the bowl in front of her.

So she probably missed the panicked look on Beau's face.

"Why did you send her up there?" He was already moving toward the stairs and abandoning the still-warm-from-the-oven double chocolate chunk cookies. Which probably would have told his mother how serious this situation was without his sharp tone of voice.

"Why not?" Heather asked.

His boot hit the first step that led up the backway to the second floor. "She doesn't work for you."

"She's sweet and offered to help me get ready for the big dinner tonight."

His mother's bed and breakfast was sold out for the next three nights. That wasn't uncommon, but it always meant things were extra busy.

"And she's deathly afraid of spiders," Beau said, starting up the stairs.

He didn't really need to explain any further. The attic was... an attic. It was clean, and Heather used it to store any number of supplies in plastic storage containers and on metal shelves that lined the old wooden walls. But it had spiders. As any attic would.

Jesus. Becca would be freaking out by now. He took the stairs two at a time all the way to the third level, stomping across the floor and yanking open the door that led up the final set of ten steps that would take him to the attic.

"Bec?" he called. "You up here?"

"Uh...yeah."

Her voice was shaky. Fuck.

He bounded up the stairs. "You okay?" he asked before he even hit the top.

"Well, I figure your mom's bed and breakfast isn't a *bad* place to die," she said.

He located her standing in the center of the floor, her head covered with the lacy white tablecloth. It dropped nearly to the floor and, for a second, reminded him of a bridal veil.

"You're not gonna die," he told her, crossing to her.

He knew exactly what she was talking about. She'd seen a spider and was having a panic attack. He glanced around. Or *several* spiders. There were cobwebs everywhere.

"If I was going to haunt somewhere, I think I'd pick this place," she went on as if he hadn't just reassured her that her death was *not* imminent. "For one, it always smells great. Even way up here. And I can't imagine there are any nasty ghosts here. I mean, no one's been murdered here. There haven't been any suspicious deaths here. Sure, the house has been here for a *long* time, but we would have definitely heard the story if something weird had happened here. So, at best, I figure there are some other just regular ghosts. Maybe even some friendly ones. I could learn some history while I drift around."

"Bec," Beau said, fighting a smile as he took her upper arms in his hands and gave her a little squeeze. "Nobody's dying here today."

"And hey, if I'm stuck here for eternity, I'd still get to see a ton of people I really love. I mean, yeah, strangers stay here, but your mom is related to a lot of the town and knows everyone I know, so they'll be in and out, stopping by. My mom will come over sometimes and I'll be able to see her even if I can't talk to her. And they'll gossip in the front hall, or I can listen in on your mom and Hannah and Crystal talking in the kitchen and keep up with all the news from town."

Yeah, she'd been stuck up here thinking for a while. Beau shook his head. "Where is it?"

"Do you think I'll be able to leave the attic? I mean, are ghosts stuck to the exact room where they die? 'Cuz I won't be able to hear the gossip from the kitchen up here."

Beau put a finger under her chin and tipped her face so she was looking up at him. He waited until she really focused on him. "Where is it?"

"It?"

"The spider."

Her eyes widened and her voice dropped to a whisper. "*Everywhere.*"

He would *not* smile. But this woman was confident and sassy except in two instances: Spiders. And when she was naked with him.

Beau felt heat pump through his bloodstream, and he cleared his throat. This was *not* the time to be reminded that Becca Bollier had been a virgin and that *he'd* been the one to teach her...fuck, so much. She'd been an enthusiastic student and had caught on quickly, but yeah, she'd been a little unsure at first when it came to getting naked and touching and being touched.

He dropped his hand and stepped back. Dammit. These memories and feelings snuck up on him all the damned time and he hated it.

"Okay, let me get you out of here," he said. He took her hand and started for the steps.

"I haven't found the tablecloth yet," she said, tugging on his hand to stop him.

He looked back, his gaze going to the tablecloth she was wearing. "No?"

"I grabbed this so they wouldn't get in my hair." She gave a full-body shudder. "But this isn't the one she wanted."

"Okay." He blew out a breath. "So, where have you looked?"

"That trunk." She pointed to the left. "And that box." She gestured toward the box next to it.

"And it's not in there?"

"No idea. Remy is in there." Again she pointed at the trunk, then at the box. "And Damon is in there."

Beau opened his mouth, then shut it. "You named the spiders?"

"I always name spiders."

"After people you don't like." He knew Remy and had heard stories about Damon.

She hugged her arms around her body. "Well, people I never want to see again anyway."

"Got it." He sighed. "I have to dig through the trunk and box, Bec."

"What if Remy bites you?"

"It will be the last thing Remy ever does."

"What if he's poisonous?"

"I'll go to the clinic."

"What if he burrows under your skin and lays eggs and they invade your body and..." She looked a little green even as she failed to complete whatever horrifying thought she had going through her pretty head.

"Well, that would make Remy a girl, I guess," Beau said.

She frowned. "It's not funny."

"Okay, if that happens, I'll still go to the clinic, and I'll have a hell of a story to tell."

She moaned. "*Beau.*"

He finally chuckled. "Bec, that is *not* going to happen, and other than taking a blowtorch to the place, I'm not sure how else you want me to handle this."

"Let's just leave. Buy your mom a new tablecloth. Just leave Remy and Damon and the rest up here alone," she said.

"But then they'll think they won. They'll invite more friends. They'll take over the entire attic. They'll be using my old skateboard and having dinner parties with mom's China. They'll grow to the size of dogs. We can't have that."

She was staring at him.

Okay, so maybe that wasn't the way to deal with a person with a phobia. A little understanding and tenderness would probably be appropriate. But that might involve standing closer to her and, God forbid, hugging her.

If he hugged Becca Bollier, he might never let her go.

He might kiss her.

He might tell her that he was still in love with her.

And all of that was way worse than feeding into her irrational fear of a creature barely the size of the tip of her finger.

Probably.

No one would accuse him of being an expert on human emotion. Or human psychology, for that matter.

"How much do you want to punch me right now?" he asked her.

"On a scale from one to ten?"

"Yeah." He felt the corner of his mouth curl up.

"Seven point five."

"Ah, I have some wiggle room then," he said. He inched toward the trunk. "You gonna be okay if I open this thing?"

"Absolutely not."

"You can go downstairs by yourself," he offered. He was right next to the trunk now.

"I can't."

"Why?"

"Emmaline lives up there." She pointed.

Beau almost choked on a laugh. He definitely knew who Emmaline was named after.

Sure enough, there was a big web right above the steps, and a spider—that was, in Becca's defense, much bigger than the tip of her finger—hung right in the middle. Well, fuck. Emmaline was also black and could very well be a black widow. Those were common in Louisiana.

"And you think she's gonna drop on you if you try to leave?" Beau asked.

"Obviously."

"She didn't drop on me when I came up," he pointed out.

"She didn't drop on me when I came up either. Clearly, she's the one in charge of *keeping* us up here."

Beau nodded as if that made complete sense. "To what end?"

"We die, and they can feast on our carcasses."

"Do spiders eat human carcasses?"

"After they suck out our souls." Becca's tone indicated this was common knowledge.

"I see." He squinted at her. "So, we're like Oreos?"

She frowned. "How do you get Oreos from that?"

"They..." He realized how this was going to sound just a beat before he said it, but he'd already started. "...lick our middles out first and then eat the rest."

She lifted a brow. "They *suck* our souls out as any good demon would. It's not *licking*."

"So they suck us before they eat us."

He watched as the pink stained her cheeks. He'd known it would happen. He'd spent three months of his life thoroughly enjoying saying playful and sometimes downright filthy things to this woman and watching her blush. The best three months of his life. He knew her buttons.

He also knew how much she liked sucking and licking. Doing it and having it done...

And suddenly his jeans were fitting tighter.

You dumbass. You started this and now—

"Yes. It's definitely *sucking*, then *eating*. And not a lot of *licking*," she said, crossing her arms.

Dammit.

He should have seen that coming.

Becca had gotten quite good at the vixen thing. *He'd* urged her on and given her that confidence. The sweet, not-sure-of-herself-with-the-naked-sexy-stuff hadn't lasted long. And she'd loved to make him squirm with her dirty talk.

Of course, that had been a year ago. *More than* a year ago. They were friends now. Just friends. Friends didn't talk about sucking and licking and eating. At least not with the images Beau currently had running through his mind.

"Have they already done that to you?" he asked, forcing

himself to focus on the fucking spiders instead of how damned easy it was to flirt with this woman. "You look a little thinner."

Finally, *finally*, she cracked a smile. "I don't think souls take up physical space that way."

"You sure?" He stretched to his full height, bracing his feet apart. "Because I'm definitely the bigger of the two of us and I've got *way* more soul than you."

She mock-gasped. "How do you figure *that*?"

"Please," he scoffed, bending toward the trunk. "I'm an *artist*. Artists are full of soul." He was a woodworker and he built custom furniture. That was his niche. He also did cabinets and other more basic projects, but he'd made a name for himself over the past couple of years for producing some of the most beautiful, unique, and high-quality furniture in the South.

"I'm a *teacher*," Becca protested. "That takes so much heart and soul, you don't even know."

But he did. She was fucking amazing with kids. Everyone in Autre was thrilled that Becca had decided to come home.

Except him.

Okay, that wasn't entirely true. The kids and families in Autre were lucky she'd come home to teach Kindergarten.

But fuck, he'd hoped she'd go somewhere else after graduating. At least for the first few years.

Sure, that sounded crazy, considering he was in love with her. But he didn't want her stuck here. He loved their little town. But it was...little. Things didn't change much here. It definitely wasn't as exciting or as progressive as a city like Baton Rouge, which he knew Becca had loved. And she was now working for her dad. Kind of. Jonathan Bollier was the high school principal and Becca was an elementary teacher, so she didn't report to him directly. Still, he was part of the administration at the school where she was now teaching.

Jonathan was a great guy. He'd been the high school principal in Autre as long as Beau could remember. He was well-respected and Beau knew both her mom and dad had influenced Becca's decision to go into education. She looked up to them and felt that their work was important. But Beau was worried that working with her dad might not be as easy as Becca was hoping.

Hell, he was worried about a lot of things about Becca being home in Autre.

That she'd get bored. That she'd feel held back. That she'd want more eventually. That she'd feel stuck. That she'd wonder about bigger, or just different, opportunities.

That he'd fall deeper and deeper in love with her and it would hurt even more when she left.

She'd only ever lived in Autre and Baton Rouge. She'd only ever considered being a teacher. She'd only ever dated Beau. She hadn't even gone to parties in Autre. Her first real taste of any kind of social life had been in college when she'd met Savannah and Toby. She'd been a quiet, nerdy, bookworm while in Autre. Really living and having fun had happened *away* from Autre.

Why did she want to settle down here for good?

And would that desire actually last?

What if he fell for her completely and she left?

He wasn't going anywhere. Autre *was* where he was going to live his life. So it made no sense to get involved with her until he was sure *she* was sure this was where she wanted to be long term.

But living next door to Becca and leaving her alone after touching her, tasting her, knowing what it was like to hold her, to talk with her all night long, after being the one she looked for across a room, after making her laugh, making her moan, making her come was the hardest fucking thing he'd ever done.

He cleared his throat and put on the I'm-just-your-friend façade he'd been wearing ever since they'd broken up. "Yeah, yeah, okay, I'll agree you have some soul. Maybe more than most. But if it comes down to you or me, Remy and Damon and Emmaline are gonna come for me, so you can make a break for it." He grabbed the handle of the trunk.

"You'd sacrifice yourself for me?" she asked. "That's sweet."

Beau made the mistake of glancing at her. She looked almost touched by that. But fuck yeah, he'd sacrifice himself for her. They were joking about some stupid spiders, but suddenly the moment felt weightier.

Dating her had changed their relationship completely.

It was why they'd been *extremely* careful about keeping things strictly platonic since she'd been home. At least he had. They hadn't talked about their past. There was no reason, really. The break-up had been a mutual, amicable decision.

His car accident had freaked Becca out. It had freaked him out too. It had pissed him off more than anything, but after the ER doc had dismissed him and he'd *finally* made it home to Autre *nine* hours after the burst pipe rather than five, he'd admitted it could have been *much* worse. He could have been killed. He could have killed someone else.

He'd agreed that he couldn't keep burning the candle at both ends.

He'd always vowed that he would let Becca end things whenever, however she chose to do it. So when she'd said, "I don't think this is good for you. I don't think we should keep doing this," he'd said, "You're right."

And that had been that.

He'd seen her when she'd come home to visit but it had

always been in passing, or when her mom asked him to come over to fix something. It was so obvious that Maureen always needed something fixed when Becca just happened to be home. But he always showed up and he and Becca were always friendly to one another. But not *too* friendly.

And he very carefully avoided being alone with her. Something she seemed very happy with as well.

They had an unspoken agreement to pretend as if those three months of being more than friends hadn't happened and to try to transition back to what they'd had before.

Which was fine. Great even. They'd tried being more, it hadn't worked out, and they didn't want to entirely fuck everything up between them forever. Especially with her living here now.

But it wasn't working. Being her friend only was nearly impossible.

Since she'd moved home permanently and taken the job as the third kindergarten teacher in Autre, they ran into each other all the time. Literally every day. They had friends in common. Their mothers were friends. They lived next door to one another.

Well, their moms did.

Beau lived in a cabin behind his mom's place so he could help her out with maintenance at the B and B and just generally be around if she needed him, while Becca was living at her mom and dad's until she could afford a down payment on a place of her own.

She'd only been home for a little over three months, so the torture of living next door to her was going to probably go on for a few more months.

"I'm gonna open this trunk, Bec," he warned. "You ready?"

"No."

He gave a low chuckle. "Gotta do it."

"You're going to lose at least one finger."

"I sincerely doubt it." He paused. "You wanna go downstairs?"

She looked up at the spider hanging above the steps. "Yes."

"Okay." He straightened and looked around.

He spotted what he needed on the shelves by the window that overlooked the front yard. His mother's canning supplies. She didn't can much anymore, since the bed and breakfast stayed full so much of the time, but she still had boxes of glass jars and lids. He crossed the space and grabbed a jar and a long piece of plastic tubing from another shelf. He wasn't sure what that was for, but it would work perfectly.

He moved to stand under where Emmaline hung. "Sorry about this," he apologized to the spider. "I know you're not doing anything wrong and you're just minding your own business and not bothering anyone, but this one needs you to be somewhere else." He inclined his head toward Becca.

"What are you doing?" Becca asked.

"Fixing this for you." Beau reached up with the plastic tubing and twirled it in the spiderweb. Emmaline was obviously concerned and started wriggling right away, but he quickly dropped her into the jar and covered the top with the lid.

Now up close with her, he could see that she wasn't a black widow. That was very good.

He turned to face Becca. "Problem solved."

Her eyes were wide. "That was... awesome."

It wasn't. He'd put a spider into a jar. He'd been putting creatures into jars since he'd been a kid. From tadpoles to lightning bugs. But if she thought it was amazing, he'd take it.

"Now you can go downstairs."

Becca glanced toward the stairs, then toward the trunk, then focused on him. "I feel bad leaving you up here alone."

He huffed out a laugh. "I'll be fine. I'm not worried about Remy or Damon."

"Okay. But scream if you need me."

There was no way in hell he was going to scream.

She started for the stairs, the tablecloth still clutched around her head.

He set the jar with the spider on the floor by the top of the steps. He'd release her outside. He supposed that removing her from the attic wasn't a terrible idea. While she hadn't really been bothering anyone, his mother would appreciate having one less spider up here as well.

He moved toward the trunk, then realized he didn't know what the tablecloth he was searching for looked like.

"Becca?" he called.

"Yeah?"

Her voice came from right behind him. He turned. "What are you doing?"

"The door's locked."

He frowned. "What door?"

She sighed. "The door at the bottom of the steps."

"What do you mean? It locks from the outside so no one can get up here."

"I don't know what to tell you." She shrugged. "It's locked. I can't get it open."

He blew out a breath. "What does the tablecloth that you were sent up here for look like?"

"Red with white trim."

He lifted the lid of the trunk.

Becca gasped and took several steps backward.

He started to reach inside to move the quilt that was on top out of the way, but he immediately met Remy. Damn. The fucking spider was big. Beau actually jerked his hand back. The spider dove into the trunk, and Beau swore.

"Told you," Becca said.

Okay, so Remy was running—or diving—for his life. Beau quickly tossed the quilt out of the way, then two tablecloths, then another blanket.

"I don't see anything red."

"Maybe it's in the box?" Becca asked. She was standing as far away from the trunk as she could get. The toes of her tennis shoes were hanging over the edge of the top step, in fact.

Beau moved to the box, pulling the top off. He pulled back the top blanket and sucked in a quick breath as Becca squealed.

"It's just a piece of lint," he said of the black blob on the top of the next blanket. This must have been what she thought was the spider she'd named Damon. He turned with it pinched between his fingers. "See—"

She was white as a sheet and two steps down from the top.

"Becca?"

"He got out," she whispered and pointed.

Beau looked down. There was a black spider on the floor about a foot from his shoe. It was either Remy, escaped from the trunk, or a friend.

"Well, fuck." Beau lifted his foot and moved to squash the little bastard.

"No!"

He paused. "*What?*"

"You can't kill it!"

"Are you kidding? I can't kill the man-eating spider that you're deathly afraid of?"

"Can't you put him in with Emmaline?"

Beau sighed and put his foot down. This woman...

Of course, Remy made a break for it just then. Becca gasped and backed up, even though the spider was not heading in her direction. Beau looked around, grabbed another jar off the shelf and quickly plunked it down over the top of the spider, trapping him.

Then he saw a pile of old menus. Plucking one off the top, he slid it under the jar and the spider. He looked up at Becca. "To get him in the jar with Emmaline, you'll have to hold her jar and open the top."

"Um...no," Becca said simply.

Yeah, that's what he'd figured. He grabbed another lid, turned the Remy trap upside down, and screwed it on.

Now they had two jars with spiders inside. They could end up with two dozen at this rate.

Not that he was going to mention that to Becca.

She stood studying the jar. He crossed to set it next to Emmaline's. Becca backed up. But then she said, "We should punch holes in the lids."

He lifted a brow. "You're afraid of the spiders suffocating?"

"Well..." She lifted a shoulder. "Yeah."

She was...sweet. Sunshine. Goodness. Optimism.

Unexpected.

She confused him. Made him do things completely out of character.

He crossed to the shelves to find something to use to punch holes in the jar lids.

And he was crazy about her.

four

ANOTHER NOT-TERRIBLE THING about dying up here and haunting the place was that she'd be able to keep seeing Beau, Becca decided. This was his mother's B and B and he did all the maintenance and handyman work. Which meant he was around a lot.

With his shirt off.

They were past the point of him having his shirt off around her on purpose, but hey, if she had to be a ghost, at least she'd have that.

The guy was *meant* to have his shirt off.

Beau Hebert was hot. Period. Muscles for days, beard, crooked grin, deep green eyes, a growly gruff attitude that went all soft and sweet for a handful of people—his mom, his grandma, his aunt, his mom's best friend, and *her.* It made Becca feel special that she could get past that gruffness.

But now, the hotness was also made more potent by the fact that she knew the guy had a dirty side. A *very* dirty side. He talked it and walked it. The things his tongue and those big, working-man's hands could do...

Becca felt herself flushing. That happened all the time

around Beau and she hated it. It was ridiculous. She'd known him since she'd been ten. She hadn't even liked him for a good year or so. Probably longer. Then she'd...tolerated him. Then she'd liked him. But she'd *never* wanted to kiss him. Until...

It didn't matter. It. Did. Not. Matter. They'd been there, done that, and were past it. It hadn't worked out.

"You know when we were kids, you would have thought this was all ridiculous."

He paused in the process of punching holes in the lids of the jars with a nail he'd found on the shelves. He nodded. "Yeah. For sure."

She smiled. "And you would've told me so."

He nodded again. "Definitely."

She crossed her arms. "So why aren't you telling me that now?"

He blew out a breath. And she suddenly had the feeling that she had said something she shouldn't.

Things had changed between them when they dated. She supposed that was natural. When you dated someone, your relationship changed, of course. But her friendship with Beau had always been built first and foremost on total honesty.

The fact that they had developed softer feelings for one another had brought them closer in many ways. Physically, for sure. Again, she felt the warmth wash through her and she had to shut down those feelings before her mind wandered down a very dirty and probably inappropriate-for-the-moment path. Or inappropriate for *any* moment now. He wasn't her boyfriend anymore. And that was for the best. She had to just keep telling herself that.

But their relationship had changed in other ways. They'd stopped being fully honest about everything. In fact, that was what had finally caused their breakup. While they'd been fully open with one another about a number of things—like her virginity and the things that she was discovering about herself and her sexuality that he'd happily and eagerly helped her explore—he'd stopped being honest with her about the toll the relationship was taking on his career and life here back in Autre.

The five-hour drive and just being in totally different places in their lives had been harder to navigate than they'd expected. But they'd never talked about it. He'd never told her how he felt about it. And in the end, it had caused the car accident that had finally led her to telling him they needed to break up.

God... she could still feel the shock and fear that had hit her when she'd found out about the accident. He hadn't told her about it. She'd found out from one of his cousins. Who had assumed that she'd known. She should have known. But he hadn't called her from the ER. He hadn't called her when he'd gotten back to Autre—having driven himself *after* ending up in a ditch and then having to rent a fucking car because his truck had been totaled. He hadn't called her for over twenty-four hours. He'd been consumed with the problems at the B and B, which she understood. But he'd also gone home after dealing with all of that and gone to sleep with *broken ribs* before calling her.

So now she was keeping one of the biggest secrets from him of all—that she was still in love with him.

"I guess I've realized that I kind of like being your hero," he finally said in answer to why he wasn't telling her she was being ridiculous.

That made her heart flutter in her chest.

"You're good at it," she said simply as he punched three more holes in the top of the jar he held.

He didn't respond to that.

Instead, he set the jars down. Then headed down the steps.

She heard the door rattle.

As if he was suddenly in desperate need of getting out of the attic.

Yeah, same.

"Dammit," she heard him mutter.

He stomped back up the steps. "Why the hell is the door locked?"

"I have no idea." She'd *told* him it was locked.

"It locks from the outside."

He'd mentioned that.

"You're saying someone locked it?"

He ground his back teeth together. "Yes."

This seemed very obvious to her, but she wasn't sure if he'd had the same realization she'd had yet.

She'd realized what was going on about three months ago.

"So...someone locked that door," she said, slowly. "On purpose."

He shoved a hand through his hair. "Yeah."

"Knowing we're up here."

"Well..." Then he muttered a "fuck" under his breath, and said, "Yeah."

She pressed her lips together. His frustration was palpable. But he'd come up here, knowing she was up here. He wasn't opposed to being with her. Even alone. In a small space.

But he was definitely suddenly restless.

She decided to just put it out there. "You know your mom did this, right?"

He finally made eye contact.

"You think so?"

"You don't?"

He sighed again. "I'm afraid so."

Becca looked around and noticed three wooden chairs that looked like they'd once been a part of a kitchen set.

"Yes, I think you can sit on one of those safely."

She glanced back at him. "How did you know that's what I was thinking?"

"I know you."

Those three words made her stomach swoop, but she tamped the swoony feelings down. The way she'd been doing with all of her feelings about Beau for the past three months.

She'd been able to *kiss him* during the community production of *Barefoot in the Park* and hadn't blurted out her feelings. She could resist the urge to throw herself into his arms because he could read her so easily. That was friendship, not romance. He knew her well. So what?

She crossed to the chair. She inspected it carefully but didn't see any cobwebs or signs of any Remy relatives. She pulled the chair across the floor until it was in the middle of the attic space, away from the walls and other furniture and boxes where creepy-crawlies might be hiding. From here, she'd be able to see attacks coming from any direction.

She sat down, crossed her legs, propped her elbow on her knee, her chin on her hand, and regarded her best friend. "You realize your mother is a part of the group of people who've been matchmaking us for the past three months, don't you?"

"At least up until now, they've been subtle."

So he did know. "Yeah, well, subtle for Autre anyway," she agreed. "I mean, our moms have been throwing us together ever since we broke up."

Every time she'd come home from college to visit, something in her mother's house had magically broken or needed to be replaced. Beau had been over to fix the garbage disposal three times that she could think of. He'd replaced a ceiling fan in the middle of February. Sure, it never actually got *cold* here, but people didn't need ceiling fans in February, even in southern Louisiana. He'd not only had to re-shingle their garage over her spring break—not that she'd minded because that had required a lot of shirtless time and muscle bunching —but her mom had even called him over to fix their blender.

Their blender.

A twenty-dollar appliance that Maureen could have easily just replaced.

Becca was also aware that her father was in on all of this. Sure, he was a high school principal, not the guy to be found under the hood of a car or with a tool belt around his waist very often, but he could have put that ceiling fan in. And he would've happily gone to the store for a new blender.

"I'll be honest, I didn't catch on for sure until they cast us in the play," Beau told her. He sat down on the top step and leaned against the wall behind him.

He was far braver than her. One thing she knew about spiders, was they hid well and were sneaky bastards. There were probably two plotting Beau's demise from behind and above at that very moment.

"Yeah, that was definitely less than subtle," she agreed about the casting decision.

Of course, their mothers had been co-directors of the show and in charge of all casting. Their plan was so obvious in retrospect, Becca was actually embarrassed she and Beau hadn't realized it right away.

The town had decided to put on a community play for the first time in at least five years. They'd chosen *Barefoot in the Park*, a romantic comedy with a small cast that told the story of a newlywed couple in New York City. The husband, played in the 1967 movie by Robert Redford, was an uptight grump, while the new bride, portrayed by Jane Fonda, was a perky sunshine.

There were a few other characters, but the majority of the show involved just those two together.

And lots of kissing.

But the biggest clue that the town was actually using the play to throw Beau and Becca together was that neither Beau nor Becca were actually any good at acting. Oh, and neither of them had auditioned.

Their mothers had begged and pleaded with their children to take the parts when, strangely, no one else auditioned for the roles either.

Becca had been *certain* there was no way in hell Beau would say yes, so she'd agreed if they could get Beau to take the part of Paul.

Apparently, Beau had told his mother something similar.

Maureen and Heather, knowing their children very well, had also decided that all proceeds from the play would go to charity. A children's literacy charity. Something near and dear to both Beau and Becca's hearts.

Basically, they'd been completely manipulated by the two people who knew them best, and who had a common goal in mind.

But neither of them had backed out.

Rehearsals had often been just Beau and Becca. Even their mothers didn't show up much of the time.

Becca had seen the movie as soon as her mom mentioned directing the play. She'd read the script after Maureen had asked her to audition. And when she'd found out Beau had agreed as well she'd been...intrigued. Okay, excited. Okay, actually *really* into it.

So, yeah, they'd played the parts—not terribly, but not to any acclaim—and the entire town had turned out.

The town had also donated four thousand dollars to the charity, and Becca had gotten to kiss Beau a lot.

In general, it had turned out pretty well, in her opinion.

"I guess since the play didn't result in us falling madly in love and getting back together, they've decided to get more direct," Becca told him, inclining her head toward the locked door.

He nodded, his lips set in a grim line. "Obviously."

"And now that there's a trophy, of course they're going to try even harder."

Beau frowned. "Now that there's a *what?*"

"Apparently, there's a trophy now."

"You've got to be kidding." He swore. "Of course, you're not kidding. That's exactly something they would do."

She laughed lightly. "I guess Leo and Ellie came up with it," she said of the heads of the Landry family who were also owners of the bar in town. "It's a golden alligator standing on its back legs. It's got big lips pursed like it's ready for a kiss and a sash across its body that says '"Master Matchmaker'"."

Beau groaned and dragged a hand over his face. "Holy shit."

"Well, you didn't think they'd settle for a plain old gold cup or something, did you?"

Their hometown was nuts. Delightful, and mostly well-meaning, and a lot of fun. But nuts.

Beau looked at her. "So it's not just our moms playing matchmaker and everyone else watching? If there's a trophy, that means more people are in on it."

She nodded. "Oh, for sure." She also couldn't *quite* bring herself to be upset. She wasn't sure if she would have gotten a chance to spend so much time with Beau if they hadn't been rehearsing for the play together. And she *was* sure she would not have kissed him so much. Or at all.

Beau ran a hand through his hair. "This is..." He sighed. "Typical."

He wasn't wrong.

"The way I understand it, the trophy and bragging rights

107

go to whoever comes up with the plan that finally gets us back together," Becca said. "But it was the school secretary talking about it around a corner with the P.E. teacher, so I might have missed some key bullet points."

Beau shook his head. "Doesn't matter. It means there's a competition now. Everyone is going to think this is hilarious and even more fun. And it'll be coming at us from multiple directions, not just our moms." After a beat, he said, "Now I want to see this trophy."

"It's probably big, don't you think?" she asked.

"Autre wouldn't do anything that wasn't over-the-top," he agreed.

She wouldn't be surprised if the thing stood two or three feet tall, in fact. And whoever won it would carry it around proudly for at least a month after. And would bring it to their wedding...

She shut *that* down immediately. There wasn't going to be any wedding.

"So I guess that just leaves the question of what are we gonna do about it?" she asked.

"The door?"

"Their scheme."

He met her gaze and held it for a long moment. Finally, he asked, "What do you want to do about it?"

That was a loaded question. There were things she wanted to do about it. Her knee-jerk reaction was: Get back together. Get married. *Thank* whoever won the trophy by naming their first child after him or her.

"I'm not sure," she admitted. "I feel like it won't do any good to *tell* them to stop or to push back. They'll think they know best. And refusing to be in the same place or spend time together seems..." She sighed. "Sad. I don't want that."

He was quiet for several long seconds. Finally, he said, "I think we play along."

She lifted both brows. "Play along?"

He shrugged. "You're right that they're not going to stop if we just *tell* them to. We have to *show* them that when we say we're just friends, we *mean* it."

"How do we do that?"

"We just let them do their thing, but we keep doing *our* thing too."

Her stomach flipped in spite of knowing that he didn't mean that to sound dirty or send her thoughts spinning back to all the things they'd done when they'd dated. The things that were *their things* in her mind. The things she'd never done before or since with anyone else. The things she couldn't imagine doing with anyone else...

"What's *our* thing?" she asked, hoping her voice didn't sound funny.

"Being friends." He gestured to the attic. "For instance, we stay locked in up here together until they decide to let us out. Then we go about our business as usual, proving nothing changed."

She watched him, trying not to let on that her heart was squeezing hard in her chest.

"We let them put their plans in motion," he went on, clearly thinking out loud. "We don't protest or argue. We pretend to not even really notice. They throw us together as much as they want. We do the plays. We hang out in the attic. We do...whatever. But things between us stay the same. Over time they'll get bored, or they'll finally realize that it's not going to happen." He shrugged. "But we can't fight with them or push back. If we protest, they'll read into it."

She swallowed hard. He seemed to think it would be no big deal to spend a bunch of time alone together and then just go on like usual. While she was very afraid this crazy plan of throwing them together to make them realize they had bigger feelings was going to work quite well on her.

"So whatever crazy plans they come up with—and you know they will—we just play along. And eventually, after all of their ideas fail, they'll give up," she summarized.

"Yeah. It will be a giant game of chicken," he said with a small grin.

She thought about that. And could admit that his grin was part of what made her more inclined to go along with this. She loved seeing him smile.

It was a Beau smile, so it was more of a half-smile, but it still made her heart trip.

He wasn't a smiley guy. He had a very dry sense of humor, and was sarcastic more than outright funny, but she could get him smiling and even laughing. There was a soft side to him that she saw that no one else did. That always made her feel really special.

Kind of like his dirty side.

She knew that people wouldn't be shocked by that side, though. Her friend Savannah had mentioned more than once that she bet Beau was dominant and growly in the bedroom.

She'd been right about that. But he'd also been sweet. In a growly way. But he'd absolutely made sure that Becca had as much fun, if not more than he did. He was very attentive. And demanding. But only in the ways that brought the most pleasure.

They might've only had actual sex that one night, but he got to know her body very well. He taught her things about her body that she hadn't even known.

Again, Becca had to distract herself from those thoughts.

Okay, this plan *could* be some fun. Who knew what the town would come up with? And hanging out with Beau was...

well, it was hard on her libido and heart in some ways, but she would rather fight the urge to beg him to kiss her—or worse, fall in love with her again—than to *not* spend time with him. He'd been avoiding her since right after she'd moved back to Autre. It had been obvious. So, would she take some help from her hometown in getting his cute butt in her personal space, even if it was only platonically? Yes.

"Even better," she said, leaning in with a conspiratorial smile. "Whenever they suggest we do something together, we *happily* agree. I mean, that will just emphasize that we are *friends*. If we seem reluctant, they might take that as a sign that we're *not* friends. You know people wondered about our break-up. They might think we're bitter toward one another. Or...that we're fighting bigger feelings."

That was as close as she was willing to get to asking if he was fighting anything bigger than feelings of friendship for her. Because he had definitely tried to avoid spending time alone with her.

He simply nodded. Which didn't really tell her anything.

"Okay, I'm in," he said, nodding again. "It's the only way to actually get the point across to them. They'll want to go through with their crazy plans no matter what."

She laughed. "I'm sure. I'm envisioning them meeting down at Ellie's, or even just right downstairs, and coming up with this stuff and assigning roles. Our moms have put a lot of effort in, what with directing the play and all. Everyone will be so disappointed if they come up with some fun plans and don't get to even *try* them. They'll always be convinced that if they'd just tried *their* plan, everything would have worked out."

He shook his head. "They're all nuts."

"But they're *our* nuts," she said affectionately.

He met her gaze and she saw a mix of emotions there. Most

she couldn't name. He almost seemed sad. Which made no sense.

She took a breath. "So how long do you think they're going to leave us locked up here?" she asked.

"That is a very good question," he answered. He had a thoughtful look on his face. "You know, as long as we're playing along with all of their crazy plans, I think we should punish them a little."

"Punish them?" Becca asked. "What does that mean?"

"Give them reason to think that things are going well with their plan. Before we crush their hopes."

Her eyes widened. *Crush their hopes* sounded kind of intense, but she liked the idea of having a secret project together. She wanted to re-establish *some* kind of relationship. She wanted to feel close to him again. Partners in crime could work if they weren't going to be hot, up-all-night lovers.

"What do you have in mind?"

"What are you supposed to be doing after this?" he asked.

"I was going to help your mom set up downstairs. Then I was going to stop by my mom's."

"Awesome. I'm sure they're waiting for us to text or call them asking why the hell the door is locked, and for someone to come help us."

Becca nodded.

"Instead, text your mom that you're going to be a little late. Tell her something came up. She obviously knows that we're locked in up here."

Becca felt her smile widen. "Very nice. She'll be wondering why I'm not freaking out."

"Exactly. We'll make them think we're happy about this."

He pulled his phone out and started typing.

"Who are you texting?" she asked.

"My mom. I'm going to tell her that we're gonna be up here for a little bit and not to worry."

"You're going to pretend that you don't know that she locked us in?"

"I'm going to pretend I didn't even try to get out."

Becca felt her stomach swoop again. She was imagining the look in his eyes. She had to be. That hot, flirty look was probably just excitement about this fun little game they were going to play with their entire hometown.

She texted her mom at the same time Beau sent his message.

Then he stretched to his feet. He crossed the attic to the far end where she had *not* explored. It was way too dark, and she was sure that Remy had a number of relatives shacked up over in that corner.

When he emerged from the shadows, he was carrying an old cassette player and had three cassettes in his other hand.

"Oh my gosh," Becca laughed, getting to her feet.

"My mom's. She has a huge collection of tapes back there. My dad at least upgraded to CDs."

He set the cassette player on the chair where Becca had been sitting. He stretched the cord over to an outlet and plugged it in. Then he popped one of the tapes in and pressed play. An old 80s love song came from the speakers. Becca couldn't have named it, but she'd heard it on the radio with her parents.

"Let's dance," Beau said.

Her eyes widened. "What?"

"Let's give them some noise on the ceiling to wonder about. Plus, what else are we going to do?" He held out his arms and wiggled his fingers in a *come here* gesture. "They'll sneak up here to try to figure out what we're doing. They'll hear romantic music. But they'll also unlock that door. There won't be a reason to keep it locked, and then Mom won't worry about me being pissed about it being locked later."

All of those points made total sense to her. Or at least to her heart—and body—that really wanted to dance with him.

He had come up to go to one dance with her at LSU. She'd known at the time that it was ridiculous. She'd been in college, going to parties, ballgames, worrying about her exams, while he was back in Autre building a business, helping his mom run hers, and hanging out with other people who were grown adults, with bills, responsibilities, and real jobs.

Still, he'd humored her. He'd sat through a couple of basketball games, had gone to a few parties, and that one dance. But it felt weird. He hadn't fit in. He'd done it for her, but she knew he'd been internally rolling his eyes.

Now, though, when she stepped into his arms, and he put one big hand on her lower back while tucking her head under his chin, it felt really good.

He didn't keep any space between them, he pulled her against his body as if it was completely natural and very familiar.

Which it was. They'd been up against each other countless times during those three months. It was a fraction of the time they'd known one another and been friends, but it was deeply imprinted on her. She melted into him, and they started moving to the music, and she let out a big, contented sigh.

He chuckled, the deep sound rumbling under her ear, "You like this song?"

"I wasn't even paying attention to the song."

For just a second, she wondered again if she'd said the wrong thing.

She shouldn't keep hinting at, or admitting, that her feelings were more than friendship.

But he didn't say anything, and his arms tightened around her slightly.

They swayed to that song. Then another. Then another. She didn't know what band this was or what album it was, but she appreciated so many slow songs in a row.

By the time Beau's phone dinged with a message, and he stepped back from her, Becca realized she was far too comfortable in this man's arms for them to be friends only. This might be a problem.

Still watching her, he pulled his phone from his back pocket, glancing down.

He chuckled. "My mom is wondering if we're coming down to dinner."

Becca shook her head. "So, she locked us in up here and is now wondering what's taking so long?"

"Well, we have been up here for an hour without protest, and when they came up to listen at the door—which you know damned well they did—they wouldn't have heard anything to give them a clue as to what's going on. Their curiosity is finally getting the better of them." He grinned. "Of course, if I tell her no, that we're staying up here a while longer, she'll be thrilled."

Becca's eyes widened. "We've been locked up here for an *hour*?"

He nodded. "I don't know when they locked the door, but we've been up here for an hour."

It had really felt like just a few songs. So, she had just been pressed up against Beau Hebert, swaying to love songs for an hour without realizing it?

Yeah, convincing everyone once they were done being locked in together that everything was just fine and they were friends only, was maybe going to be more difficult than she'd expected.

"So, are we going down to dinner?" she asked.

"I think we should definitely get dinner. Together. But I think we should go to Ellie's. No doubt, my mother has already told several people about this whole attic thing. If we walk out of here, grinning as if nothing unusual is going on, and then head down to Ellie's for burgers, it will really make everybody wonder."

She liked that idea. Not only because it would torture all of these people who thought they knew so much, but because it would be easier to hang out with him in public, rather than sitting around his mother's dining room table with his mom, her best friend, and maybe even Becca's mom watching every single move, gesture, and expression for signs of romance.

"And we need to get something with onions, and something with garlic," she said, grinning. "Really make them wonder how this night will end."

He chuckled. "I think this game of ours is going to be fun."

Fun. That was probably one word.

Torturous might be another.

five

BEAU WATCHED as Becca stopped at the table just inside the door to Ellie's to give Toby and his fiancé, Sam, each a hug. They were at a table with two other teachers. Beau had said hi to them all on his way in as well, but he and Becca had decided to arrive separately and a few minutes apart. Unlike two people on a date. More like two friends grabbing a casual dinner together.

She'd also stopped at home to change clothes and dress down. Thank God. She was now in a simple t-shirt and denim shorts instead of the dress she'd been wearing earlier. Not that she didn't look amazing in the shorts as well, but her dresses... well, those reminded him of when she'd been his. She knew he loved her in a skirt and she'd always worn a dress or skirt for him when they'd been together.

He smiled at her as she crossed to the table where he was already seated but didn't greet her with too much enthusiasm. He didn't pull out her chair. And he hadn't waited for her to order his own beer and an order of onion rings for them to share.

"Everyone's watching us," she said, taking her seat across from him.

"Of course they are." He picked up his beer and took a long swallow. "You ready for the show?"

She slung her purse strap over the back of her chair and studied him. "It's not a show though, right? It's us. The real us. The show was pretending to not be annoyed being locked in the attic together."

Right. He'd been annoyed by that.

Except he hadn't been. Not even a little. He'd been worried about it when he'd first discovered the door wasn't budging. Because he knew that there was only a fifty-fifty chance that Becca was leaving that attic unkissed. But he hadn't been annoyed.

The dancing had been good, though. Tempting, difficult to rein in his feelings, and very hard to ignore how much he'd missed having her in his arms, but good. Nice. And she *had* gone unkissed. He was proud of that. He'd been able to remember that all of the reasons not to kiss her were still valid.

If he thought she was staying forever, it would be a different situation.

"Have you decided what you want?"

Beau looked up at Ellie, the owner of the bar. "Hey, Ellie. Um, yeah, I was thinkin' a burger with garlic sauce." He glanced at Becca. "But are you ready?"

Becca picked up a menu and scanned it. "That sounds good."

Ellie propped a hand on her hip. "I'm not asking about food."

Beau blinked up at her. "You're not?"

"'Course not." She waved her hand. "You always get a burger. It's already bein' prepped. No garlic sauce though."

"What if I want garlic sauce?" Beau asked.

"I don't have garlic sauce."

"You do. I've had it."

Her eyes narrowed. "I don't have garlic sauce tonight."

"You sure? Maybe I should check with Cora," he said of Ellie's best friend and the main cook.

"Cora's not giving you garlic sauce either," Ellie said. "Get over it. And give me the intel I'm over here for."

Beau rolled his eyes. "What about Becca?"

"She's getting the shrimp and grits. That's her favorite."

Beau looked at Becca. She shrugged. "I do really like the shrimp and grits"

"We don't even get to place orders here?" Beau asked Ellie. "Isn't that how restaurants work?"

"I don't really care how 'restaurants work'," Ellie informed him. "This is *my* place, and when you're here, it's like you walked in the front door of my house and you get what I've got on the stove."

Beau knew that. Ellie's bar and "restaurant" was essentially an extension of her home, and she'd opened it more so she'd have room for her big and expanding family than because she wanted to run a restaurant. Now she had the ability to feed all the people she loved according to their various crazy schedules.

However, she also happened to serve lots of people who lived in Autre, and handfuls of tourists who happened in after they got off the swamp boat tours her grandsons conducted from the docks across the street or when they left the animal park that more of her grandkids ran just to the south of the docks.

"What about those people?" Beau asked, nodding toward a table of tourists. "Did they get to choose what they wanted?"

"Sure. I don't know them," she said.

"That matters?"

"Of course. Food is one of my love languages. I want you to leave here feeling loved, so I want you to have what you like best. Them? I don't care if they order something that's not quite right."

Beau liked that answer. But he narrowed his eyes. "Isn't all of your food wonderful?"

"Absolutely. But certain things are just right for certain people." She leaned in. "And garlic sauce is *not* just right for you tonight."

He leaned in too, fighting a smile. "Why not?"

"Because I also love Becca."

He chuckled and glanced across the table. Becca was watching them with amusement and affection.

"Becca doesn't care if I eat garlic tonight, El."

Ellie sighed and leaned back. "Well, dammit."

Beau and Becca shared a grin.

"So you *haven't* decided what you want," Ellie said.

Actually, Beau knew exactly what he wanted. It just wasn't on the "menu".

"Don't know what you're talkin' about," he told the older woman.

She nodded. "Okay. Good. I was thinkin' you were goin' to take all the fun out of this."

"What do you mean?" Beau asked.

"Well, that trophy is really pretty. And I haven't even gotten to play yet." She gave them a wink, then turned and headed toward the bar.

Oh...crap.

Ellie Landry was even getting in on this "competition" to throw him and Becca together? The Landry family did two things big and loud and better than pretty much everyone else: bullshitting and falling in love.

"Okay, so..." he said, turning back to Becca.

Becca leaned in, elbows on the table. "Why do I feel like our plan just backfired?"

Beau shook his head. "No one's getting kissed in here, and there are no rings on anybody's fingers. Nothing's backfired."

She nodded. "Right. That's the ultimate win," she said. "For us to officially be back together there will have to be some kind of public gesture or acknowledgment."

He nodded. "Grand gestures are the thing around here. It won't count until that happens."

She nodded. She seemed thoughtful.

"What?"

"I guess it just hit me, they actually expect us to end up together. Like married. Together forever."

He watched her for a long moment, not trusting himself to speak. That made his entire chest feel tight. He wanted it. And the fact that the rest of the town wanted it too did not make that any easier.

Beau cleared his throat. "Yeah. I mean, I guess if I just laid a kiss on you in the middle of the bar like I did the first time, they'd probably try to count that." They'd gone to Baton Rouge for New Year's Eve as their first official "date", but they'd been in Autre the following weekend, and he'd kissed her right in the middle of Ellie's. That's when everyone here had known they were officially a couple. "But yeah," he said, "I think they're all hoping for a diamond ring."

She nodded. "Whoa."

He gave a little laugh, that was completely unamused. "Don't worry, Bec, I'm not going to propose."

She frowned. "I wouldn't say I'm *worried*."

He swallowed. He had to say this. If they were going to be continually thrown together with the whole town hoping it would turn romantic, they needed to have a few things out in the open.

"I would never do that to you," he said.

She frowned. "Do what to me?"

"Make you say no to me. To that."

She stared at him. "I..." She took a deep breath, then blew it out. "You're so sure I'd say no?"

Surprise and heat rocked through him, but he clung to reality. And the fact that he cared about her way too fucking much to mess around with this. "You'd *better* say no to me. If I get drunk some night, and that comes out of my mouth accidentally, you better say no."

She leaned in. "You better not say that to me and not mean it, Beau. Because *I'll* mean whatever I answer, and you can't take it back."

He leaned in further. "Becca, you better—" He sucked a deep breath in through his nose, clamped his teeth together, and sat back. "Jesus." He scrubbed a hand over his face. "We're actually arguing about this? Neither of us is going to be talking about that or saying any of that anyway, so this is a stupid conversation."

"It's *stupid?*" she repeated, looking angry. "The idea of all of that is *stupid?*"

"Look," he said firmly. "We tried the more-than-friends thing, right?"

"Yes, and it was awesome."

"The *sex* was awesome," he said, lowering his voice, but making sure she saw how serious he was. "Yes. It was. And I don't regret any of that. I wanted to be your first and I'm damned glad I was. I wanted to be sure you knew what you wanted and how to ask for it and *demand* it. But we got all of that checked off."

That was an asshole thing to say. It wasn't *entirely* untrue. That had been a definite priority for him, but that had not been the entire reason he'd been with her. He hadn't believed they would last, but he'd selfishly wanted *some* time with her. Still, he was okay with her believing it had just been about sex. Her not liking him all that much would make them getting thrown together repeatedly by their hometown and families a lot easier.

But she was studying him intently and Beau realized that he'd forgotten something very important.

She knew him.

He'd been open and vulnerable and loving and all in with her. For three months, but still... she'd gotten a look at his soul.

"Okay," she said, sitting back. "Fine. No diamond rings tonight."

Had she emphasized "tonight"? Surely not.

"I'm not tying you down," he said. "Because that's exactly what it would be. I'm not leaving Autre. This is it for me. I know what my future looks like. It's not fair for me to ask you to make my future yours."

"But...I'm home. This has always been my plan."

"You don't know that. You're just getting started," he argued. "You can go anywhere. Teaching opens up a lot of doors for you. You're not stuck here."

She studied him. "Is that how you feel? Stuck?"

Yes. No. Not really. He just...wondered sometimes. If he'd missed something. If he was doing what he was supposed to be doing. He loved his life. He loved this town, the people here, being here for his mom and his family. But he *was* stuck in the sense that he couldn't leave. "I'm just lucky I don't want to be anywhere else."

"Maybe I don't either."

She was so damned stubborn. "Fine," he finally said. "If you're still here, and happy, and want to stay in ten years, we'll go on a date."

Her eyes widened. "Ten years? That's how long you think it will take for me to figure out what I want?"

He shrugged. "That's how long it will take to convince *me* that you're sure you want to be *here*."

She sighed. "You can be such an asshole sometimes."

He couldn't help but smile at that. "Glad to see some things are getting back to normal between us."

She actually cracked a small smile.

"I honestly didn't think it was possible for you to be a bigger bitch than you were in high school, but you've done it!"

Beau and Becca both turned at that. They weren't the only ones. Everyone had turned toward the commotion.

Which was coming from Toby and Sam's table.

"Oh, great," Becca muttered.

Emmaline Morris was standing next to the table of teachers. And Landon Gilroy, the high school math teacher—and once a classmate of Emmaline's—was the one who had delivered the remark.

Emmaline crossed her arms. "You can blame me all you want, but it's not like I'm the only person in favor of it. And I'm not even on the board."

"No, but your husband is and all your behind-the-scenes campaigning did this," Landon said, glaring at her. "The worst part is you won't even *try* to understand the other side."

Emmaline rolled her eyes dramatically. "You're acting like it's coming out of your salary."

"Believe it or not," Toby interjected. "We care about more than that."

Emmaline looked at him. "You're not even from here. You don't understand how important the field is."

Toby nodded. "You're right on both counts. I do *not* understand how that field can be *that* important."

"Do you know what that's about?" Beau whispered to Becca.

She sighed and leaned closer. "Remember how the football field got all torn up in the tropical storm in July?"

"Yeah."

"And how they miraculously raised a bunch of money to repair—and *upgrade* it, and the bleachers and the scoreboard —really quickly so it would be ready to go in time for the season?"

"Sure." Of course he did. Autre was a very small town. The high school football field getting torn up so close to football season was a big deal. Even if Autre hadn't been predicted to have a huge season this year. Led by none other than Emmaline's youngest brother, Mason, the Senior star quarterback. This was Louisiana...football was always a big deal here.

"Well, they used Mr. Shadwick's money."

Beau lifted a brow. Mr. Shadwick had been the long-time music and band teacher in Autre. He'd died three years ago and in his will he'd left a large chunk of money to the school. "I thought that money was supposed to be for music, and band, and the arts programs."

Becca nodded. "Exactly. But it was never *legally* stipulated. I guess Mr. Shadwick let his family know his wishes and trusted that the school would honor them. So Emmaline, and a few of her friends, pressured the school board, and they voted to dip into that fund for the field when the school budget didn't have enough and their fundraising efforts came up short. None of the teachers knew until earlier this week. The school is putting on the musical *The Music Man* and planned to involve the band and the music program, and, as always, have the shop class and art kids help make the sets. But they needed more supplies."

"And there's no money left?" Beau guessed.

"The way the fund is set up, there's a limit to how much they can take out each year so that the bulk of it remains invested and earning," Becca said. "They took out the max amount."

Beau blew out a breath. "Wow, that sucks."

Becca nodded, frowning. "It does. The fact that money from the arts programs went to a sports program instead. But also that the board and the administration kind of did it behind everyone's backs."

"Is there a process where they have to tell you all?" Beau asked.

She shrugged. "No. Not really. The superintendent makes up the budget. The board approves it. Parents and teachers can definitely weigh in, but it's all pretty boring and I guess most of us assume that they know better than we do and will do the right thing for *all* the kids and the school as a whole and that they won't give preferential treatment to one group or program."

She was chewing on her bottom lip and Beau wanted to reach over and smooth it with his thumb. He wanted to hug her. He wanted to say something that would make her feel better.

All of that was a very typical reaction to seeing Becca upset about something.

He'd always wanted to make things better for her. Even before he'd been into hugging and kissing her, even before he'd known constructive ways to make things better, he'd hated when she'd been upset.

Beau opened his mouth, not completely sure what to say—and aware that in the past when he'd tried to make things better for her his words hadn't always come out perfectly—but Toby swept up to their table just then.

"Wow, *she* is a piece of work." He was clearly annoyed. He

slapped his hand down on their tabletop, then leaned in, focusing on Becca. "Have you talked to your dad?"

Beau felt trepidation crawl up his spine. He watched Becca's face.

She swallowed hard and shook her head. "I haven't."

It seemed this wasn't the first time they'd discussed her talking to her dad about this.

"You need to, Bec," Toby said. "This is bullshit."

"It's not like they can *undo* the field now," she said. "The money is spent. I'm not sure what he can do."

"He needs to know we're upset."

"He knows," she said. "We all walked into his office and *told* him we were upset. Just before we walked into Mr. Clark's office and told *him*."

"He didn't listen," Toby argued. "You can make him understand."

Beau felt his gut tightening. Toby was asking Becca to further the discussion. With her *dad*. Not just as a teacher, but as his daughter. At home. And it was a discussion they'd clearly already had. That was a tough spot to put her in.

Becca sighed. "He's a smart man, Toby. He understands."

"If he did, he wouldn't have let it happen."

"He can't override the school board."

Toby just stared at her for a long moment. "You're defending him?"

Becca frowned and sat up straighter. "I'm not defending him. I'm just saying that there's nothing he can do at this point."

"So you won't even try to talk to him? To be our voice?" Toby asked.

"I didn't say that!" Becca protested. "It's just complicated."

"You're in a unique position," Toby said, softening his tone slightly. "He has to listen to you. He'll care more if it comes from someone he *loves*."

Beau saw Becca grimace slightly at that and his chest tightened. It wasn't that Becca thought her dad didn't love her. Of course he did. But he'd always been tough on her. Strict. With high standards. And he wouldn't play favorites. Her talking to him might not make a difference.

"You're his daughter and a teacher at this school. The decisions he helps make affect you directly now," Toby said. "That has to matter to him. It will make him think about things differently. That's powerful. You have to use that."

Scowling, Beau shifted forward. "Okay, enough." He lifted Toby's hand off the table, causing the other man to straighten and step back. "You've made your point."

Toby frowned. "I'm just saying."

"Yeah. You did. Now stop," Beau told him.

"This is a big deal," Toby informed him.

"I get it."

"And I'm sure you agree that the football field is of the utmost importance, but there are twenty kids on the football team. The arts programs includes actual art classes, band, choir, drama, dance. And our art classes include everything from painting to photography to graphic design. And yes, we're '"just"' elementary teachers and this is a '"high school problem'," Toby continued, using air quotes. "But our kids will be those high school kids one day. I want my second graders to *have* an art program. I want to know that Alexa will be able to sing and dance on a stage with her parents in the audience applauding just as loudly as they do for the football team. I want to know that Mason will be able to play a saxophone like his favorite jazz musicians, even if he also puts on a football uniform. I think we should *all* care about the *whole* school!"

Beau and Becca weren't the only ones staring at Toby after

that impressive rant. Several tables nearby had also stopped eating and had heard every word.

Beau watched Toby for several seconds before asking, "Can I go now?"

Toby drew in a deep breath. "Okay."

"Okay, so I did play football and was damned good and had a hell of a good time. But because of Mr. Taggart, our shop teacher, I learned to use tools and realized I love woodworking and became an *artist* who has made that into a business right here, about five blocks from that football field. So I'm *on your side*," he told Toby.

Toby opened his mouth.

"And I did just *star* in the community theater's summer production of *Barefoot in the Park*, if you remember."

Of course he remembered. Toby had played the eccentric upstairs neighbor and had delighted in giving Beau and Becca director's notes after every "rehearsal".

Toby closed his mouth.

Then Beau looked at Becca. "Bec is fully on your side too, of course." He looked back at Toby. "But you need to back off of her. I'm not gonna have you making her uncomfortable and butting into things with her and her dad."

Toby crossed his arms and looked at Becca.

She just sat staring at Beau.

"I'm sorry, Bec."

She focused on Toby. "It's okay. I understand why everyone wants me to talk to him."

"It's just that—"

Beau cleared his throat.

Toby sighed. "I know you get it," he said to Becca. "I'm sorry."

"Thanks," Becca replied.

Toby looked back and forth between Beau and Becca, then asked her, "You okay?"

She looked at Beau. He didn't say anything. But she nodded after a second. "Yeah. I'm good."

"Okay. Then...I'll leave you guys to...this." It was as if something had just occurred to Toby. He started backing away. "Sorry to interrupt. You two go back to...whatever."

Beau sighed as Toby turned and headed back for his table with Sam and Landon.

"Of course, Toby and Sam know all about the trophy and matchmaking competition, right?" he asked Becca.

She finally smiled. "I don't know how they could miss it."

"Well, I'll take consolation in the fact that he's probably going to get scolded by someone for interrupting our 'date' that way," Beau said.

Becca laughed and the tightness in Beau's chest eased a little. "You're probably right."

Beau took a breath. He wanted to let this all go, but he couldn't just yet. "They're all expecting you to talk your dad into...what? Funding the art program somehow?"

As expected, her smile faded. "I'm not sure exactly. Dad was...less than receptive to all of us crowding into his office after we found out about the money. He really only listened for about five minutes before telling us we had to leave and could schedule meetings with him or come to the next board meeting. But he also commented about how the elementary teachers needed to take their issues up with *their* principal. Which is ridiculous, of course, since it's not an elementary school issue, but...I guess that was kind of his point."

"That you shouldn't all have an opinion about this?" Beau asked with a frown. "That's kind of bullshit though."

"I know." She sighed. "So they said, "well, you can talk to him about it at home." I guess that's what they want me to relay? That we all care about everything having to do with making Autre's school great for all the kids. He should *like* that."

She was frowning and Beau finally gave into the urge he'd been fighting and reached out and took her hand on top of the table, giving her fingers a squeeze.

She squeezed back.

"You know he won't listen to me," she said softly.

"You don't know that. You're a teacher in the school now. Your input matters."

"He can't play favorites." She lifted a shoulder. "You know how he is. He was always *harder* on me. I got detention twice in high school. Just twice. You know what a good kid I was."

Beau laughed. Calling Becca Bollier a "good kid" was an understatement. "Yeah."

"Both of those detentions were *from* my dad. One was because he caught me in the hallway without a pass. That was something that he'd let a dozen other kids get by with just a warning. But, with me, because it was school policy, he had to write me up. He said he could never let me get by with something, or people would scream favoritism. You remember Mrs. Johnson, the science teacher?"

Beau nodded.

"She was so hard on me. It was like she would always push just to see if Dad would ever come to my defense."

"And he never did?"

"Never. Even when she was blatantly unfair. My mom went to those parent-teacher conferences. Dad would never intervene."

"And you think this is the same? He's purposefully not going to take your opinion into consideration because he feels like it would be showing favoritism?"

She shrugged. "I mean, he can't help but hear me. We sit at the same dinner table every damn night."

"But you don't want to bring it up at dinner?"

"I want to be professional. I want to be his *colleague* in education. I don't want to rant and rave about how things are unfair and give long monologues about how important the arts are and how the number of kids who are going to go to college to play sports is tiny but the number of kids who can find a passion for writing or design or music or drama and use that talent in future professional endeavors is huge..." She stopped and pulled in a breath. "He *knows* that. I know he does. I've heard him and my mom talk about those very things at that very dinner table. I'm torn between wanting my dad to see me as a professional who respects him and a true advocate for what I do and believe as an educator."

And *this* was the kind of crap that Beau had been worried about when Becca had chosen to come home to teach. It sounded so easy, but having a history, baked-in assumptions, established patterns, could complicate things.

A fresh start would have been better for her.

"We'll figure it out," he told her.

"*We* will?" she asked, a smile tugging at the corner of her lip.

But he shrugged. Something was bothering Becca. Of course, he was going to get involved with fixing it. Somehow. "Yeah."

Emotion flickered in her eyes.

Thankfully, Ellie arrived with their food and they shifted to lighter topics, one of which was how interested the entire bar still seemed in their dinner together.

"So, we haven't convinced anyone totally yet," Becca said as they paid separately for their dinners and walked to the front door.

The whole place had seen them together and made their assessments, so Beau opened the door for her and ushered her through with a hand on her lower back.

They stood outside on the front walk.

"I didn't think it would be that easy. We can probably expect some additional matchmaking shenanigans."

"Hanging out with you has been fun," he told her, wanting to soften the things he'd said earlier. He couldn't—wouldn't—date her for real. But he couldn't deny that the idea of being "forced" to spend time with her because of the town's crazy matchmaking plan was appealing. "I can't say that I'm upset about the idea of doing it some more."

She smiled up at him. "Same. And since we're reverting back to our old friendship where we could say anything and be completely honest and blunt with one another..."

He lifted a brow. "Yeah?"

"You need a new hoodie. That thing has so many holes in it it's pathetic."

"It was supposed to convince people we weren't on a date," he said with a chuckle.

"Well, it's probably convincing people that you don't have enough money to buy yourself a new hoodie. That isn't a good look for your business."

He nodded. "Fine. I'll wear a different hoodie next time."

"What about me?" She spread her arms wide. "I'm ready for critique."

There had definitely been a time in their lives when he had critiqued her outfits, her shoes, her hair, and her general attitude.

Damn, what he wouldn't give to have Becca Bollier be just slightly less than amazingly fucking gorgeous and perfect.

"I don't like that lipstick," he finally said.

She pressed her lips together. "I'm not wearing any lipstick."

Damn, her lips were just that color.

He'd been lying anyway. The only thing he didn't like about the color was that it made it impossible for him to stop looking at her lips.

"Well then maybe you need to get some," he said.

And that would've been a pretty good, nonchalant, almost rude thing to say.

If she hadn't had that knowing look in her eye when she said, "Noted. 'Night, Beau."

"'Night, Bec."

six

Two weeks later...

"EVERYTHING OKAY?" Beau answered the call after only one ring.

Savannah Lee, Becca's best friend, didn't call him often and she was with Becca tonight so of course, he was going to answer the second her name popped up on his phone.

"Um, mostly."

They were in New Orleans tonight at a wedding and reception with their other college friends, Daniel, and Toby, and Toby's fiancé, Sam. Sam was a cousin to Beau's cousins, the Landrys, which made Sam...not Beau's blood relation at all. Still, Beau loved the guy, and they'd grown up together, and hell, in Autre, everyone felt like family.

Beau frowned at Savannah's response. He set his saw down. "Where's Becca?"

"She's here. Well, she's in the restroom."

"Why are you calling me?"

"Yeah. There's a...situation. And I think you're the best one to handle it."

"What situation?" He was already pulling off his work gloves and heading for the door of his shop.

"Okay, so you're gonna be pissed, but just listen."

Beau blew out a breath. Savannah was one of Becca's best friends and had been her roommate during their years at LSU. For the most part, Beau liked her. Savannah was smart and sassy and had definitely matured over the years since she'd come to Autre to visit with Becca. But she liked to push buttons. And she seemed to really like to push his.

"What's going on?" he asked shortly.

"Okay, we're at the wedding reception in New Orleans."

"Yeah."

"So we set her up with someone Daniel knew. Paul was coming to the wedding too and we thought, since Becca was the only one of us without a date, that they might as well come as each other's plus one."

Beau stopped in the middle of the dirt parking lot between his shop and his truck.

"Okay." He hadn't known Becca had a date for the wedding. Or that she'd wanted one.

Not that it mattered. She hadn't asked him, so what she was doing tonight was none of his business.

"Well, the guy's being kind of a jerk. I mean, it's a blind date. But he's all over her, won't leave her alone or give her any space. I can tell she's sick of him but doesn't want to make a scene or make things awkward for Daniel. So I was thinking..."

She trailed off and Beau blew out a breath. "*What*, Savannah?"

"Maybe you could come up here? Play the jealous boyfriend? Cut in?"

Beau narrowed his eyes. There was something off about this.

Mostly that it was Savannah calling him and not Becca.

"She should tell Daniel and he should tell his 'friend' to back off," Beau said.

He started for his truck again. A reason to prove to Becca that she could always call him no matter what situation she found herself in? Yeah, he was going to New Orleans tonight. But damn, he wished she'd been the one to call. That was all he really wanted. To be the person Becca could always turn to.

"Yeah. She should," Savannah agreed slowly. "But you know how sweet Becca is."

She was. Unless she needed to be not sweet. She knew how to say no in no uncertain terms, how to throw a punch, and how and when to get help. She could hold her own.

So could Savannah. If she wanted a guy to back off—from her or from someone else—she'd put her sassy self right in front of him, point one of her perfectly manicured fingernails in his face, and lecture him until he happily took himself out of the situation. Or she'd knee him in the balls.

He was happy to help, but he wasn't entirely convinced they needed his help. Or that Savannah was telling him the whole story.

"Where are you? I'll come get her and bring her home."

"The Marriott on Canal. But she shouldn't have to leave!" Savannah exclaimed. "She's having fun with us. And we haven't seen Daniel in two months."

Beau agreed that a woman shouldn't have to leave a space she wanted to be in because a man wouldn't leave her alone.

"Well, then you can point this guy out to me, and I'll make sure *he* leaves. But Becca doesn't even need to know I'm there."

Yes, he was testing Savannah.

"No, no. That won't work," Savannah replied.

Uh-huh. He'd expected that answer. "Why not?" Beau started his truck.

"Because he's...a good friend of the groom. They'll notice if Paul leaves. He won't want to do that."

"Then I'll just be sure he *fully* understands that he needs to leave her the fuck alone. I can do that without coming inside. Send him out to the hotel lobby. I'll meet him."

"But then she'll be alone."

"She'll be with you guys."

Savannah was telling him everything he needed to know. Savannah wanted Beau there *at* the party with Becca. He didn't think it was because she was actually concerned about this guy. She didn't have any kind of panic or worry in her voice.

She was trying to set them up.

Like everyone else they knew.

He should have expected it. Her friends had been the ones to start the entire *ask Beau his opinion on your Halloween costumes* thing had led to him feeling jealous and turned on by Becca in the first place. That had led to them kissing for the first time. That had led to them dating.

He shifted on the truck seat. Going to this party to scare off another guy could be complicated. Because he really wanted to scare off this other guy.

But being there for Becca? Making sure she was safe and had a good time? Yeah, he'd do that.

Which Savannah, Toby, and Daniel knew very well.

"But it's not the same when we all have dates," Savannah protested. "She'll feel left out or like a third wheel. Or a seventh wheel. I want her to have fun tonight and not be worried about some creep being clingy and gross. I want her to relax and be treated like she's special."

Damn. Savannah was good. Not only did she truly care about Becca, but she knew *him*. She was definitely pushing all the right buttons.

"I'm halfway there," he admitted. "But I'm in jeans, a t-shirt, and work boots. Not really wedding reception attire."

"It won't matter," Savannah said quickly. "You being here is the important part." She paused. "But..."

He rolled his eyes, waiting for the rest.

"Sam has an extra button-down shirt you could borrow."

How convenient. Sam was the only one of the group who was even close to Beau's size. Daniel was tall but thinner and Toby was both shorter and slimmer. Sam was about the same build as Beau, but he was smaller through the shoulders and arms. No, if there was a shirt in that hotel that was going to fit Beau it was because these people had specifically bought it, knowing this was all going to happen.

Yeah, they'd played it pretty perfectly.

Had they picked a jackass to set her up with? That was...risky.

No, it wasn't. He sighed. They'd known he'd come. They'd stick close to her, so nothing bad happened with this guy. But they'd let him get annoying. Then they'd call Beau. And he'd show up.

He'd definitely been protective and a little possessive of Becca while they'd been dating. He wasn't an easy-going guy. Not when it came to Becca. In most other things, yes. But there were three things that could get him riled up in the blink of an eye: when something bothered his mom, when something messed with his business, and Becca.

Becca topped the list.

And it didn't matter that they were no longer dating.

But did this mean that they were in on it with the town, or was this just her three closest friends coming to the same conclusion that he and Becca belonged together?

Toby and Sam were definitely in on conspiring to get them

back together. Toby would have definitely passed that on to Savannah, and she would have wanted to run with it.

"Savannah," he said firmly. "Is Becca actually in trouble?"

"No. I mean, this guy is just a little too interested and isn't taking no for an answer. But I knew that I could call you, and you'd be there for her, so it seemed like the easiest answer."

Fuck. Savannah had no way of knowing that hit him directly in the chest. That had been some of the problem when they'd dated. He *hadn't* been able to be there when Becca called every time. He'd been too fucking far away.

Now she was here. Right next door. Where he *could* be there for her. She could depend on him, turn to him, as a friend every time.

He wanted that.

Even if it never turned into anything more. For however long she was in Autre.

"Let me talk to her," he said.

"She's in the ladies' room. I think she figured that was the best place to go to avoid him for a little while."

"Let me talk to her," he repeated.

"Fine. But she's going to be mad that I called you."

Yeah, maybe. Too bad.

He heard movement on Savannah's end of the phone and then her saying, "Becca? Hey, Beau is on the phone for you."

"What? Why?"

"Just talk to him."

There were several beats of silence. Beau turned his truck off the main highway and into New Orleans. He'd be there in ten minutes.

"Beau?" Becca asked a moment later.

"Hey. Everything okay?"

"Yeah. We're having a great time. What's going on? Are *you* okay?"

Right. She'd think he called Savannah. "I was just checking in. I'm in New Orleans. Remembered you guys were up there tonight. Thought maybe I'd stop by."

"Savannah left the room," Becca said. "Why are you really calling?"

"I really am on my way over there."

"Why?"

"Your friends set you up with the creep, hoping that when he made you uncomfortable, you'd call me."

There were several beats of silence. Then Becca sighed. "They're in on all of this?"

"I think so."

"Of course they are. Savannah is so competitive. You know the second she heard about the trophy, she'd be in. Now that there's a reserved table, I know she's determined to win."

"A *what*?" Beau asked.

Becca sighed. "Yeah. There's now a reserved table at Ellie's up for grabs. Winner gets it for a year. Any time they come in."

"What about the trophy?"

"That's still part of it too."

"They get both things?" Beau asked.

"Yep."

"Well...fuck."

She laughed. "Yeah. Things just got more serious."

He groaned. "Yeah. We're screwed."

"So...what's the plan here? They want you to come get me?" she asked. "I'm having fun, in spite of Paul."

"They wanted me to come, interrupt your date, and then take his place because you deserve to have a great night out with someone who will treat you well," he said.

She was quiet for a moment. Then she said, "Well, I do deserve that."

"You do," he agreed as he pulled up in front of the hotel and the valet moved toward him. "Which is why I'm right outside."

"Oh." Her voice was soft. "You don't have to do this. I can deal with him."

"Sure you can. But I can deal with him better. No offense. But...I can convince him very effectively that his attention is not welcome."

She was quiet for a beat. Then she said, "But you're working tonight."

"This is much more impor—" He broke off.

Becca was definitely more important than work, but in the past, work had gotten in the way. Like the night they'd broken up.

He handed his keys to the valet and looked up at the front of the Marriott. "I'm here. Just tell me where you are."

"Third floor. The Rosalie ballroom."

"Be there in a minute." He started inside.

There was a long silence on her end, then she said, "Well, maybe this will be good. I mean, if we want to get everyone's hopes up and then go on about our business as if nothing's changed, you rushing up here, still in your work clothes, and making a big scene of saving me, and me swooning at the whole thing, is exactly what we should do, right?"

He let that sink in. Right. They were playing this big game with their hometown. The two of them on one team and everyone else on the other. There was something fun about that. No matter how much he wished the claiming her and making-her-swoon thing was real.

"Yeah, exactly. Let's play this out the way they imagined it. Make it dramatic."

Besides, that might lead to some kissing...

Bad idea, Beau. Really bad fucking idea. You and your hand already spend enough intimate time together, don't you?

"I'm going to head back into the reception so you can make a grand entrance," Becca said. "Oh, I'll see if he wants to dance, and maybe his hands will wander, and you can come in and make a big deal out of being jealous."

Beau felt his teeth grinding together. Yes, that would be a good scene. But that would mean this jerk got to be close to her, and have his hands wander.

"How about you just go talk to him? I'm like two minutes away."

"Okay, sounds good. This'll be fun."

"Yeah." Fun. Sure.

Beau headed for the elevators and worked on not frowning at every other person who got on. He was only going to the third floor. They wouldn't slow him down much.

He was striding down the long hallway toward the Rosalie ballroom four minutes later.

"Beau!"

He turned at the sound of his name.

Savannah was hurrying toward him. "Hey! Glad I caught you." She was carrying a white button-down shirt and a brown suit jacket.

"Hey."

"Thought you might like to borrow these."

She hadn't mentioned the "extra" jacket. But Beau and Becca had decided to play along with everyone and their matchmaking plans. So he gave her a grateful smile. "Thanks. I appreciate it."

"Thought the brown would go with your boots."

They both looked down. He was still in his work boots. They were a little scuffed and clearly worn. They were, well, *work boots*. But they weren't covered in mud or anything. He shook a little sawdust off of one and nodded. "Good thinking."

"If you just want to duck into the—" She gestured at the doors to the men's and ladies' rooms behind him.

But Beau simply grabbed the bottom of his t-shirt and pulled it off.

Savannah's eyes went wide. "Or...that works."

Beau held out his hand for the shirt she'd brought him. Instead, she handed him a travel-sized stick of deodorant.

He grinned. "You thought of everything."

"Just lucky Sam and the other guys had extras." She also handed him a travel-sized tube of toothpaste and a tooth-brush. And a comb. And a bottle of cologne. "You can't keep the cologne."

Sure. The guys had extras of all of this just by chance. He shook his head. They had to know how obvious this all was, right? But he took everything from her, including the clothes, and said, "Wow, this is great. Thank you."

"Tuck the cologne in the inside jacket pocket and return it tomorrow," she said. "You can toss the rest."

"She okay for a couple more minutes?"

"I'll make sure," Savannah promised.

Yeah, she could have made sure of it all night. But he was glad he was here. "I'll be just a minute then," he said, turning toward the men's room after all.

He used all the products, shrugged into the "borrowed" shirt and jacket—he had to pull the sales tags from the shirt—and had to admit that Savannah and the guys had done a good job shopping. He was keeping the clothes. He liked the fit and the look of them. And—he took a sniff of the top of the cologne bottle—this stuff too. He liked it. If they were going to mess in his relationship with Becca, it was going to cost them.

Beau straightened the jacket and then headed for the ballroom.

Inside, it was a very typical wedding reception—a big room

with tables and chairs scattered throughout and lots of people —so it took him a few seconds to locate Becca.

But when he did...he was pretty sure he wasn't going to be looking at anything else for the rest of the night.

Had he had a moment to stop and think, he probably would've expected to be punched in the gut by how amazing Becca looked. But he hadn't given what she'd be wearing much thought.

This was a friend's wedding. She wasn't dressed in her typical blue jeans and t-shirt that was her usual attire around Autre. She also wasn't in her sundresses, Capri pants, or khakis that she wore to work as a kindergarten teacher.

No, tonight, she was in an emerald green dress that had wide straps crossing her shoulders, dipped low in the back, was fitted at the waist, then flared below her hips, hitting at midcalf. The color was amazing, as were her curves inside the sleek, shimmery material.

She was also wearing heels. He loved her just as much in her converse tennis shoes, flip-flops, boots, or flat shoes she wore to school.

But damn, the girl looked good in heels.

It only took him two seconds to decide how this scenario was going to play out.

He stalked across the room toward her, vaguely registering the fact that some guy was leaning onto the bar, facing her.

He assumed the guy was the creep, but he didn't really care. Whoever it was going to get the full experience of Beau Hebert showing up to sweep Becca Bollier off her feet.

He expected the story would circulate no matter who the witness was.

He approached from the side, so she might have seen him coming in her peripheral vision, or perhaps she just sensed him, but he was about ten feet away when she looked over. Her eyes widened. Obviously, it wasn't shock. She'd known he was coming. But it could have been the look of possessiveness in his eyes. Beau didn't even try to hide it. Sure, she might think he was faking it, but no one else in that room would think so.

"Oh," she said, putting surprise in her tone.

The man leaning on the bar next to her straightened. He frowned.

Beau barely spared him a glance.

Without a word, Beau crowded close to Becca, put one big hand on her ass, cupped her face with the other, and pulled her in for a deep kiss.

seven

BEAU DIDN'T GO EASY. The kiss was deep and hot from the very beginning. He opened his lips, tasting her fully, sliding his tongue along her lower lip and then into her mouth.

She immediately opened, as her hands grasped the lapels of his jacket and she gave a little moan he suspected only he could hear over the sound of the music and conversation around him. But no one else needed to hear that. He was an audience of one for Becca's *true* reaction.

The way she arched into him and completely accepted the kiss without pushing him away was all everyone else needed to see.

But he definitely took note of the way she softened in his arms, pressed against him fully, and met every stroke of his tongue with her own.

Fake, his ass.

"Um, excuse me," the guy she had been speaking to interjected.

Beau very much wanted to just ignore him. He wanted to throw Becca over his shoulder and ask for her room number.

But that was a *bad* idea. For one, he knew exactly what

would happen if they were shut together inside that hotel room. He could keep hold of his emotions when they were out and about in Autre, surrounded by people they knew, or even when they were working on the community play together and having to kiss as characters in the story.

But one-on-one, with no one around, a big old king bed, and no part to play, he was very afraid that every single emotion he felt for this woman would be front and center. He wasn't sure what to do with that.

Avoiding it, and ignoring it, seemed best.

Besides, this was a game. They were here to mess with her friends, who thought they were setting them up. Everyone wanted to manipulate the situation, and Beau and Becca were teaming up to tease them right back.

That's what he had to remember. This was all for show.

Which meant staying here in the ballroom. Yes, kissing her, acting possessive, acting like he couldn't stop touching her—which was far too real—but for an audience.

He lifted his head and loosened his grip. He stared down at her. Yeah, those dilated pupils and flushed cheeks were not fake.

He shouldn't feel the thrill that he did with that.

What good did it do for them to have an actual attraction? That was just going to make everything more difficult. He hadn't been kidding when he said that she had to stick around Autre for a *long* time before he'd trust that was what she really wanted.

Finally, he looked at the man next to them. The one Becca had been in the middle of a conversation with.

"Oh, hey Toby," he greeted.

Okay, so not the creep.

"Beau," Toby said, tipping his head. "Good to see you."

"Am I interrupting something?" Beau suddenly realized

that Toby seemed tense. Shouldn't he be happy? If he was in on this little plan to throw Beau and Becca together, he should be thrilled with this kiss. Instead, he looked annoyed. Like Beau had interrupted something.

"Yeah, actually," Toby said. "But it's a good thing. This isn't the place for this discussion. I'm going to go slam back some champagne, stuff my face with cake, and dance with my hot fiancé." He turned and headed across the ballroom.

Beau frowned and looked at Becca. She was watching Toby go, looking upset.

That wasn't okay.

Beau took her hand. They were going to dance. Out there, they could stand close and talk quietly without anyone interrupting.

He pulled her onto the dance floor. She followed willingly.

"So tell me what that was about with Toby," he said as he turned to face her and pulled her in close.

With her heels, she was at an even better height for dancing and she looped her arms around his neck and pressed close.

They started moving and Beau rested his hands on her hips. Okay, lower than her hips. They were right above the curve of her ass. He appreciated that this was great for the show. Because it was exactly where his hands wanted to be. They'd always fit along those curves perfectly.

She looked up at him. "You don't want to hear that."

"I don't?"

"No. You're here as my pretend jealous boyfriend. This is supposed to be hot and sexy." She frowned. "And there is nothing hot or sexy about any of *that*."

"On the outside to everyone looking in, I'm here as your jealous boyfriend. If they watch us, it can seem hot and sexy. But I'm actually here as your friend, Bec. I want to know."

"How are we going to talk about something like that? Something that is depressing and upsetting, and still make it seem hot and sexy?"

"Are you challenging me?"

She laughed softly. "No. Honest question."

He moved his hand a little lower and spread his fingers so that his palm encompassed most of her left ass cheek. Then he pulled her up against him more tightly. Her breath hitched. Then he leaned in, putting his lips against her ear.

"Kinda like this." He took his other hand and rested it on her bare shoulder blade. He stroked the pads of his index and middle finger up and down. He felt the goosebumps break out and couldn't help but feel satisfied.

"Now nuzzle your temple up against my chin."

She did. He caught a whiff of her shampoo and breathed in deeply. "Now talk."

"I'm not sure how I'm going to be able to keep my train of thought."

A little groan rumbled from his chest without warning. "It's just for show."

"It feels pretty real."

"Focus. *Toby*," he said for himself as much as for her. "What happened?"

It was one thing for him to hold back. She was right that it was distracting as hell to be dancing like this, but knowing it was affecting her was another thing. His cock said *let's affect her a whole lot more* and he was sure she didn't miss that fact.

They were dancing but really barely swaying. They were more or less pressed up against each other in the middle of the floor. But at least they were in public. They were putting on a show and that was keeping him from doing anything stupid. Like sliding the strap of her dress off her shoulder to press his lips there. He kept simply stroking his fingers over her skin instead. But fuck, she smelled good, felt good, and he was sure tasted as good as he imagined. Like everything he ever wanted.

"Toby made an appointment to go in and talk with my dad about the arts funding."

Beau forced himself to concentrate on her words. "And it didn't go well?"

Becca nodded, her temple grazing against his beard, some of her hair catching on his whiskers. "Right. Dad said it was a done deal and that the school budget was tight and there was nothing they could do. So Toby suggested that the money from the gate at the games and the concessions should come back to the arts program."

"That's a good idea."

Becca nodded again. "It is."

"And your dad said?"

"That the money is already earmarked. Then Toby said that we should have some other fundraising at the games then. A bake sale. Auction something off. People could buy tickets to try to kick a ball through the uprights. People could buy tickets to see the teachers do a dance routine at half time."

Beau kept them moving but he was frowning. People shouldn't have to work this hard and put in extra time to fund the basic programs at the public school. "What did your dad say to that?"

"That the teachers shouldn't have to humiliate themselves in front of the town begging for money."

Beau pressed his lips together. So, he agreed with Jonathan. Though he wasn't sure how Becca's dad had *said* the words. Or how that was a productive answer to give a frustrated teacher trying to solve a problem.

Becca pulled back. "He's right."

Beau nodded. "He is." Beau put his hand on the back of her neck and stroked his fingers up and down the side of her throat. It was supposed to look sexy, but he also meant it to be comforting.

"I think Dad actually meant it to be supportive, which is what I told him just now. But Toby took it as dad shooting down yet another option to fix the problem."

"And he thinks you're defending your dad again instead of siding with the teachers."

"Yes."

"Why is Toby the one meeting with him?"

"He's only one of several. But he's the one talking to *me* on behalf of the other teachers because we're friends. Landon and Toby have gotten close. And hell, we're a small school. Just because someone teaches high school doesn't mean all the elementary teachers don't know them. They want me to be the mediator. It's all..." She sighed. "I feel like I'm letting them down, and I feel like there's this tension with Dad because he's *expecting* me to come and talk to him. It's like there's this elephant in the room whenever we're together. And I tell myself it's just a minor thing. We're all upset over a football field and a school musical. A lot of schools have much bigger issues. But it *is* a big deal. On principle. And for the kids who are seniors this year and wanted to do a musical. And I hate that the teachers I want to work with and be friends with are judging me, in my first year, because my *dad* is upsetting them, and they think I'm not advocating for the kids and programs that are important." Her voice had risen slightly and her cheeks were pink.

"Okay." Beau pulled her closer, tucking her head against his shoulder again. It was an instinctive reaction to comfort her, but it resulted in pulling her more firmly against his erection.

She didn't seem to mind and she cuddled closer. He felt her

hand stroking over his lapel. *She's just playing along,* he told himself. But it seemed absent-minded.

He loved the idea that she might get comfort from touching him, but he knew that reading anything into any of this was stupid.

"That's a tough position to be in, Bec. I'm really sorry. That sucks," he said honestly.

He was. He hated when she was upset.

But dammit...if she'd gone to teach somewhere else, she could go storming into the administrator's office with her friends and raise hell about cutbacks to the arts program. No one would look at her and think *she's just scared of her dad,* or, *dad must have told her no at dinner last night.* And she wouldn't be walking on eggshells around her dad at home.

Sure, once she moved out of her mom and dad's place, some of that would get better. But she'd still see them a lot, of course. Sunday dinner or a birthday celebration could still be tainted by school politics. The other teachers would still see her as a possible intermediary with the administration.

"Yeah, it does," she agreed. Her arms tightened around him, as if she was hugging him.

"Doesn't Toby understand this is hard for you?"

"It's not about me," Becca said. "And Toby reminded me of that *clearly* tonight."

"Did he?" Beau felt a streak of protectiveness. Did he need to have a talk with Toby about how he spoke to Becca again?

She stroked her hand over his back as if sensing his sudden tension. "Yes. But I'm fine. He's right. My discomfort and friction with my dad shouldn't be more important than a whole bunch of kids missing out on opportunities they deserve from their school."

Funny, for Beau it was all about Becca.

No, that wasn't true. He did care about the kids. He was

eternally grateful to Mr. Taggart for seeing that not only was Beau a natural with tools, but he had an artist's eye.

The 'tech and trade' program in Autre was a partnership with other schools and a community college in New Orleans that allowed students to explore things like engine repair, construction, welding, electrical work, and plumbing, along with computer skills and other vocational tracks. Beau had hated the traditional classes like history and English but had loved the tech and trade classes.

He was sure the same was true for a lot of the students who enjoyed and excelled in the music, art, and drama classes. And sure, they could still go to class as things stood, but didn't they deserve to show off those skills as much as the football players did?

Of course they did.

But mostly he cared about Becca.

He stroked his hand up and down the bare skin of her back and loved the little shiver that went through her. "I'm sorry," he said softly. "What can I do?"

"You can keep doing that," she said, her voice soft as well.

He smiled slightly and ran his hand over her back again.

"Hmm." Her sigh was contented.

"Excuse me."

They were interrupted by a man in a navy-blue suit. He was wearing glasses, had perfectly styled hair, and a deep frown.

Becca pulled back and Beau had to resist the urge to tug her back up against him. Tightly.

"Yes?" he asked the man, giving him a frown in return.

"You have your hand on my date's ass," the guy said.

Ah, *this* was Paul. The creep.

"Paul, this is—" Becca started.

"Her *boyfriend,*" Beau interjected. "So, you're not excused."

"Her boyfriend?" Paul repeated, looking at Becca.

"We've been...on a break," she said weakly.

Beau snorted. A two-year breakup but sure, "a break" would work.

"It was a misunderstanding," Beau said smoothly. "When I said I was working tonight, I sure as fuck didn't mean that she should bring someone else to this thing." He pulled Becca up against his side, very purposefully keeping his hand on her ass. Not that he minded.

"I see." Paul's eyes narrowed, then he looked at Becca. "She didn't mention you. Maybe she wasn't as upset about you not being here as you think."

Beau wondered if Savannah and Toby had informed Paul that he was supposed to come with Becca to make Beau jealous. It would be nice to know if Paul was in on the set-up and was acting or not, because the way he was looking at Becca right now seemed concerned and a little protective and Beau did *not* like that.

No one needed to be protective of Becca. She had *him*.

Does she? Thought you were just friends.

Friends could absolutely be protective. He wanted to know everything about her and help her through anything she went through. He hated the idea that she was having trouble with Toby and with her dad. He wanted to make all of that right. He had every intention of talking to both men and doing what he could to smooth things over.

And she sure as hell didn't need protecting *from* Beau.

Paul could fuck off.

"She wasn't upset about me not being here, because she knew all she had to do was call and I'd be here in a heartbeat."

That was true enough.

"So why'd she ask me?" Paul asked.

Beau made a point of looking the other man up and down. "Felt sorry for you?"

Paul stepped forward and reached for Becca's hand. "Hilarious. Now my *date* and I are going to—"

Beau's hand clamped around Paul's forearm before he could touch Becca. "I don't think so."

Paul jerked his arm back and glared at Beau. Then he looked at Becca. "Well?"

"Well, what?" she asked.

Beau almost laughed. Becca clearly wasn't used to men fighting over her. Which was crazy. Becca should have men falling over themselves just to buy her a drink.

Paul sighed as if she was being slow. "Him or me. I don't appreciate you not telling me you were involved with someone, but if there's an issue between you two, I'm happy to have someone show him the door and continue our date."

Beau lifted a brow. Paul would have him thrown out? Well, if he really was here harassing Becca, he could respect that.

"But if you want to be with him, then I'll back off," Paul finished. "This is our first date. I like you. But I'm not going to get in the middle of something."

"Well..." Becca said slowly, looking up at Beau.

She was enjoying having two men vie for her attention. She deserved that.

Maybe he should let this go on for a little bit.

She looked fabulous and if it would make her smile and feel confident and sassy to have two—or more—men lining up to twirl her around and compliment her and look at her like she was the most gorgeous thing they'd ever seen, then maybe he needed to let it happen.

Though he sure as fuck would be in that line.

"You want to dance with him, sweetheart?" Beau asked her, meeting her gaze directly. "Fine by me. But I'm not goin' anywhere. I know who's unzipping this dress tonight and who's buyin' you coffee in the mornin'." He put extra Louisiana-boy-drawl in his voice.

Her eyes widened.

He was playing a role, he reminded himself. *They* were playing roles. For the purpose of good-naturedly torturing their friends.

"I just..." She shook her head and cleared her throat.

Beau let himself enjoy affecting her a bit, though. He wasn't unzipping this dress tonight. But no other man would be either.

She turned to Paul. "Do you want to dance—*just* dance —with me?"

Paul looked from her to Beau and back. "I would really like to dance with you, yes," he answered.

Yeah, Paul liked her.

Beau let go of her and immediately wanted to pull her back. But he took a deep breath as Paul took her hand and tugged her close.

Beau made himself turn and head to the bar. He ordered a drink and leaned onto the bar to nurse it, forcing himself to act nonchalant and cool about everything. But his eyes were on Becca the entire time.

She was smiling as the song she and Paul were dancing to ended. Yeah, Savannah had oversold the "clingy-creepy" thing.

Another man, who had been hovering on the edge of the dance floor watching them, stepped out and spoke to her. Becca nodded and Paul moved to one of the tables nearby as the new guy started dancing with her.

Beau kept his eyes on them, but he realized he wasn't upset about Savannah's exaggeration or about being here.

And that was the whole problem, wasn't it? He *wanted* to be with Becca. He wanted to be her plus-one. He wanted to be the one making her smile as she danced. He wanted to be the one stroking his hands up and down her back. He wanted to be the one she told about her issues with her dad and Toby. He wanted to be the one she looked up at with bright, hopeful eyes when she realized that he was firmly on her side and would support the same efforts and causes that she believed in.

That had made his heart squeeze as hard as seeing her in that dress.

She affected him—*all* of him.

"She's dancing with Eric now?"

The casual observation came from Daniel. Beau looked over at the other man and nodded. "Is that his name?"

"Yeah. Eric Franklin."

"Nice guy?"

Daniel shrugged. "Sure."

"Okay." Beau lifted his glass of whiskey for a sip.

"Thought you were here because you didn't want her with anyone else," Daniel said.

Beau looked over again. "She's not *with* anyone else. She's dancing. She's feeling beautiful and realizing she has admirers. She's having fun and smiling, and her cheeks are a little pink."

Daniel narrowed his eyes, then looked out at the dance floor. "That doesn't bother you?"

"That Becca is happy and feeling appreciated?" Beau shook his head. "Of course not."

"That other men are making her feel beautiful and appreciated?"

Beau turned and set his glass on the bar, then pinned Daniel with a direct gaze. He hoped that Daniel would repeat this to Savannah and Toby. "The things I make Becca feel are a bit... different from what those guys are making her feel."

The corner of Daniel's mouth curled up. "Is that right?"

"Yeah, very."

"How so?"

"Why don't you watch us dance and see if you can tell the difference?"

Daniel looked back out to where Becca and Eric were just finishing their dance.

Beau picked up his glass, tossed back the rest of his whiskey, then set it down with a *thunk*. He gave Daniel a wink, before crossing the dance floor.

"My turn," he said as yet another man approached her.

Becca smiled up at him, and sure enough, her grin was much wider for him than her previous partners. "Good."

The other guy turned on his heel and went back to the tables without saying a word.

Beau gathered her close. His hand splayed wide across her lower back, and he pulled her up against his body fully. Her breath hitched, and her eyes widened.

"Arms around my neck, Bec," he said gruffly.

His other hand settled on the bare skin between her shoulder blades.

"Who are we showing off for?"

He leaned in, putting his lips against her ear. "Everybody."

She nodded. "Okay. What are we showing off exactly?"

"How you dancing with me is different than how you dance with everyone else."

They started swaying. "And how is me dancing with you different?"

"Well, none of them did this." He lifted his hand and dragged the strap of her dress off her shoulder. He pressed his lips to the bare skin. "If they had, I would've stomped out here and smashed them in the face."

A shiver went through her body. "Oh. Well, I probably would've kneed him in the nuts before you got here."

"You feel like kneeing me in the nuts?" His voice husky and low.

She shook her head. "Not what I'm thinking about doing with your nuts, no."

That surprised him, and for just a second he paused before chuckling. He kissed her shoulder again. "Nice."

"What?"

"Good answer. That will convince them."

"Convince them of what?"

"That we're actually here together."

"No one can even hear what we're saying."

"No, but they can see the effect what we're saying has on each of us." He lifted his head and met her gaze. "They can absolutely tell that you're turning me on. And vice versa."

He stroked his hand over her shoulder where he'd just put his lips. "When you were dancing with the others, you're smiling, your cheeks were a little pink—I assume they gave you compliments—and you were having fun."

Her voice was breathless when she asked, "And now?"

"Now you have this pretty flush on your neck," he said, running an index finger down the front of her throat, where she always got red when she was turned on. "Your smile is softer and more affectionate than just outright happy." He lifted his hand and ran the pad of his thumb over her bottom lip. "And we're hardly moving. This is a lot more about being up against each other than about the music or even where we are."

Her breaths were coming a little more rapidly now. "And they're all noticing?"

"The important people are. The ones who brought me here wanting a reaction." He dragged his thumb over her lip again. "And they're definitely seeing a reaction."

Her eyes dropped to his mouth and Beau realized that he

was playing with fire. He'd started this. This was all part of the show. But damn, it felt real.

"It's probably helping that I'm thinking about the line earlier," she admitted. "The thing about unzipping my dress and buying me coffee in the morning."

"That one came easily to me."

"Yeah?"

"I want to be sure that whatever we say to one another in front of other people gets repeated."

She blinked. "Right. Paul might say something to Savannah."

He nodded. But his gaze went to her lips too.

"But now...you have to spend the night," she told him.

Those words sent a ripple of panic through him. "What?"

She nodded. "We all got rooms here at the hotel. We knew we'd be drinking, and that we shouldn't drive home. We're planning to get breakfast with a few people from out of town tomorrow before everyone leaves. So we have rooms. What you said to Paul means you have to spend the night with me."

Well...fuck.

eight

BECCA WATCHED Beau process that information.

Yeah, he hadn't known that.

She knew that what he'd said to Paul had been part of the act. He had to act possessive and crazy about her. And she suspected that he'd intended for Paul to repeat his words to Savannah.

But now... they were kind of stuck.

Not that she minded.

His hand was hot and heavy on her lower back, and it made everything in her stomach and pelvis feel hot and heavy as well. Her nipples had been tight since he'd walked in and kissed her at the bar. Her pulse had been erratic since she'd seen him stalking toward her. And her panties had been wet since he'd kissed her.

Damn, he was convincing as a jealous boyfriend.

And he looked hot in a button-down shirt and jacket.

And he'd been sweet, gruff, possessive, sexy, and funny all at the same time.

Just like he had been when they'd been dating.

This was making it very difficult to remember that they

were trying to get back on firm footing as *friends*. And that this was really just one big game.

Honestly, if people were watching them and trying to figure out if they had feelings for one another, this would absolutely convince them.

"You're staying here tonight?" he repeated dumbly.

She nodded. "You're going to have to go upstairs with me. And stay. And take me for coffee in the morning."

Suddenly, she liked this idea. Sure, a million different things could happen on the other side of the hotel room door...

Okay, not a million. There were maybe four or five things that could happen on the other side of that door.

Okay, two. There were basically two things.

Either nothing would happen.

Or... *something* would happen.

Something that would change everything.

"I can't stay," he finally said.

He'd been acting cocky and confident and completely in charge since he'd walked into the ballroom. Now he looked freaked out.

"Why not?"

"I..."

She lifted a brow as he trailed off. "Have an early project in the morning? Promised to be back tonight? Left the stove on?" She offered him a few different excuses.

His eyes dropped to her mouth again. "Because that would be really fucking dangerous."

She blinked in surprise. He was going to be honest.

Okay then.

Of course, that was the reason he didn't think he should stay. Because he thought something would happen too. Which would complicate everything.

Her heart, of course, flipped. And the area between her thighs got warmer.

"Dangerous? Why?"

He gave her a look that said, *seriously?* But she really wanted to hear this. For some reason.

Probably because she was a masochist.

But hearing Beau talk about wanting her was just so...delicious.

"Okay," he said, "if we can tell each other our hoodies look ratty, we can be honest about this, right?"

She nodded. "Right."

"If we spend the night in a hotel room together, I'm going to fuck you. And if I do that, it's going to make it really hard for us to just be friends."

Heat arrowed through her and she had to take a deep breath. "Have you heard of friends with benefits?"

"That won't work for us."

"Why not? We both know the benefits will be great. And we both know that we want to stay friends."

He stopped moving, but he did not remove his hands from her body. In fact, he seemed to draw her closer. He pinned her with a direct gaze. "Because friends with benefits are for people who like each other but *only* want to fuck."

She swallowed hard. "And that's not us?"

"I would want to consume you. I would want to tangle you up in everything I've got. I would want to be tangled up in everything of yours. I would absolutely want to tie you down. But I told you, you have to make these decisions on your own. If you decide to stay, you have to stay for *yourself*. If you decide to leave, you have to be free to do that. You've been here *four months*. It's not enough. I can't sleep with you without wanting everything else and you can't promise me everything else yet. I won't believe you."

She knew she was barely breathing. *Intense* was definitely one of the top five adjectives she would use to describe Beau Hebert. Especially when it came to her. But she had not expected this tonight.

"We clear?"

She wet her lips and nodded. Everything he said rang true.

And she appreciated it. He wasn't wrong. She did *think* she wanted to stay in Autre, but this was her first year teaching. Her first time out on her own and she wasn't even actually on her own yet. She was living with her parents. She was working for her dad. And that was more complicated than she'd expected. They'd been in class for six weeks and she was already feeling pressure and disappointment. Did she think things would get better? Sure. The first time doing something was always hard. But damn, shouldn't coming *home* be one of the easiest things?

Beau was right. Getting involved with him would mean committing to Autre too. For good. All of that at once was probably too much.

"Okay. Fair enough."

He pulled a breath in through his nose and let it out, almost in relief. "But I could throw you over my shoulder, and carry you out to my truck, and take you home," he said.

Yeah, they'd come this far. Obviously, she couldn't go to the room by herself. "You can't sleep on the floor or something?" she asked.

His heated gaze bore into hers. "No."

"Oh." Her heart rate kicked up.

"I could lie to us both," he said. "I would go up there and *intend* to. But no, I don't think I'd spend the night on the floor."

Damn. He needed to stop. She was feeling very...horny. She was turned on and swept off her feet by his "show" and he'd turned her down for sleeping together, dating, and definitely for anything more. But even pretending had made her heart race, and her skin heat, and her whole body tingle.

Because Beau wanted her.

He didn't want to want her. He was convinced he couldn't —shouldn't—do anything about it. But he wanted her.

And that was, apparently, enough to send her libido into overdrive.

"I, um...need to go upstairs," she said suddenly, stepping back.

He frowned. "You okay?"

"To...get my stuff," she said. "I'll... um, change. And get my stuff. And we can go."

"You're ready to go now?"

Well, she was definitely ready to go upstairs now. "Yeah. For sure."

"Just like that?"

"Yep."

"You're ready to leave the party that you needed me to come to so that you wouldn't have to leave—"

"Hey Beau?" she interrupted.

"Yeah?"

"Why don't you go get some cake and I'll meet you back down here once I get my stuff and change my clothes?"

"I'll just go up with you."

"No!" She said it way too quickly and emphatically, she knew.

"No?" He looked confused. "Why not?"

"Because...you said we can't be in the hotel room together alone."

"Overnight. I can probably control myself for ten minutes while you pack."

Yeah, well, this might take longer than ten minutes. Though not much. "Just...let me go alone."

He frowned and took her elbow. "Are you sick?"

"No."

"Then why can't I go up with you?"

"I just need to be alone."

His frown intensified. Then his eyes dropped to her stomach. "Oh."

Now she frowned. "Oh?"

"Do you need...privacy?"

"Yes."

"Got it. No need to be embarrassed."

She leaned in. "What are you talking about?"

"If you need the bathroom..."

Her eyebrows arched. She should really just let him think she suddenly needed to rush to the bathroom because of something she'd eaten. But she couldn't.

"I don't need the bathroom," she snapped. "I need my vibrator."

His mouth fell open. Then snapped shut. Then fell open again.

She pulled her elbow from his grip. "I'll be back in...a little bit." She took two steps. Then felt his hand on her arm again. She turned back.

"Your vibrator?"

She smirked at his stunned expression. "Yeah."

"Because of...me?"

"Yep."

He swallowed. "And this will just take a little bit?"

She grinned. "Setting three is *really* good."

"I um..."

"You wanna come with me?"

His eyes heated. "Yes."

"Okay."

"I..." He coughed. "Jesus. I can't."

She shrugged. "Okay."

He let go of her and she took another couple of steps. But she looked back. "Room twelve-fifteen. If you change your mind."

"You're killing me."

"Good. I'll think about that...while I'm upstairs."

He groaned. Loudly.

This time she took four steps before he stopped her. He turned her but didn't say a word. He simply cupped the back of her head and drew her in for a long, deep, hot kiss.

When he let her go, her heart was pounding and it took her a second to take a full breath.

"Think about that too," he said gruffly.

"Yeah." She pressed her lips together. "I will. Thank you."

She only needed twenty minutes in her room. And that included packing and changing her clothes.

She texted him from the lobby.

He joined her at the front doors five minutes later.

His jaw was tight as he approached. She gave him a big smile.

"Much better now," she told him.

"So glad," he said dryly as he grabbed her suitcase and headed for the valet stand.

She giggled.

"Glad you're enjoying this."

"Well, I'm not enjoying it as much as I enjoyed—"

"Don't," he said firmly.

"Just making conversation."

"Not about that."

The valet pulled his car up at the curb, and Beau moved to open the door for her. He stored her suitcase behind the seat, then shut the door and rounded the front of the truck.

Becca watched him the whole time. He was *not* happy.

No, that wasn't true. He wasn't unhappy. He was...tense.

She, on the other hand, felt great. Not as great as if he'd come up to the room with her, but the vibrator she'd packed was good. It wasn't fancy and didn't have any extras. It was basically a clit stimulator with ten speeds. But she never needed to go past three.

He pulled out onto the street and they drove for five minutes before either of them said anything. She'd already texted Savannah that Beau was taking her home, so she settled back and sighed.

"Stop it."

"Stop what?" she asked.

"The happy sighing, the contented looks, the relaxed body language."

She laughed. "I need to act upset and worked up? Even if I'm not?"

"You're rubbing it in."

"You could have rubbed it in."

"Becca," he said, his voice low and firm. "Stop."

She looked over at him. "Why didn't *you* take the edge off?"

He met her eyes. "Just head into the public restroom and jerk off in the stall?"

She shrugged. "I don't know how it works."

"You do know how it works."

Memories and images slammed into her. Beau's big hand wrapped around his thick cock, stroking while his hot eyes were on her...

She cleared her throat and shifted on the seat.

He smirked. "That's better."

"That wasn't very nice."

"Not sorry."

Well, damn, it looked like she and her vibrator were going to have a double-header tonight. And she was definitely going to be thinking about Beau right next door thinking about her.

~

Three weeks later...

BEAU HAD AVOIDED her for three weeks.

Mostly.

He couldn't avoid her entirely, of course. She lived next door. He saw her car pulling in and out of the driveway. He'd run into her at Ellie's twice. And they'd had to make conversation and smile and laugh and act friendly.

Because they *were* friends.

Even if he thought of her every single night when he was in bed alone. And he was *not* thinking friendly thoughts. No, he was thinking very dirty thoughts. He remembered every sound she made. He knew her scent, her *taste*, even a year and a half later. And he let himself fall into all of those memories every night while he jerked off in his bed like a horny teenager.

But they hadn't been alone together since he'd walked her to her parents' front door with her suitcase and stoically avoided kissing her goodnight the night of the wedding in New Orleans. Or even tucking a strand of hair behind her ear.

Because if he'd touched her *at all* he would have pressed her up against the side of the house, put his hand down the front of the shorts she'd changed into for the drive home, and checked to see if she was wet for him even after getting off with her vibrator.

He'd resisted. Barely.

Then he'd spent the next three weeks on edge, bracing himself for the moment when their crazy hometown would lock them in a room together, or sign them up for some project together, or come up with some other way to get them alone together for more than ten minutes.

He figured that was about how long he'd be able to resist saying or doing something really fucking stupid.

Like telling her fuck it, he didn't care if she left in a year, or a month, or a week. He had to have her again.

But nothing had happened.

No one had set them up. They hadn't even been left alone in his mother's kitchen together when Becca had stopped by to pick up cookies for some teacher appreciation something-or-other at school. He'd met her on her way out and had held the door for her as she gave him a wobbly smile.

That was it. His mother hadn't even *tried* to get him inside while Becca was there.

They'd been at Ellie's together twice and Ellie hadn't asked him to go into the storeroom to grab something on a high shelf and then sent Becca in after him. Cora hadn't come up with a reason for him to follow Becca out to the parking lot when she'd left.

She'd gone out with her friends to the bar in Bad two weekends ago and no one had called to ask him to come get her. Or to intercede when another guy got too flirty. Or even just to join them.

He'd gone fishing with his buddies last weekend and when he'd sliced his finger open, they'd just bandaged him up. No one had sent Becca over to help him make dinner since he was one-handed or to re-dress the wound.

Nothing.

All of those missed opportunities for their friends and family to throw them together. But no one had done a damned thing.

And that was making him itchy too.

Being around Becca made him antsy. But *not* being around her felt...wrong.

Had they been wrong about the matchmaking? Was that *not* what had been going on?

Or had *their* plan already worked? When he'd brought her home from the wedding reception and dropped her at her mom and dad's, had everyone gotten the message?

Maybe believing that he and Becca were only friends was easier than he'd thought.

He was in the B and B's driveway loading up the lawn-mower when he heard the front door at the Bollier house slam. He looked over and straightened when he saw Becca stomp out onto the porch and brace her hands on the railing, staring out at the yard.

She looked upset.

Well... shit.

Why was she home? It was Friday morning at nine a.m. She should be at school.

He immediately started in her direction.

"Bec?" he called when he got close.

She looked over and straightened. She swiped at her cheeks. "Oh, hey."

Hell. She'd been crying.

"What's going on?"

"Nothing. I'm fine."

"Why aren't you at school?" He stopped in the grass in front of where she was standing at the porch railing.

"First day of fall break. We have today and Monday off."

"Ah." He tucked his hands in his back pockets. "So why are you crying? Isn't a break from school good?"

"Um..."

Her eyes were not on his. They were on his chest. And shoulders. And stomach. And Beau became aware that he was shirtless. He'd pulled his shirt off while he mowed. And that shirt was still over in his mom's driveway.

His skin heated as her gaze roamed over him. He coughed and pulled his hands from his back pockets, tucking them into his front pockets and slouching a bit.

Jesus, he was self-conscious? With *Becca*? Really? She'd had her hands, and *tongue* on every inch she was now studying.

He shifted, trying to surreptitiously pull his fly away from his cock that was saying *yep, I remember*.

"Bec?" he said.

Her eyes finally came up to his. "Huh?"

"Why are you crying?"

She pulled in a breath and seemed to collect herself. "Oh. Um...it's nothing."

He frowned. "Tears are not nothing."

Her shoulder slumped. "Just..." She looked over her shoulder at the front door. "My dad and I had a fight."

Fuck.

"Wanna go get coffee?" he asked before he thought about it too hard.

She was on fall break, which meant her dad was on fall break as well. Which meant they were home together. If they'd just had a fight, she probably didn't want to go back inside.

Were there a dozen other places she could go with a dozen other people? Yes.

Did Beau want to be the one that helped her with whatever this was? Yes.

"Coffee?" she asked.

"Since you're off today, we could drive over and get coffee at Bad Habit," he said of the quaint little coffee shop that was a favorite of Autre residents even as they maintained that Bad, Louisiana, was their "rival". That might be true on the football and baseball fields, but honestly, the two towns already shared some resources and would probably share more in the future. And truly, the people in Bad were good people. Who had a lot in common with the people in Autre. And everyone in both towns knew it.

Becca pressed her lips together, considering his invitation. Then she nodded. "Coffee sounds great."

"Let's go." He turned on his heel and started for his truck.

"You're going to put a shirt on, right?" she asked. "Or should I take mine off?"

He made himself keep walking. It was going to be a long fifteen-minute drive to the next town if she was feeling flirty. "I'll put mine on, but you do you," he tossed back casually.

She laughed and he felt his gut tighten. That's what he wanted—to turn her tears to laughter.

Jesus, he was feeling poetic this morning? That was just great.

She was right behind him, still with her shirt on, as he grabbed his t-shirt from the front seat and pulled it over his head. She climbed up and he slid behind the wheel.

"Text your dad to tell him you're with me."

She opened her mouth, no doubt to protest, but then simply muttered, "I really need my own place." Still, she pulled her phone out and typed in a quick message.

Beau turned them toward Bad. As soon as they were up to highway speed, he said, "Okay, what happened?"

She sighed and turned a little on the seat to face him. "I finally tried to talk to him about the arts program. I wanted to know what had gone down in that school board meeting where they'd decided to use the money for the football field."

"And it didn't go well?"

"It did not."

She sighed and Beau looked over. She looked sad.

"Did he tell you about the meeting? Or did he not want to talk about it?"

"Well, both. He tried to put me off. He said it didn't concern me and that it was over and done and why did we have to keep discussing it? But finally I pushed hard enough and he told me that they discussed it all for only about fifteen minutes. The Superintendent brought up the fact that Mr. Shadwick had clearly intended his money to be used for the arts programs. But the board felt that the storm tearing up the field was a special emergency, one-time situation and that if Mr. Shadwick was around he'd understand."

Beau wasn't so sure about that. Mr. Shadwick would have been sympathetic, certainly, but he would never have chosen a sports program—with lots of parental and community support —over the other, often overlooked, and underappreciated programs like choir, band, and the speech team.

"We all know that's crap," Becca said. "Those board members know it too."

Beau nodded. "Yeah."

"There was only one board member who seemed uncomfortable with it. Mrs. Robbins. She wanted to at least talk to the Shadwick family about it first, and wanted them to name the field after him or something in exchange, but they said there was no requirement to involve the family—which legally is true —and they voted down the motion to name it after him too."

Becca was scowling when he glanced at her again.

"Because they didn't want to have to explain to everyone *why* they were naming a football field after a guy whose only involvement with that field was the marching band and why they're doing it three years later."

She nodded.

Beau blew out a breath. "Sorry, babe." Then he winced. He

really shouldn't call her babe. "What did your dad say about all of it?"

"That's the problem. Sounds like he didn't say much of anything in the meeting."

"Really?" Beau frowned. "I don't see your dad thinking football is more important than the arts programs."

"Yeah. I know. I don't think he does, but it sounds like he just kind of let them do whatever they wanted. He said his job is to listen to all sides. That he answers to the school board, which is made up of parents and community members. He has to keep their issues and concerns in mind."

Beau couldn't help it. He reached across the seat and took her hand, lacing their fingers together.

"But it's really crappy that the board discussed this without letting the music and art kids' parents even know it was up for discussion so *they* could participate or protest or whatever," she went on. "Then I asked him for ideas about how to make the musical happen. He said they'd have to make do with what they have—which just isn't enough. I mean, they can fake the instruments and I suppose get creative with costumes, but the set? I mean, how do you do that without supplies?" She paused. "And worst of all, he seemed unwilling to even try to come up with anything. He just kind of threw up his hands."

"So you're disappointed in the school board, *and* your dad."

"I'm *pissed* at the school board. I'm disappointed in my dad. And I let Toby and the other teachers down. I didn't get anywhere with him."

"Toby can't expect you to constantly be the mediator with your dad."

"It's not Toby. It's me. I mean I should have some sway, shouldn't I? I *should* be able to talk to him in a different way.

I'm his *daughter*. Shouldn't he care more what I think than what Emmaline Morris thinks?"

"He does, Bec. You know that. I know it's tough working for your dad, but it's tough on him too. He can't treat you differently than the other teachers and he does have to listen to the school board."

She shook her head. "I know. I just hate how tense things are at home."

Beau squeezed her fingers. "I'm sorry."

"Thanks."

They pulled up in front of Bad Habit. The parking lot was nearly full, as usual. The coffee shop was incredibly popular.

"Thanks for trying to cheer me up," she said, looking over at him with a smile.

"I'll always be there for you."

"I know."

And that meant the world to him. No matter what else had happened between them and what their current status was, he *needed* her to know that he always had her back.

They went inside and got their coffees. They chatted with several people as they stood in line, but when Beau asked if she wanted to stay or take their order to go, she chose to go.

She was quiet during the first few miles on the way back to Autre.

"What's going on in that pretty head?" he finally asked.

"I don't know..." She sighed, then looked at him. "Just being at the coffee shop, I realized that I don't know many of the people from Bad and the ones who are familiar from Autre...I just realized..." She blew out a breath. "You know I didn't have a *ton* of friends in high school. All the nice girls, like the ones your cousins are with, are older. And Alexis and Sarah don't live here anymore."

He nodded. His cousins, Josh and Sawyer, were married to

great girls, but Tori and Juliet were a few years older than him and Becca. The other Landry cousins, like Fletcher and Zeke and Zander, were also married to amazing women, but they too, were older.

Alexis and Sarah were two girls Becca had hung out with in high school, but they'd gone to college out of state and were working in Texas and Wisconsin respectively.

But Becca had been a homebody as a teenager. She'd loved to stay home with her books. She hadn't gone to parties, and ballgames, and sleepovers. That had all happened once she hit college and was why he'd tried to make those things a priority when they'd been dating.

"I mean, I have Toby here, of course, but he's got Sam. And Savannah comes down a lot but she doesn't live here and..." Becca blew out a breath. "The other teachers are all annoyed with me because of my dad anyway."

She was staring at her coffee cup, playing with the lid.

"So you're lonely."

She looked over at him. Then nodded. "Yeah. I am."

And he'd been avoiding her for three weeks. Well...fuck.

They should go out. Catch a movie, or find a bar with music, or something. He'd been avoiding time alone with her because he couldn't get the thoughts of her and her vibrator and setting three out of his head. But they were supposed to be *friends*, dammit.

"Do you—"

His phone ringing cut him off. It was connected to the Bluetooth in his truck and MOM popped up on the screen. He glanced at Becca.

"Take it," Becca said with a nod.

He *was* going to make the last three weeks up to her. She wasn't going to be lonely anymore. Not with him right next door, for fuck's sake. But her sweet ass was in his truck with him right now and he could just keep her with him...some-how...for the rest of the day.

He hit the button. "Hey, Mom."

"Hey. I need a favor."

"That's my specialty," he told her.

"A bunch of new plants and bushes that I special ordered just came in. But there's a lot and I need you to run and get them for me."

"Sure. I happen to be done with everything else. I can do it right now."

"Excellent. Would you mind picking a couple of things up for Ellie and Cora too?"

"'Course not. Like, what?"

"They've ordered some new glassware for the bar, and it all came in, but they need someone to make sure that it's going to look good before they haul it home, and they don't have time to make the run up there themselves."

Beau frowned. "Ellie and Cora are going to trust me to decide if their new glassware looks good?"

"Actually, we were hoping that Becca could go along with you. I think she's off today."

Beau looked over at Becca. She met his gaze with a smile and a shake of her head.

"Well, *coincidentally*, she happens to be with me right now." He didn't believe for one second it was a coincidence that his mom was calling right now, but he suddenly loved their matchmaking attempts. "We just grabbed coffee."

Beau wondered if his mother had seen Becca get in the truck with him at the B and B or if someone at the coffee shop had called or texted her.

"Oh, that *is* convenient. Hi, Becca."

Beau rolled his eyes. "Just give us a second. I'm muting

you." He pressed the mute button before his mom could protest.

"So what do you think?" he asked Becca. He *really* wanted her to spend the day with him.

"I don't have any other specific plans today," she said.

"It might be good to get away from Autre for a little bit. Not be hanging at the house with your dad."

"Good point."

"You realize this is very likely another set up?" he asked.

"One hundred percent," she said with a grin. Then she added, "I was starting to think they'd given up."

"Me too."

She just pressed her lips together.

He unmuted his mother. "Hey, Mom. Yeah we're good to go."

"Oh, wonderful. I'd love Becca's opinion on the bushes and flowers as well."

"Great, happy to help," Becca told her.

"You two are the best."

Beau felt a funny kick in his chest. Set up or not, he was suddenly feeling really good about the day ahead.

"I'm texting you the address right now."

Beau glanced at the screen as the text came in. Then he frowned. "Mom, this says Evendale."

"Yep, that's right."

"You're sending Becca and me to *Evendale*?"

"Well, that's where the plants and glassware are."

"That's four and a half hours away."

"Isn't it great that they called early and let us know everything was in so we could get there today?"

Beau didn't have a response. A four-hour road trip. Eight hours round-trip. Not to mention the hour or two actually in

Evendale. They'd probably have to grab lunch and maybe even dinner. That was a lot of time alone with Becca.

But they'd be on the road. In the truck. Driving. So there would be no kissing or touching or temptation to do more.

Yeah, this was good. Just this little bit of time with her this morning had made him realize that he'd missed her over the past three weeks.

He looked over at her. "Still up for this?"

She shrugged. "Yeah. You?"

"Yeah. I'm gonna stop at home for a shower though," he said, plucking the shirt he'd worn to mow the lawn away from his chest.

Becca nodded. "Great. I can get road trip snacks then."

He laughed. "Awesome."

As she got out of the truck and started for her house a few minutes later, she turned back, "Hey."

He looked over the truck bed. "Yeah?"

"I'd be happy to go along today even if it *wasn't* another set-up."

His chest squeezed. "I'm glad."

"And even if I *did* have other friends."

He gave her a grin. She did have other friends. Things were just a little rough right now. But he said again, "I'm glad."

"Just wanted you to know that." Then she pivoted and headed up her mom and dad's front porch.

And Beau finally felt like he could take a deep breath.

Ten hours straight with Becca.

That was going to be way too much, and far too little, at the same time.

nine

"YEAH, looks like we're stuck here overnight. He said he couldn't get the part until tomorrow at the earliest," Beau told his mom.

"Oh, no. That's too bad," Heather said.

Becca covered her mouth with her hand. That was a *terrible* acting job.

"Yeah. I don't know what's going on. The truck's been running perfectly. But while we were inside looking at the glassware, something happened," Beau said.

His acting job wasn't much better. His tone was dripping with sarcasm. His truck had suddenly "broken down" once they'd gotten to Evendale. The truck that had gotten them four hours away from home without so much as a hiccup. The truck he personally maintained. The truck that was now missing some part—she didn't know truck parts so even though he'd told her, it hadn't sunk in—that he said could only be missing if someone *took it out.*

Seemed a lot like an attic door that would only lock if someone intentionally locked it.

"Well, honey, don't worry about a thing," Heather said.

Beau glanced at Becca across the small table in the café where Jack, the mechanic the folks at the glass supply company had recommended, had dropped them. Beau had Heather on a video call, but he still gave Becca an eye roll.

"I mean, we're a little worried," Beau said. "We're stuck here overnight. For at least one night. Where will we stay? What are we going to do?"

As if they both weren't full-grown adults. Though Evendale was a *tiny* town. They didn't have a motel or a Target or similar store to pick up toiletries or basic clothes. So it was...inconvenient...that this was where their families had decided to strand them overnight together.

Because *clearly* that's what was happening here.

"Well, as luck would have it, I happen to know Maggie. She runs the bed and breakfast there. I'll just give her a quick call and see if she can put you up for the night. I'm sure she also has extra toiletries, so you won't have to worry about toothbrushes and things like that."

Beau actually let his mouth drop open as he stared at Becca.

She just shook her head.

"Well, that really is a convenient coincidence," Beau said.

Becca stifled a laugh. If Heather didn't notice her son's sarcasm, it was because she was choosing to ignore it.

This was actually funny. They were playing along with this quite obvious game of matchmaking and Heather *had* to know that they were on to them.

"And that's so interesting because Jack mentioned that *he* happens to know *Leo*," Beau said.

Jack had pulled up in his tow truck and asked where they were from. When they'd said Autre, Jack had perked up and asked if they knew Leo Landry.

Jack was a terrible actor too, so it was about that time that Beau had caught on.

"No kidding," Heather commented.

"Yeah, we're definitely among friends over here," Beau said with an eye roll to Becca. "So, if you could give Maggie a call and beg her to help us out with a couple of rooms, that'd be great. You can just give her my number. She can call us direct."

"I'll do that. I'm sure it will be no trouble."

Becca was sure it wouldn't be.

"We'll talk soon," Beau told Heather.

They disconnected and Beau scrubbed a hand over his face. "Either they think we're idiots, or they've caught on to the fact that we've caught on."

"Well, it is a game in a game of chicken. Everyone knows everyone else is playing, right?" Becca asked.

Beau sighed. "I guess. But if they know that we know that they're matchmaking, do they still expect that we're gonna fall for it?"

Becca leaned in, elbows on the table. "It's not so much about getting us to spend time together. They're betting on the fact that if we do that, we won't be able to help but fall in love."

Beau's jaw tightened.

She ignored it. "Twenty bucks says Maggie's bed and breakfast only has one room… with one bed…open tonight."

Beau slumped back in his chair and groaned. "Oh my God, you're right."

"So what do we do?"

He lifted a shoulder. "There's nothing we *can* do. They literally took part of my truck out. And until they put it back, it's not going to run."

"Do you think Jack took it out?" Becca asked as the thought occurred to her.

"Yes. Now that I know he's a friend of Leo's. He could have

done it while we were inside picking up the glasses. Or he got someone else to do it. Either way, several people in *this* town are in on this too."

Becca giggled.

He lifted a brow. "It's funny?"

"Kind of. My college friends obviously tried and struck out. You know they had to slink back to Ellie's and admit that their plan didn't work. So the older generation now stepped up. And they're using their connections out of town to get it done. Kind of impressive."

"Well, and their plan is a little more effective. We are actually stuck here. Unless we rent a car or something to drive home. And I'm not even sure this town has a car rental place."

She studied him across the table, and he shifted on his seat, seemingly uncomfortable. "Is it really so bad to be stuck here with me? We'll hang out. We'll walk around town and see what's going on. We'll talk and laugh and watch TV and..."

He nodded. "Yeah, it's the *and* that I'm concerned about."

"You mean what you said at the wedding dance?" she asked. "The thing about being stuck in a room with me alone?"

He sighed. "Yeah."

"I've missed you the last three weeks."

His gaze met hers. "Same."

"I don't want that to happen again. So if we need to be on our best behavior, and be super diligent about not letting this get out of hand, then we will. I don't want to risk not having you around."

He took a deep breath, then blew it out "Okay."

His phone chimed with a text. He looked down. "I have the address. And, shocker, there's only one room open tonight, but we're welcome to it."

Becca laughed. "I almost would've been disappointed if

they'd missed an opportunity to stick us in "'the only room'"," she said, using air quotes.

"Maybe the room has a couch."

"Or maybe we're two grown adults, who are good friends and know where we stand and can share the bed with nothing happening."

He looked at her for a long moment. A long moment, that seemed heated. At least to her. Her stomach got warm, and she finally shifted on her seat.

Finally, he said, "Yeah, maybe."

That did not seem absolute at all.

They went up to the cash register to pay, but the café owner told them that their sandwiches and sodas were on the house.

Beau shook his head as they stepped out on the front side-walk. "Mom, Ellie, Leo, and who knows who else really thought this through. They called ahead to everybody."

Becca shrugged. "Let's just enjoy it. Free food, a free bed and breakfast, and time away from the disappointment and disapproval at home."

"Your dad is not disappointed or disapproving of you."

"No, *I'm* disappointed in *him*. But I know he's disappointed about the fact that we're having problems."

"Yeah, you moving out will be a good thing for all of you. There's just a point where you can't live with your parents anymore."

She nodded and they started up the sidewalk toward the bed and breakfast.

"Hey, there's something we could do," she commented, pointing to a sign hanging from one of the lampposts. There was a fall festival going on.

"Awesome," Beau said with surprising enthusiasm.

"You're in the mood for carving pumpkins?"

"I'm in the mood to not be stuck in a quaint bed and break-fast, with a big, comfy bed and the woman I want more than I've ever wanted anything."

Becca stopped walking and spun to face him. "You can't say stuff like that."

He seemed chagrined. "Yeah. I know. Slipped."

"You can't let things like that slip."

"I know. Sorry."

She stood studying him for a moment. She loved affecting him. She loved knowing that everything she felt was recipro-cal. Except that she hated it too. It made it very difficult to ignore. It made it very difficult to not act on it. She wanted him. She wanted to have a relationship. And even though she'd spent most of her life in Autre with him *not* being her boyfriend, ever since she'd fallen in love with him, it just felt wrong to not be able to hug him, hold his hands, kiss'him, climb into his bed at ten o'clock at night when she was cold or had a bad dream. She'd never done that *in* Autre, but it felt like she should be able to.

He felt like hers.

Yes, she'd broken up with him. But she'd never expected the break-up to actually last. She'd really thought when she came home, everything would be good. That they would start over.

He thought she was leaving eventually. She understood that. He thought she could be happier somewhere else. And until a few weeks ago, she thought he was crazy. Now she wasn't so sure. Things with her dad were uncomfortable. Things with the other teachers were tense. And none of that would change. This football field thing would pass, but there would be other issues. And her dad would never listen to her.

Which was why she couldn't get over the conversation she'd had with Sarah, one of the girls she'd gone to college with. Becca had called to get an objective perspective on what was going on in Autre.

Beau, Toby, and Savannah were her closest friends, but none of them were objective about this situation. So she'd called Sarah.

Not only had Sarah commiserated and given her some good advice, she'd also informed her there was an opening coming up in one of the kindergarten classrooms in Houma. Houma was only an hour away from Autre and was a much bigger district with a more diverse community, student body, and faculty with a lot more resources. And the position would be permanent.

Sarah had offered to put in a good word for her with the principal and Becca had said yes.

Every time she thought about it, Becca's stomach swooped and knotted.

Did she want to leave Autre? Not entirely. But she wouldn't have to leave entirely. She could live in Autre and commute to Houma.

And now looking at Beau, she realized there was another good reason. If she left Autre the way he was expecting her to, they could date.

He was afraid that Autre wouldn't be enough for her. That they would start something, then she would decide to leave, and not only would they break up, but she knew it would break his heart that their hometown wasn't enough for her.

This would fix that entire situation. She could be somewhere else where she didn't have all of this pressure and disappointment, and that other shoe he was waiting to drop would have already fallen.

But she couldn't tell him about it yet. It was only a simple conversation she'd had with a friend. It wasn't even a conversation with anyone who could hire her. It certainly wasn't a job offer.

"Yeah, let's go to the fall festival," she decided. That would keep her from saying anything she shouldn't about the job. Or about her feelings for him.

"Sounds good. I saw pumpkin bars and apple cider on that poster. That's all I need to know."

She forced a smile. "Great."

They stopped first at the bed and breakfast to check-in.

As expected, Maggie was delighted to see them. And not at all convincing in her apology about the single room.

Because they didn't have any luggage, they simply stopped upstairs, used the bathroom to freshen up, then stood next to one another, staring at the bed.

"We can get extra pillows and build a little wall between us," Becca suggested.

"Yeah, pillows will totally keep me from wanting to reach across and—"

Becca turned swiftly and slapped a hand over his mouth. "No. You can't talk like that. Not unless you plan to act on it."

His eyes flared with heat. His hand came up to circle her wrist. She started to pull away but he pressed her palm against his lips and kissed it. Then *he* pulled her hand away. "You know I want to."

She narrowed her eyes. "Knock it off."

"What?"

"Talking about it."

"I just don't want you to think I don't want you. That's not it."

She blew out a breath. "Shut *up*, Beau."

"I just don't want you feeling rejected or something."

"Argh!" she groaned. "How do you not get this? This is..." She cast about for an analogy. "It's like you having a huge hot fudge sundae, me starving for it, and you continually waving it around in front of me, while telling me I can't..." She regretted the analogy at that point. Because ice cream made her think of words like "lick". Because sure, yeah, you could "take a bite" of ice cream. But did you really? Even when it was on a spoon, there was a lot of tongue and lip involved.

He cleared his throat. "Got it."

Okay, so she maybe hadn't needed to use the words "huge" and "starving" either.

She pulled herself together. Sort of. "So the nice thing to do would be to toss the hot fudge sundae in the garbage and stop talking about it."

"But you have such a great sundae," he said. "I can't get away from you."

She knew him. Well. He'd meant that to come off as flippant and funny. *Not* as hot.

But he hadn't quite gotten his voice out of the gruff, sexy range and he definitely hadn't gotten the heat and want out of his eyes.

She felt like he'd poured hot fudge over her—warm and very much like she'd have liked to have his mouth on her.

"Stop," she said softly.

"Yeah. In a minute." He pressed her hand to his mouth again and kissed her. Except that it was more of a lingering press of her hand against his mouth and less of a kiss.

She swallowed hard. "You know, I only eat hot fudge sundaes once in a while. I can go a long time in between them, because I know I shouldn't have them more often. But sometimes I just can't help it."

His chest rose and fell with a deep breath, and he dragged her hand from his mouth to his cheek. She cupped his face, rubbing her palm over his beard.

"If you really were a hot fudge sundae, I might be able to

say that I could just have a taste once in a while," he said, his voice rough. "You're more like a drug. One taste and I just want more and more. I'll get to the point where I simply can't go without you. And I'll do anything to have you. Even make really, really bad decisions."

"Like tying me down? Trying to keep me in Autre even when you think it's bad for me?"

With her hand still against his cheek, he slid his hand down her arm. Goosebumps erupted, dancing up her arm to her shoulder and spreading. She felt the tingles over her scalp and cascading across her chest, tightening her nipples.

"I just wanted you to have options. As you've learned, Autre isn't always so perfect."

"The place has to be perfect?"

"For you? It needs to be as fucking close as it can get."

She believed that he felt that way. She believed that he wanted her to have the best of everything. She also believed that he would give up what he wanted to be sure she had what she needed.

"And if I decide that Autre is what I want and that it is perfect for me?" she asked, ignoring the little niggle in the back of her mind that said, *you're already afraid it's not.* "Then what?"

"I told you, if you're still there and happy in ten years, we'll talk."

"I want more than a talk."

"Okay. I'll propose."

She sucked in a little breath. That was what she wanted. It hit her suddenly and hard. "And I'll say yes."

Heat and desire flared in his eyes. And not physical, chemical desire, but desire for *her*. All of her. All that the proposal would signify.

"But ten years is too long," she added.

His hand continued along her arm up to her shoulder and around the back of her neck. "Becca, you're testing me."

She wet her lips and nodded. "I don't want to wait ten years to have you."

"Seven years."

She shook her head. "Two years."

He frowned. "Five."

"Three. If I'm still in Autre in three years, I'll know what it's all about—what living there, teaching there, everything is like in three years. Come on."

He studied her face for a long moment. "I'm such an idiot."

The next thing she knew, his mouth was on hers. He was kissing her deeply, his tongue stroking urgently against hers. She arched against him, going up on tiptoe, needing to be closer.

Three years felt like an eternity. Three minutes felt too long.

"There's no fucking way I can wait three years for you."

The gruff confession made her heart flip, and she realized that the idea of teaching in Houma was a really good one. If he needed her to be somewhere else, somewhere that he didn't have to wait to see if Autre would drive her away, then that was the answer to this.

But that thought was only able to flash through her mind briefly before his hand slid down her back to cup her ass and bring her forward, against his erection. His very big, very hard erection.

He didn't hesitate to deepen the kiss. She met him stroke for stroke. The hand that had been on his cheek slid to the back of his head and into his hair as she gripped the front of his shirt with her other hand.

He walked her backwards until the backs of her knees hit the bed. He followed her down onto the mattress. Her fingers immediately went to the hem of his shirt and she stripped it up and over him. Her fingers greedily traced the lines of his chest and abs. God, she'd missed touching him. He was always so hot, hard, so real and rough. He made her feel hot and safe, sexy, and loved all at the same time.

He rolled so that he was pressing her into the mattress with his body. One leg came up between her knees. As his thigh pressed between her legs, she ground against him unabashedly. One big hand coasted under the edge of her shirt in the back and then around to one breast. His thumb played over her nipple and she gasped.

"Yes, Beau," she said against his mouth.

"Jesus, Becca, you feel so fucking good."

"Make me feel even better," she pleaded.

Her fingers dug into the muscles of his back and she thrilled at the feel of them bunching as he touched her. He played with her nipple as he kissed her deeply, then dragged his mouth down her throat.

"Such a bad idea. I will never get enough of you."

"I'm not over you," she said. "Even as long as it's been. Even though we've tried to stay away from this. I want you. I'm still in love with you."

He froze.

Dammit.

She reached up and cupped his face, forcing him to look at her. "You know that. Don't act surprised. Don't act like this is some shock that changes everything. I love you. And you're still in love with me."

He closed his eyes and sucked in a breath through his nose.

"Beau, look at me."

He opened his eyes. There was a mix of emotions in them. Heat, resignation, affection, but yes, love.

"Say it," she said. "Tell me that you're still in love with me.

Or tell me that you're not. Tell me you're over me. Tell me this is just a quick fuck—that's fine, by the way. But you have to say something. Tell me where we're at here."

"Jesus, Bec," he said, his voice hoarse. "Of course, it's not a quick fuck. Of course I'm not over you. I will never be over you. I'm crazy, madly, deeply in love with you. That's the entire problem. Having you right there, in Autre, next door, within reach every day, is tearing me up."

Her heart swelled as heat and love and *relief* burst through her. She arched against him. "I'm in reach now."

He gave a short laugh, then pressed his forehead to hers. "The town's winning."

She laughed. "No. They're trying to get us back together, to fall back in love. But we never fell out of it."

He gave a groan, and kissed her again, deep and hot, but this time it was slow.

He dragged his hand down her side to her hip, then around to undo the snap and zipper on her jeans. He slid a big hand into the front of her panties without preamble.

"Beau!" She gasped.

"I've got to have you like this."

"You can have me any way you want. You can *totally* have me."

"Just like this," he said again. His middle finger moved over her clit, circling, making sparks shoot out through her body.

She gasped, and arched closer. "Take them off, I want you too."

"I need to feel and hear you come. It's been too long."

"Yes, agreed," she said, reaching for his fly. He grabbed her hand, pressing against the mattress over her head. "Like this. Just you."

"But why?"

"I need to make you lose your mind. I need to hear and feel it."

"So hear and feel it with your cock," she said, wiggling against him.

"I can get off in a number of ways, and have, but I haven't gotten you off in way too long. Let me do this."

"Oh," she started to protest, but he moved quickly, kneeling above her, straddling her thighs. With a hand on either side of her hips, he pulled her jeans and panties off in one smooth move.

Breathing heavy, he just stared at her for a long moment.

"Beau," she started again.

He shifted back. "Spread your legs, beautiful," he said, his voice gruff.

Heat streaked through her. Like him, she'd been getting herself off for a year and half. It had been while thinking of him, remembering the dirty words, and the touches. But yeah, it wasn't the same.

She got it. She'd love to make him lose his mind. But the look on his face was determined. And hot. She knew she wasn't getting her way. At least not until he got this.

She wet her lips and parted her knees.

He stroked a hand up her inner thigh. "Good girl."

"I've missed you," she said. "I haven't even wanted to kiss anyone else. And my vibrator isn't enough."

His eyes were nearly black as he looked down at her. "You haven't been with anyone?"

"I so wanted to," she said with a little laugh. "But none of them talked like you. No one touched me like you. I didn't even want to dance with anyone else."

She heard a soft growl come from what seemed like the back of his throat and his touch on her inner thigh turn from a stroke to a grasp. He spread her thighs wider. "Do you have any idea what that does to me? To know that you're mine? That you've always only been mine?"

She nodded. "I hope it makes you hot and wild and unable to keep from—"

His mouth was on her a moment later. He licked her with one long lick, his tongue flat against her clit. He circled, then sucked and she nearly came off the bed.

He ate at her for several minutes before sliding two thick fingers into her.

It took him less than ten minutes to send her shooting over the edge, crying out his name.

When he lifted his head, wiped his mouth, and gave her a wicked grin, she got hot all over again.

"All mine," he said.

She could only nod.

Just then there was a loud knocking on the door.

They both jumped.

"Yeah?" he called out.

"It's Maggie. Dinner's ready."

Beau looked at Becca. "Hungry?"

For some reason, she felt her face flush. "Yeah."

She was hungry. For him. For more of what he'd just done. All the things he made her feel and want.

He pushed back on the bed and stood. He pulled his shirt back on. "Let's go eat."

Her eyes widened. "Really? Just like that? After what just happened?" Her gaze dropped to his fly. Where he was clearly still hard. "And what *didn't* happen?"

"You're not satisfied?"

Again she flushed. Why? Lord, after what they'd just done —which was almost nothing compared to things they'd done and said in the past—why was she blushing? But was she satisfied? Hell yeah. She felt very good. "Well, yeah."

"Then get your sweet ass off the bed and let's go have some dinner."

"So, what does this mean?"

He took a deep breath. "Can we...talk about that later?"

Uh, she didn't like the sound of that. Why did that feel like "hot fudge sundaes aren't good for you every day, Becca".

"Yeah, okay." She pulled her panties and jeans back on, then slid off the bed. She ran her hands through her hair. The looked up at him. "But I'm not waiting ten years to talk about it."

He slapped her on the ass and gave her a little grin. "Deal."

ten

THIRTY MINUTES LATER, they were half-way through their meal of roasted chicken, potatoes, vegetables, and some of the best dinner rolls he'd ever had. Which he *did* not intend to tell his mother. Ever.

At the Hebert bed and breakfast you gathered around the big dining room table with all the other guests and shared breakfast every morning. Dinner was only served on Friday and Saturday nights.

At Maggie's bed and breakfast, she offered breakfast and dinner every night, and her dining room was big enough that there were multiple tables and chairs.

Which meant that Beau and Becca were at their own table near the window. It was cozy, and yes, romantic.

"So I read that the festival is still going on tonight. They have a few activities and then a dance."

"You want to go up to the festival tonight?" Beau asked.

She shook her head. "Not necessarily. But it's something to do. I was just laying out options."

Beau shifted closer, leaning in and pinning her with a

direct gaze. "No, you're asking me what's going to happen if we go back upstairs."

He knew her. It was going to be very hard for her to hide any thought or feeling from him at this point. And vice versa. The dam had broken. The wall he'd erected between them had crumbled. Any distance he'd successfully put between them was gone. He hadn't intended for any of that to happen—okay, that wasn't entirely true...he'd known if he and Becca were alone in a room with a bed, all of what had happened was possible. Very possible. But he hadn't gone upstairs with her, *intending* for that to happen.

He couldn't quite bring himself to regret it, though.

He'd been holding himself back, barely, ever since she'd moved back to Autre.

He'd known it was only a matter of time before he lost control.

But it did complicate things.

They weren't going to rush. They weren't going to get married or even move in together. He still felt like she needed more time to actually live and work in Autre to be sure it was where she wanted to stay.

He believed she had feelings for him. Their chemistry was incredible. He knew he would never feel this way about anyone else. But he needed to be sure about her. He didn't want to simply be her only option.

She had to *choose* to be in Autre and with him. Not just fall into it. Or get stuck.

"Yeah, I'm wondering what will happen. We've stepped over this line now."

"Yeah." They sure had. Not all the way, but it was enough. He was addicted all over again.

"Friends with benefits," he said. "That's probably the best thing."

"Meaning we don't tell anyone? We're not officially dating?"

"Yeah, I think that's best."

"Does that mean we date other people?"

He immediately scowled. "Fuck, no."

"Well, that sounds like a boyfriend then."

"Do you want to date other people? Who?"

She shook her head. "I don't. That's part of the problem. I've never really wanted to date anyone else. Not since you."

That hit him directly in the chest. He felt the same way. He wished like hell he could feel this way about someone else.

"I can't stay away from you," he admitted. "But I also won't propose. I'm not going to move you into my house or knock you up. I am not going to tie you down in Autre. Not until you are absolutely a thousand percent sure."

She looked at him for a long moment. Then she swallowed. "Well, actually there's something I wanted to talk to you about."

Just then her phone rang. She frowned. It was a Friday night, around seven. Everyone who knew them knew where they were. And all of them were thrilled they were together, stranded hours from home.

She reached into her purse and pulled the phone out. Then her eyes widened as she looked at the screen. "I should probably take this," she said.

Beau nodded. "Go ahead."

"Hello, this is Becca." She paused. "Yes, hello." Another pause. "That's no problem at all." She listened for longer this time. She seemed surprised. Then she smiled. "I understand. Yes, I'd be interested."

She was quiet for several seconds. "Yes, I can make that work," she answered. She finally looked up at Beau, but she nodded. "That will be great. Thank you."

She listened again. Then she smiled. "Okay, great. Thanks for calling. I'll see you on Monday."

She disconnected and took a deep breath.

"Everything okay?" Beau asked. But it seemed obvious that it was. She seemed very pleased with the phone call.

She nodded. "Yeah. Actually, this is what I was going to talk to you about."

"What's going on?"

"I was talking to a friend of mine. Sarah. We went to college together. She's a teacher too. I wanted to talk about everything that's happening in Autre. I needed another teacher's perspective and I'm used to talking to Toby about everything. But obviously that's a little awkward right now."

Beau nodded.

"Anyway, as we were talking, Sarah mentioned that there might be an opening at her school. Soon." She paused. "In kindergarten."

Beau felt his heart leap into his throat. He swallowed hard. "Oh."

Becca leaned in. "It's in Houma. So just an hour away. But a much bigger school district. There are *multiple* elementary schools serving that area."

Beau just nodded. It was definitely a bigger area than Autre. It was an old city with a lot of history and a strong Cajun culture.

"One of the current kindergarten teachers in the school where Sarah teaches first grade just had a baby and she's decided coming back was too hard and she wants to stay home instead. She plans to finish the semester and then not return after Christmas."

Beau felt his stomach knot as Becca took a breath.

She held up her phone. "That was the principal. He wants to talk to me on Monday."

Beau stared at her. "You might leave Autre in December?"

"Yes. I could do the second semester in Houma. They'd have to cover me in Autre, but that won't be hard." She sighed. "Emmaline's sister could do it. She graduated in May too and isn't working anywhere right now."

"But I..." Beau had no idea what he was going to say. He frowned. "I had no idea you were thinking about leaving so soon."

"I wasn't really. It just came up in conversation. But it's worth considering. Things in Autre are tense. And of course, there will be issues in Houma too. No place is perfect. But it will be different somewhere I didn't grow up. Where my dad isn't my boss. Just like you said."

Beau tried to process all the information. His thoughts were spinning and his heart was pounding.

This was good. This sounded great for Becca. It would get her away from all the tension that was making her unhappy.

So...she'd leave.

Exactly as he'd expected.

"It sounds great," he finally said.

She leaned in. "It's only an hour away. We could date. I could easily make that commute."

"Long-distance again? Didn't we learn from that?"

"One hour and five hours are very different. Hell, I could live in Autre and drive to Houma."

"Come on, Bec. You'll have parent-teacher conferences and activities. And don't you think it would be good for your kids, and *you*, for you to live there and really get to know the community and the families?"

"I'm a kindergarten teacher. It's not like I'll be at ballgames and science fairs. Sure, there might be meetings and things once in a while, but it's not that far, Beau."

"Yeah."

But there was a huge pit in his stomach. It wasn't that far and that road was good. But his hours were crazy. And there was no promise that she would stay in Houma. Yes, it was bigger than Autre, and maybe more progressive. There were more kids for her to interact with. A bigger staff to learn from and share with professionally.

But it could be a steppingstone to something even bigger. She had no idea if she would like it there. She'd never spent time in Houma, didn't know anyone there except for this Sarah. She could get there and not make any friends, not like the school board or the administrators, a million things could make her want to move on from there.

"Beau," Becca said. "Look at me."

He did.

"This can work. We don't have to be friends with benefits. We can actually be together."

"Are you doing this because of me?" The thought occurred to him as he said it out loud.

"Sure. Of course. You're part of all my considerations."

He frowned. "Becca, that's not okay."

"It's not okay to consider how I can make a relationship work with the man I'm in love with?"

He leaned back, oxygen rushing out of his lungs. They'd just said it to one another upstairs, but hearing her confess that she was keeping him in mind while she was making huge life decisions suddenly made him feel cold. He did not want to be responsible for her making decisions that might be wrong. He'd made his choice to stay in Autre because of other people and he didn't *resent* it, but he did wonder if he'd done the right thing. He didn't want Becca wondering about anything. Not about anything having to do with him anyway.

"We need to head back to Autre," he said.

Her eyes went wide. "What?"

203

"We need to head back. Tonight."

"How are we going to do that? We don't have a truck."

"We do. They're gonna put the part they took out of my truck back *in* my truck. Tonight. Now." He shoved back from the table and stood.

"Beau—"

He slapped his hand down on the table. "They're gonna fix the truck, Becca. We're going home."

BEAU WAS RIGHT. Jack fixed the truck.

Sure, it took some growling from Beau. And a phone call to Leo. And a threat to just take the part out of another, newer, truck and put it in his truck himself.

But eventually Jack fixed the truck.

Then they took the four-hour road trip back to Autre that felt like it took four years.

Beau didn't want to talk about their relationship. He did not want to talk about her new job. He didn't want to talk about much of anything. And when she tried, he cranked up the new Jason Young album to a level she couldn't talk over.

So she let him stew. She researched facts about Houma and the school system on her phone. And forwarded several to Beau's phone.

Every time his phone dinged with a new text from her, his jaw clenched.

At least that part was fun.

That ride home was only slightly more pleasant than the following six days. It was shorter, for one thing. And it had a great soundtrack to it at least.

The almost-week following that trip was annoying, sad, frustrating, and lonely. Because he avoided her. Completely.

And when she listened to Jason Young without him, she oscillated between wanting to cry and wanting to punch someone. Well, okay, wanting to punch *Beau*. But he wasn't around so that just made her even more angry.

She'd been by his shop, but he'd been "way too busy, Becca, I have a business to run" to stop and talk. She'd gone to his house after hours, but he hadn't answered. Because he was a chicken. Which she'd told him—by yelling at his front door, on the note she'd taped to that front door, in the three texts she'd sent, and in the three voicemails she'd left.

He also wasn't returning texts or voicemails.

Even the ones where she'd sexted. And included a video.

She hadn't been proud of that. In fact, she'd been pretty embarrassed when even the video of her *naked* in bed telling him how much she missed him failed to get a response.

Finally, desperate, she did something that she *really* wasn't proud of.

But dammit, it was his own fault.

She texted again. With the thing she knew he wouldn't ignore.

I'm at Ellie's. Don't feel good. Need a ride home.

She knew he'd assume she was drunk, but she hadn't actually *said* that, so she wasn't lying to him—and if he'd just return her phone calls, she wouldn't have to resort to this—but she also knew that he would definitely come if he thought she really actually needed him.

She watched the little bubbles pop up showing that he was typing.

They disappeared.

They popped up again.

Then disappeared with no message coming through.

It was *possible* he would try to call someone else to come pick her up, but she didn't think anyone else would. They all still wanted to throw her and Beau together. And, honestly, Beau had this thing about being the person who was there for her. The one to be her hero. The one she could depend on.

But just to be safe, she texted Toby, Sam, Mitch, and Zeke telling them that she needed *Beau* to come pick her up. None of them.

She didn't bother texting any of the other Landry cousins. They were all sitting in the back of Ellie's at the family table, eating dinner, laughing and talking, as usual.

Typically, she would join them. They always welcomed her as one of their own. But they also respected a good pout, a straight shot of whiskey, and a "No thanks, I'm in a shitty mood tonight."

So, she was sitting at the end of Ellie's bar alone—or as alone as anyone really got in Ellie's—when Beau walked through the door less than ten minutes later.

"Okay, let's go," he said, stopping next to her.

She picked up her glass of soda—the only thing she'd had since that first shot—and took the final swallow before setting it back down.

"Okay." She turned on the stool and slid to the floor. She wobbled, but not because of intoxication. Because she was wearing heels. Which was also a stupid, desperate ploy to get his attention.

But it worked to get his hand on her elbow to keep her upright.

She was past the point of caring about being pathetic. She *had* to talk to him.

Once they stepped outside, she said, "Yes, I'm here alone."

He didn't say anything. He just started toward his truck. Thankfully there were a lot of other vehicles taking up space in front of Ellie's so he had parked several yards from the door.

"I'm in a bad mood," she said. "Didn't want anyone else around."

He sighed. "I'm not gonna ask you about your bad mood, Bec." He kept tugging her across the dirt parking lot.

She stopped, digging in her heels. He stopped with a muttered curse and turned.

"I got offered the job."

He just looked at her for a few beats, then shoved his hand through his hair. "Congratulations. I'm not surprised." He glanced toward the door behind her. "Why the bad mood then?"

"Because I can't tell anybody about it. Except you. And I have no fucking idea how you feel about it."

He moved closer to her. "I'm happy about it. Happy for you. I think it's great. You need to be in a bigger school system. Where there are more kids that you can help, other teachers you can work with, a community that will give you and the students and the programs the support you all deserve."

She lifted her chin. "The only reason I'm not yelling at you right now is because I know you actually mean all of that. I know you actually think that me being there will be better for me. And you care enough about me that that's what you want."

"Of course it is."

"I don't get it. Why are you avoiding me then? I did what you thought I should do, I looked at a new job. I expanded my horizons. I thought outside the box. I decided not to just settle for what's in Autre. And that's when you closed off. You pulled away even further than you had when I first moved back. What do you want, Beau? Do you want me here in Autre or far away? Or do you really not care at all where I am?"

He advanced on her. Quickly. "I've not been staying away this week because I don't care." His voice was gruff and firm.

There were so many emotions swirling in his eyes, Becca felt her heart begin to pound.

"Then why? You're the only person in my life who actually knows all about this. All of the different sides of what I'm dealing with here and that I'm even thinking about a new job and I haven't been able to talk to you about it."

He stared at her for a long moment, his breathing was uneven. "I've been staying away while you think it all through and make this decision because you said you're considering me in everything and...you shouldn't. This should be *your decision.*"

She felt her eyes widen. "I don't have to actually *see* you or talk to you to consider you. I'm in love with you whether I see you or not. And that's been true for over a year. Even after we broke up. That's not going to change now just because you're being a stubborn ass."

Finally, he took the step that brought him right up against her. He cupped her face in both hands. "I've also been staying away because the taste I got of you, and the realization that you might actually be leaving, has had me on the verge of buying a diamond ring for days. And if I didn't stay busy or drunk, I would lose what little control I had and do something we both might regret."

Her stomach and heart both flipped over. She looked at his mouth, then back to his eyes. "There is nothing you could do that I would regret."

"I think leaving is the right thing for you. But it's tearing my heart out."

"I'm not leaving you. I can drive—"

He lowered his head and covered her mouth with his.

The kiss was desperate. It was hot, and deep, but there was definitely an edge to it. Like he couldn't get enough. Like he wanted to drink her in and pour himself into her. And like he knew it was never going to be enough.

He kissed her for several long moments, and only pulled apart when he heard a car door slam. He stood looking down at her, breathing hard. "I don't really know how I feel. Except that I want you happy. I want you to have what you need."

"I want you."

"What you *need*," he said, emphasizing the last word.

"But I—"

"Oh my God, I'm so glad you guys are here!"

They jerked apart as Jordan Landry approached.

"Jordan," Beau said. He cleared his throat. "What's up?"

There was no way Jordan and her husband, Fletcher, who was right behind her, hadn't seen the kiss. But they acted as if they'd just come upon two friends hanging around outside the bar chatting.

"We were just talking about the two of you," Jordan said, glancing at her husband.

Fletcher was another of the other-side-of-the-family Landry cousins. He was also one of the third-grade teachers at the school. Becca saw him every single day.

"You were talking about us?" Becca asked, pulling her fingers through her hair.

Normally, she'd be surprised by that, but with the way everybody had been scheming, she assumed that they were a topic of conversation regularly.

She knew that Heather, Leo, and Ellie were disappointed by their early return from Evendale. Heather was especially disappointed because they'd forgotten to pick up the plants.

Of course, no one believed that she actually needed those plants.

With that gigantic matchmaking failure, Becca had thought everyone might give up.

She had a suspicion that was not the case when Jordan and Fletcher grinned widely and said, "Come inside. We have something exciting to talk to you about."

"Actually, I just showed up to give Becca a ride home. She's had a bit too much to drink."

She could definitely play along with that. Several people inside, including Ellie, had seen Beau come pick her up.

But her lips were still tingling from his kiss, and more, her heart was still beating hard from what he'd confessed. He was torn up about her leaving. He was mixed up about how he felt. He'd been staying away from her this week because he wanted her so much.

Yeah, she didn't want to go home. He would drop her off and leave her there alone.

Now she might get another chance to be thrown together with him?

Yes, please. Even if what happened in the bedroom at the bed and breakfast hadn't happened.

But it had.

Plus, she was maybe leaving. And if he was going to pull back when that happened, then there was now a countdown clock ticking on their time together.

She was definitely going to wring pleasure out of every second she had left with Beau.

"No, I'm feeling great. Let's go back inside."

Beau lifted a brow. "Not so drunk then?"

She knew that he knew that she wasn't. Beau had seen her drunk. She was pretty sure that the minute he'd walked into Ellie's he'd figured out that she'd lied to get him down there.

Certainly, after he kissed her the way he had, he'd known that she'd only been drinking cola.

"Nope, I'm good. And I want to hear what Jordan and Fletcher are up to."

Beau's heavy sigh was very loud.

They followed Jordan and Fletcher into Ellie's. Of course the Landrys led them back to the family table at the back of the bar.

It was actually more than one table now. Originally Ellie's grandkids had gathered around one big, long table. But now that they all had partners, and friends who had turned into family, as well as kids of their own, the tables had expanded to four long tables that were pulled together. In addition to the Landry family, there was the LeClaire family, the firefighters that worked at the local station, the group of friends and the security detail who had come with Fiona Grady when she'd moved to Autre with her giraffes—yes, there were giraffes in Autre, Louisiana. Penguins, too, as a matter of fact. And many other animals.

Becca and Beau were hardly the only non-blood relation and they settled into chairs completely comfortable in the group.

Well, comfortable except for the tension between them.

Becca leaned over and whispered to him, "Relax. Everybody's going to be able to tell something's wrong."

"They're trying to set us up for something."

"Of course they are. We knew that was going to keep happening."

"So, we keep up with it until you move?"

She turned and met his gaze. "I guess we keep it up until it's over."

He didn't look happy. "And when will that be?"

"I'm not sure. But there has to be an endpoint, right?"

Anything he was about to say, was interrupted by Jordan moving to the head of the table and calling, "Okay everyone. I have all the details."

Becca and Beau gave their attention to Jordan, but Becca could feel the rigidity in his body.

"For anyone who's missed the story," Jordan said, her gaze landing on Becca and Beau. "I have as many tickets to the Jason Young concert in Vegas as we want."

Becca smirked as Beau sat up a little straighter. He was a huge fan.

Almost everyone around here was. Jason was from Bad. He'd played football against the guys Fletcher's age. And he'd dated Jordan. For years. In fact, their break-up had been a public spectacle that had caused Fletcher to jump on a plane and fly to Vegas to be there for her.

They'd come home married.

"As you know, up until now he's been an opening act. But now he's headlining his own tour. He's also got a local girl from New Orleans, Hayden Ross—who some of you have probably seen on Tik Tok—opening for him." Jordan beamed at all of them as if *she* had discovered Hayden rather than Sabrina Sterling, the singer-songwriter from Bad who had introduced Hayden to Jason.

"And his next stop is in Vegas," Jordan went on. "He's already had a couple of shows in Nashville. Fletcher and I drove up and he was amazing. He does have a couple of dates in New Orleans, so anyone who doesn't want to go along can see him later on. But—" She gave the table a huge smile. "He's going to get us as many tickets in Vegas as we need. This show is going to be huge for him. Lots of media coverage and he really would love to have a hometown crowd there. Some people from Bad are coming too. And"—She glanced up at Fletcher—"since that's where everything changed for Fletcher and me, *at* a Jason Young show more or less, we thought it would be a really fun trip for us. And we'd love to have you all there with us."

"Oh my God," Charlie Landry said, beaming at her friend and cousin-in-law. "That is a fantastic idea."

Jordan nodded. "It can be just a quick trip. The show is Saturday night and we can all stay at the casino hotel. Flights to Vegas are super cheap and easy to get from New Orleans. I say we all hop out there, have a great weekend, and be back in time for work on Monday."

Everyone around the table started talking at once.

That gave Beau and Becca some cover to talk just between the two of them.

Beau leaned over. "No way."

"Come on, it sounds fun," Becca said to him. "And they're just including us in the group plan. It's not really a set up. I really don't think Jason Young is throwing a concert to get us together."

"No, but pretty much everyone around this table who is planning to go are couples."

Becca scanned the table. He was right of course. Most everyone sitting around was coupled up. There were a few single guys, like a couple of the firefighters and the guys who were now working private security for Fiona's ex-bodyguard, Colin.

But yes, if Beau and Becca went along there would be a lot of couples in the group.

"So what? You love Jason Young. We both do."

"This is a bad idea, Becca."

"Why? It's not any different than any of the other set ups. We go, we resist, we come home as friends, they give up."

He didn't say anything.

She looked up to meet his gaze. His eyes were hot.

"Things have changed," he said gruffly.

"Have they, though?"

"You fucking know they have. You're leaving. And we crossed the line."

She scoffed even as heat swept through her belly. "We *barely* crossed the line."

"Becca," he said, low with warning in his tone.

"So you're back to being afraid of being alone together? You think that all the reasons to keep your hands to yourself are gone now?"

"Something like that."

"And what would be so bad about that?"

His jaw was tight when he leaned close and put his mouth against her ear. In spite of the fact he was clearly frustrated, goosebumps skittered down her neck, over her shoulder, and down her arm.

"I've told you this. Repeatedly," he said, low, firm, and hot against her ear. "I don't want to cross that line because there's no coming back. I'll want it all. And then I'll spend the rest of my life thinking that I tied you down and wondering if you regret it."

She pulled in a deep breath, then leaned away from him. "Well, tell you what, Beau, if we do end up in Vegas and have to share a hotel room, with your current attitude, you don't have to worry about me agreeing to any sex." She met his gaze. "I don't sleep with assholes."

"So, who's in?" Jordan asked the table.

Becca turned back around to face everyone. And stuck her hand up in the air. "Me. Sounds like a great time."

eleven

A HOT HAND slid over her stomach, then down to settle on one of her thighs. Becca's eyes opened slowly. What registered first was that it was completely dark and she was really warm.

No, she was *hot*.

She was lying in a very comfortable bed and there was a furnace next to her.

Okay, she knew it was a person.

The calloused hand stroked up and down her inner thigh. The big body shifted, and then she felt a hot mouth press against her skin where the hand had just been.

"Got to taste you. Need this sweet pussy against my tongue."

Oh, yeah, she knew that voice.

She'd known it was Beau. Just the feel of him was so familiar. And his scent. And the way he touched her. But, that voice—that gravelly, low, dirty voice—was *definitely* him. She dreamed about that voice. She conjured that voice when she was using her vibrator.

She shifted her legs against the silky sheets.

"Beau," she said huskily.

"Yeah, baby. Need you."

His shoulders moved between her knees, and she had to spread them to accommodate him. One hand went around to cup her ass while the other splayed across her lower stomach. He rubbed back and forth as he squeezed her butt, just breathing on the spot that was now suddenly aching for him.

How could he get her going so quickly? She'd been asleep just a moment ago. But her whole body felt hot and melty and like she was straining toward him.

"Beau, *yes*."

"You know the way you say my name makes me wild," he practically growled.

She wiggled in his hands, trying to arch closer to his mouth. Even in the dark. She knew exactly where all of their body parts were.

He ran his hand from her stomach up to one breast. He cupped her, then thumbed over her nipple.

"I swear, I dream of your taste. I can conjure how you feel against my tongue. Your taste haunts me, Bec."

The total darkness made all of this hotter. She arched her neck, pushing the back of her head into the pillow. Damn, these were nice pillows.

He squeezed her nipple then rolled and plucked it. That sent shimmers of heat arrowing through her stomach to her pussy. Her inner muscles fluttered.

He knew that playing with her nipples made her hotter and wetter.

"That's my girl," he praised. "Want you hot and begging."

"Keep going," she said breathlessly.

"You want this?"

Was she dreaming? For just a moment, Becca paused. But no, she could feel the sheets under her back. She could feel cool air brushing across her skin from an AC vent. His calloused hands were real, his shoulders were spreading her wide and she could feel the stretch of her inner thigh, and his hot breath against her was definitely real.

"Yes," she said. "Please."

"I'm not stopping," he told her. "Can't. Not again. You're mine now, Bec, and I need you. All of you."

"Yes." She reached down and threaded her hand through his hair, then gripped. She pressed him closer. "Please."

"I'm gonna make you scream," he said with a dark promise in his voice. "Then I'm going to fuck you. You understand?"

"God, yes," she said, her voice needy. She was ready to beg at this point if she had to. And she might. He liked that.

"All mine," he said, again, almost in a growl. His fingers tugged her nipple as he lowered his head. The first lick against her clit made her gasp and arch closer.

His hand on her ass tightened, holding her in place.

Then he proceeded to lick, suck, and talk her into a fast, hard orgasm.

She cried out his name, pulling on his hair. He continued eating at her until the ripples quieted to slow flutters. But her body was definitely still trembling when he moved up and put his lips against hers.

He kissed her deeply, stroking his tongue against hers. He always loved doing that. Kissing her after making her come with his mouth. It was so dirty, and she loved it. She wrapped her arms around his neck, opening her mouth and wrapping her legs around his hips.

His cock pressed against her center, and she moaned.

He reached between them, running his middle finger through her slick folds and then sliding two fingers deep.

Her body responded instantly, ripples of pleasure quickly turning into waves.

He pumped deep. "You ready for me?"

"Always."

He shifted and she felt his cock against her entrance.

"Do I need a condom?"

She shook her head. Even though it was dark. "I'm still on the pill and I told you there hasn't been anyone else."

He gave another growl and lowered his head, kissing her hungrily. When he lifted his head, he said simply, "It's always only been you for me."

God, she wished there was some light in here now. "You haven't been with anyone?"

He gave a short laugh. "It's been me and my hand ever since I drove away from Baton Rouge that night."

In the dark, she cupped his face with her hands. "Oh my God."

"Need you." His voice was rough.

"Yes."

"You're mine, Becca. All mine."

She tightened her thighs around him. "I always have been."

It was as if at that moment, he realized that not only had she not been with anyone since him, she'd *never* been with *anyone* else. He'd known that, of course, but in that moment, it was like the words were hanging in the air between them.

He thrust forward, filling her, all at once. Her previous orgasm made it an easy entrance, in spite of how long it had been.

She cried out. "Yes, oh yes, Beau."

"Christ, Becca," he said, resting his forehead against hers, and just breathing.

"Yes, this is so good," she said. She had to assure him that she was good and that everything was wonderful. She curled her fingers into his back and lifted her hips closer.

He put a hand on her hip, squeezing and holding. "Just give me a second."

"Are you okay?"

"Yeah. Just want this to last longer than thirty seconds."

She smiled. "We can always do it again."

That got him moving. He pulled out and thrust back in. It was a nice, long, slow movement, stretching her. The heat was incredible. The friction, perfect.

He paused at the end of the thrust, breathing raggedly for a moment. Then pulled out and thrust forward again. But soon enough the pace picked up.

The only sound in the room was the rustling of the sheets, their breathing and groans, and the sound of skin on skin.

"God, tell me you're with me," he said after a few minutes.

She was. She actually wanted this to last even longer, but her body was having none of that. Her orgasm was coiling, tight, low and deep, and she was only a few strokes away.

"So close," she said.

He reached between them, his thumb finding her clit. "Need you there *now*," he told her.

"Beau," she said, wanting to slow it down just a bit.

But he knew her. He knew her body. He knew her buttons. He'd taught *her* all about her buttons.

"You're taking me so good, Becca," he told her. "You feel so fucking good. Milk me, baby. Take me. Take it all." He circled her clit. "Come for me. I want to feel you come on my cock."

That shot her over the pinnacle easily.

She gasped, her pussy clenching around him as sparks of pleasure and heat exploded through her body.

He was right behind her, shouting her name as he froze, then shuddered with his climax.

He braced himself over her, breathing hard. "You okay?"

"I'm so okay." She laughed. "Except for being mad at you for keeping us from doing that for the past four months."

"Can't talk about that," he said. He pulled in a long breath, then dropped down next to her. He gathered her close. "That's over."

She sucked in air and nodded. "Okay."

They lay, cuddling for a few minutes, him stroking her hair, her running her hand up and down his arm.

Eventually he pushed up and padded away, she assumed to the bathroom to cleanup. When he came back to bed, he simply pulled the covers up over them, tugged her against him with her back to his chest, and wrapped a big heavy arm around her.

"Beau," she started.

"Shhh," he said into the back of her hair.

So she did.

～

BEAU HAD WOKEN up hung over before.

He'd also woken up in a good mood before. That had happened less often, but it had happened.

When he rolled over and pried his eyes open the next morning, he realized that he was feeling a little bit of both.

And he didn't really understand either one at first.

Okay, not *a little bit* of both. He was definitely hung over. But he also felt pretty good. Like he was in a good mood. He scrubbed a hand over his face. What the hell was that about?

It must've been a great party.

Slowly, bits and pieces came back to him.

Vegas.

He was in Vegas. And there had been...okay, less of a party and more of an Autre-Does-Vegas night on the town with his friends and cousins. Of course, it had been a good time. A rip-roarin'-lots-of-liquor-over-the-top-make-bad-decisions-crazy time.

They'd had plenty of those times back in Autre, so put them all in Las Vegas and... well, anything could happen.

And probably had.

He opened his mouth and smacked his lips together. Yeah, that dry mouth and thick tongue were definitely hangover symptoms. As was the dull jackhammer at the back of his head.

The room was only dimly lit, sunlight barely filtering in through the heavy drapes.

Las Vegas knew what it was doing.

But what about this good mood? Yeah, the night had been great, but there was something just on the edge of his consciousness that was making him feel especially happy.

He stretched and reached his arms out in both directions. He was in a huge bed. Alone...

His eyes widened suddenly. He'd had sex last night.

That came rushing back to him. Sweet sighs, husky moans, his name being cried out at orgasm, the feel of hard nipples and silky skin, the sweet taste of a pussy...

He sat up quickly. And instantly regretted it. He rested his head in his hands.

Damn, his head hurt. But the rest of him felt *oh, yeah*.

It had been a really long time.

He became aware of the sound of the shower running.

And the person in the bathroom started to sing.

It was a Hayden Ross song. That was all he knew for sure. He couldn't have placed the title and he certainly didn't know the lyrics well, but it was definitely one of Hayden Ross's.

And that was definitely Becca singing it.

And the feeling of *yes* that coursed through him was

221

intense. He'd had sex last night. With Becca. And she was now in the shower. Singing. That was good. That was very good.

The next second he frowned.

Because he could not, for the life of him, conjure much more than those flashes of memories from the night before.

Oh...*fuck*.

He'd had sex with Becca and he didn't fucking remember it?

He scrubbed his face with his hands.

Noooo.

The door opened.

He looked up slowly.

Becca stepped out, wrapped in a towel.

She propped her shoulder against the doorway. "Hi."

"Mornin'."

"I wasn't sure if I should wake you. People are texting that they're going down to the buffet here at the hotel for breakfast, but they're going in shifts."

He nodded, just looking at her. She was so fucking gorgeous. Sure, part of it was her being clad in only a towel. But he found her gorgeous in anything. Making it hard to breathe right now, though, was the soft smile she was giving him.

She didn't seem upset. She didn't seem nervous. She didn't seem angry.

She seemed really, really happy.

Damn, he wanted this girl happy. As happy as she could possibly be. Every damned day of her life.

"How are you?" he asked.

Her smile grew. "Better than I've been in a long time."

He blew out a breath. That was a pretty good answer. "I'm extremely hung over," he told her. It seemed that he needed to put that out there.

She frowned. "Yeah, I've definitely got a headache. Do you..." She paused and wet her lips. "Remember last night?"

"Up until about the third casino," he admitted, thinking back. "And then...only bits and pieces from there."

She pushed away from the door. "Oh."

"I remember that..." He glanced at the bed, then back to her. "It...happened. I just don't remember every detail." He grimaced. "Sorry. Trust me, I really fucking wish I did. But I didn't want to lie to you about that."

She padded toward him, stopping about a foot away. She was clutching the towel between her breasts. "No, I'm glad you told me. I kind of woke up thinking maybe it was a dream."

"Not a dream," he said, his voice rough. "It happened."

She gave him a sexy little smile. "Yeah. I know. I don't remember absolutely everything about it either. It must've been the middle of the night. It was pitch black. You woke me up."

He winced. "Sorry about that too."

She laughed lightly. "Don't be. I was *not* upset."

"So, you were good? I made sure you were?"

"It was completely consensual," she told him. "No regrets."

He took a deep breath and blew it out. "Okay, great."

She stood just looking at him for a long moment. "So now what?"

He studied her as he thought about her question seriously. Then he asked himself if his answer would be the same if she was fully clothed. When he realized it would be, he said confidently, "I'm torn between three options."

She lifted both brows. "I'm listening."

"Option number one, we pretend nothing happened and we go about things as if everything was the same as before."

She just nodded her understanding.

"Option number two, we try this dating thing. You go to

Houma to work, but we try it. I mean, worst-case scenario, it doesn't work, and I'm as torn up about it as I will be if we don't try."

She looked mildly surprised by that. But she nodded again.

"Third option, we don't talk about any of that. And I strip you out of that towel and bring you back to bed and make sure we both remember absolutely everything about this time."

She took a big step forward. "Can we do a combo of option two and three?"

Beau accepted his fate and nodded. "Yeah, I think we can do a combo."

She dropped her towel and took another big step. Beau drank in the sight of her, then his hands settled on her hips and he tugged her between his knees. "Just one thing."

She ran her fingers through his hair. "Anything."

"Can I get some ibuprofen and maybe a toothbrush first?"

She laughed. "Probably a good idea."

And when they left the room an hour later, they both felt a lot better. All over.

BECCA COULDN'T REMEMBER BEING this happy in a long time. Sure, part of it was the amazing sex and the orgasms she'd had in the past twenty-four hours. But she and Beau were going to try dating. That was making her even happier than the orgasms. She could get those other places. Not as good as the ones Beau gave her, of course, but nothing could compare to knowing that she and Beau were going to try to make this relationship thing work.

"So are we going to admit that we're dating? Let somebody get the trophy and the reserved table at Ellie's?" she asked as they located the big table full of Landrys and friends across the casino buffet.

Beau sighed. "I think they're going to know."

"I guess we leave it to them to battle out who is actually the winner. Unless they make the trophy into some kind of traveling trophy."

"Yeah, the reserved table at Ellie's is less of a draw for them. They already have reserved tables there."

She laughed and nodded. "But that trophy is going to be something they pass around happily."

He lifted their linked hands and pressed a kiss to the back of her knuckles. "Honestly, I can't be mad."

She grinned up at him. "I'm glad."

She knew that Beau felt a bit of a sense of obligation here. Now that they'd slept together again, and she was taking a new job, he no longer had any reason to fight her on getting back together. But she also knew that he wasn't entirely convinced this was going to work.

That broke her heart a little bit. But it would just take time. A year or two from now, he'd be convinced and they could move ahead. They could get married, start a family, decide where they were going to live. Maybe they should live in a little community outside of Autre. Someplace where they could start new.

But those were all conversations for a later date. One step at a time.

They approached the table, and everyone turned to look at them at once.

Yeah, there was no way they were going to miss that she and Beau had gotten together last night.

"Well, good morning, you two," Owen Landry, one of Beau's cousins' cousins greeted, settling back in his chair and linking his hands behind his head. He was giving them a huge grin and looked very smug about something.

"Good morning," Becca said calmly taking a seat in the chair Beau pulled out for her at the end of the table. Beau dropped into the seat next to hers.

"I choose the cornbread muffins," Owen said. He was addressing his grandmother.

Ellie had made the trip to Vegas with them. She was a huge Jason Young fan and had informed them all that if anyone was going to his show in Vegas with the seats right up front and backstage passes to talk to Jason, it was going to be her.

She was wearing her tour t-shirt this morning and looking better rested than everyone else by far. She scoffed. "The corn-bread muffins aren't your favorite thing on the menu."

"No, I decided instead of naming my favorite thing after myself, I'm going to name something that people order a lot. I can't wait to hear all these people ordering Owen's Nice and Firm Sweet Corny Muffins. Sounds dirty and funny at the same time."

"We're not naming them that."

"You have to."

"You think you get to come up with the name?" Ellie asked.

Owen shrugged. "Obviously."

"That was not part of the deal. You get to choose the item, but I can name it. And why would I name it something stupid?"

"You didn't say that you get to name it. I want to see the fine print."

"There's no fine print. It's what I decide."

Becca looked at Maddie, Owen's wife. "What's going on?"

"Oh well, Owen's obviously won, so he gets to have a menu item named after him down at Ellie's."

"Won what? Menu item? What are you talking about?"

"Oh, you didn't know?" Josh asked, leaning in, with a grin. "In addition to the trophy and the reserved table, Ellie threw in having an item on the menu named after the winner."

Becca heard Beau groan. "When did this happen?" she asked.

"After you two came back from Evendale not even talkin'," Owen said.

Becca shook her head. "So I guess we're all just going to give up pretending that you all don't know that Beau and I knew all about the matchmaking competition?"

They all laughed.

"We aren't sure when exactly you figured it out, but yeah, we realized you'd caught on," Tori, Josh's wife, said with a grin.

Becca looked at Owen. "Okay, I'm curious why you think you're the winner."

"Well obviously you're together. And I was the last one of this group to see you single."

"We're officially together?" Becca asked, amused as she always was by Owen. "Do you have proof?"

"Girl, please," Owen said. "I've seen that look on many a girl's face the morning after, thank you very much."

Maddie elbowed him hard.

"From you, honey," Owen said, holding his ribs and grinning. "I meant from you."

Maddie rolled her eyes. Owen had been a notorious playboy before she'd come back to town and tied him down.

"Well, that was just a crazy, drunk moment," Becca said, feeling a little sassy this morning. "When in Vegas and all that."

"Sure, okay," Owen said, nodding. "I'll give you that. Hookups are hookups. But I've got it in writing."

"You've got what in writing?" Becca asked. Had she declared her love for Beau on a cocktail napkin or something?

God, that would be mildly humiliating. Though not surprising.

"That you're Mr. and Mrs.," Owen said.

"Excuse me?" Becca asked, her heart doing a somersault in her chest. "How do you have that in writing?"

"Well, I guess the state of Nevada technically has it in writing. But that marriage certificate is real. I made sure."

Beau had just taken a drink of coffee and he started choking. Becca just felt her mouth drop open. If they hadn't been in Vegas, of all places, she would have scoffed and chalked this up to Owen being Owen. But...they *were* in Vegas. And something was niggling at the back of her consciousness that wouldn't let her just laugh it off. And no one else at the table seemed astonished by this revelation.

Oh...crap.

She blinked at Owen for a good ten seconds.

He just let her. Grinning back.

"The what?" she finally managed.

"The marriage certificate. That definitely takes things beyond a hookup." He looked around the table. "I knew I would need proof. And when I do something, I do it right."

Multiple people around the table laughed at *that*. Owen Landry was a lot of things—some of them very good and admirable even—but meticulous and responsible were not two of those things.

"Explain yourself," Beau said, butting into the conversation.

It wasn't really butting in. Obviously he was sitting right there, and the conversation was *about* him. In part.

"I knew that we needed something official to prove that you two were back together and that *I* was there when it happened so I could get that trophy and my Corny Muffins on the menu."

"No," Ellie cut in.

Owen ignored his grandmother. "Nothing more official than a piece paper from the government that says something's true."

"We have a *marriage certificate*?" Beau said.

Owen nodded. "And a couple of rings, and some cheesy photographs, and a bouquet of fake flowers somewhere."

Beau leaned in even further. "What the fuck are you talking about?"

Owen frowned. Then he leaned in too, studying Beau's face. "Are you shitting me?"

"Talk," Beau said shortly.

"You seriously don't remember?" Owen asked. He looked around the table. "It really happened."

"It did," Maddie said. "I was there."

"We can go ask Luke and Bailey and Sabrina and Marc too," Owen said, clearly offended that people were questioning his honesty.

Flickers of memories were tripping through Becca's mind now. She remembered a wedding. But it felt like it was someone *else's* wedding. Like she'd been there as a guest.

Like...Luke and Bailey.

Becca sat up straighter. Yes, that was it. "I remember that we went to the wedding chapel. And down to the marriage license bureau beforehand." A piece of the puzzle slipped into place. "But we were there for Luke and Bailey."

Luke and Bailey were from Bad. They were friends of Sabrina and Marc Sterling.

"Yes, Luke and Bailey and Sabrina and Marc were at the blackjack table. You and Beau and me and Maddie were there too, watching them. Luke was on a roll," Owen said. "Luke told Bailey that if he won the next hand, it was fate's sign they should get married. She agreed. He won so they decided to do it that night, right then and there."

Becca suddenly remembered Luke's huge grin and the way he turned to Bailey and kissed her and then threw her over his shoulder and carried her out of the casino to hail a cab right that very minute.

It had been so romantic. He'd been so clearly thrilled. Becca had been thrilled for them.

And jealous. Really jealous.

Owen continued. "We all decided to go down to the marriage bureau with them. And I, um..." He shifted on his chair. "I filled out a license for you while we were there and talked you into signing it."

More memories rushed through Becca's mind at that. In vivid technicolor.

She remembered the license bureau building clearly. She remembered feeling jealous of Luke and Bailey. She remembered Owen suggesting they sign a certificate too. She also remembered really liking the idea.

Owen grinned, clearly not apologetic. "Then we went back to the chapel. They needed witnesses, so we all filled in. But after their wedding was over, the guy asked if you two were ready. Becca said, "I've been ready for over a year," and the guy married you."

Becca felt her cheeks flush. Yeah, that sounded very believable actually.

She turned to look at Beau.

"You're fucking with us," Beau decided. He sat back in his chair. "We got drunk, and now you're fucking with us."

Owen shook his head. "Come on, man. How long would it take you to figure that out? No way. There's a piece of paper somewhere up in your hotel room saying that you and Becca are married. It's official. You are about as back together as you could possibly be."

Becca pressed her lips together and focused on her fork.

"Becca?" Beau said, his voice low and firm.

"Yeah?"

"You remember, don't you?"

She closed her eyes. Obviously, he was reading her face. "Yeah. Maybe. Some of it."

All of it now. She remembered saying that she'd been ready for over a year to marry Beau. She also remembered turning to Beau, taking his hands in hers, and proposing.

Marry me, Beau. Please. I love you. I want you.

You're definitely the marrying type, Becca.

I am. But if it's not you, it will never be anyone. You're the only one I want.

God... Her cheeks got even hotter.

He'd been really drunk. She'd known it at that time. She now remembered thinking that that was the perfect moment to talk him into it.

I'll do anything for you, Becca.

Then do this. Just say I do.

She'd been drunk too. If she'd been sober, she would have felt *some* stab of conscience that would have kept her from using his vulnerable state against him. Probably. But she'd definitely been less drunk than he was.

She felt him grasp her chin.

"Open your eyes."

"No."

"Becca, look at me."

Finally, she did. She took a deep breath. "Sorry."

"What are you sorry for?"

"I... proposed to you. I talked you into getting married."

He dropped his hand and sat staring at her. After several ticks of the clock. He finally asked, "*You* did?"

She nodded. "I thought it was all so spontaneous and romantic. And Luke and Bailey were so happy. I was jealous. And I *am* in love with you. And they've been friends for a long time too, and fell in love, and Luke was so happy about getting married and all of that just made me so... jealous." She took a deep breath. "So, yeah, when we were at the marriage bureau, I wanted to sign that license. And at the chapel, I was ready. And I proposed."

Beau was staring at her as if he'd never seen her. "How the fuck do I not remember this?"

"I can help with that," Josh said, from two seats down.

Beau looked at him. "What?"

"Jägermeister shots."

Beau's eyes slid shut. "*Fuck*."

Jägermeister was one liquor that Beau didn't handle well. It got him very drunk, very fast.

"Beau," Becca said. Now it was her turn to cup his face. "Beau, look at me."

"No."

But his eyes opened, and he shoved his chair back from the table. "I'm going back to the room."

She knew he was going back to the room to find the marriage license. To prove to himself that it happened.

He was going to be very pissed.

Because it had definitely happened. She remembered it all now.

Becca looked around at the table as Beau stomped out of the restaurant.

No one else was moving.

She really wished someone else was moving. But yeah, she was the one who needed to go after him.

"I'm going to...uh, yeah." She had no idea what exactly she was going to do, but they got it.

She got to her feet and followed Beau out of the dining room. He was halfway down the hallway leading to the elevators.

"Beau!"

He didn't slow down.

"Beau!" She started running after him. Something that her hungover body did not appreciate. She caught up with him and grabbed his upper arm, tugging him to a stop. "Hey!"

He turned on her. "*What?*"

"Maybe we should talk."

"About what? We've talked. You know how I feel about this. I did *not* want to do this. I did not want to date. Move in together. Get married. And now here we are, in Vegas, and you talked me into it. The thing I most didn't want. While I was *drunk.*"

Ouch. She understood that this was a shock. She understood that she should have probably put the brakes on last night. She understood that he was processing all this. She even kind of understood where he was coming from. But he didn't have to be quite so adamant about being married to her being the most terrible thing that had ever happened to him.

"I'm sorry. Okay? I wasn't totally sober either. And shouldn't you be at least a little bit...I don't know... happy? That when my inhibitions are down, marrying you is what I most want to do?"

He stared at her. "No. *No,*" he repeated with emphasis. "I am *not* happy."

"Why is that thought so terrible?"

"You know what's so terrible? The fact that I am now going to have to tell you that I want to get this annulled. And that we are going to have to tell everyone in there, which is half the fucking town and most of our friends and family, that I want to get this annulled. I'm going to have to hurt you and a bunch of other people I love. I'm going to have to live with the fact that I am married to you—the thing I do want most—but that I can't *stay* that way. I'm going to have to be the asshole who breaks everybody's heart."

She stood there not sure what to say. "You want to get this annulled?"

"Yes. Vegas is set up for quick and easy annulments too. We can get it annulled before we even get back to Autre. Before our parents hear about this. Before my mother gets this in her head."

Her heart felt like there was a fist around it, squeezing hard, not letting it beat correctly. She swallowed down the tears she felt clogging her throat. "You don't think it's worth trying? I mean, so we did it. So, it wasn't exactly planned out and it was very spontaneous and we weren't entirely sober, but we did it. Why don't we just stay married? Let's give it a try."

He stepped close, grabbed her by the upper arms and stared into her eyes. "No."

"Why not?"

"Because if we go back to Autre as husband and wife, and you come into my bed as my wife, wearing my ring, you're never leaving. And I will wonder every day for the rest of our lives if that's *really* where you want to be, where you *should* be. Or if there is someplace else that's better for you." He let go of her and stepped back. He shoved a hand through his hair. "All I want is for you to be happy. I want you to have every opportunity, every chance to have everything you want and deserve."

"And if that's you?" Becca was aware that her voice was wobbly. That made sense considering she was on the verge of tears.

"If it's me, and you can say that to me, standing up in front of the church, full of our entire town, all of our family, fully sober, after two years of living in Autre, then I'll believe you."

Well, at least it had gone from ten years down to two.

"Are you guys okay?" Owen came up beside them. Ellie was right behind him.

Beau nodded, still looking at her. "We're fine. Becca and I are heading downtown."

"What's downtown?" Owen looked back and forth between them, obviously concerned.

"That's where we need to go to get this annulled."

Owen's face fell. "You're getting it annulled?"

Beau nodded. "Yes. Before we get on the plane."

Ellie crossed her arms. "You're sure that's what you want?" She wasn't looking at Beau. Her gaze was on Becca.

Becca thought about the question. Her first reaction was, no, it wasn't what she wanted. But then she looked at Beau. Her husband. Her best friend.

If this was what he wanted, then it was what she wanted. She didn't want him to feel trapped or tricked. She wanted him to choose this. If she had to *convince* him that she wanted to be with him, she would. If it took time, fine. She had to show him that what *he* wanted, what he needed, mattered too and that she would give that to him, the way he always gave her what she wanted and needed.

She took a deep breath and nodded. "Yeah, it's what we should do."

"And this is now over," Beau said. "All of it. The matchmaking, the contest, everything. It's over."

Becca felt her stomach knot, but she forced herself to keep breathing.

Ellie looked back and forth between them. Then she nodded. "You want someone to go downtown with you?"

They both nodded. "Yeah."

Becca was pretty sure Beau thought that with Ellie and Owen there, Becca wouldn't throw a fit or start sobbing uncontrollably or something. Though he had to know that Ellie and Owen would be Team Becca at this point. Maybe he thought they'd keep him from saying anything mean or harsh. Whatever his reason, Becca wanted them along because Owen and Ellie would make it all less awkward and tense.

Becca was in love with this man. But wow, he drove her crazy.

twelve

IT WAS MONDAY. The worst fucking Monday of his life. And that was saying a lot.

Beau sat at the end of Ellie's bar, nursing a beer and a bowl of gumbo.

Everyone was steering clear of him. He appreciated it, but he'd done his damned best to make sure that they did. Scowling and growling had a way of doing that.

Except of course for Ellie. It was extremely hard, if not impossible, to intimidate Ellie Landry.

She set a glass of water in front of him and then rubbed at a nonexistent spot on the bar with a towel.

"You mad at me?" he asked. If she was going to lecture him or yell at him, he wanted to get it over with.

She looked at him. It was the first time he'd addressed her since he walked through the door. She'd simply looked at him, then set his favorite beer and a bowl of gumbo in front of him without a word exchanged.

"Not exactly," she said. "I'm just trying to figure something out."

"How I can possibly think I can live without her, how I

could possibly let her go, how I'm not absolutely ecstatic to be married to the woman of my dreams," Beau guessed.

Ellie shook her head. "No. I'm trying to figure out why you think that Autre doesn't deserve Becca."

Beau's eyebrows rose. Then pulled together. "What?"

"I love this town. And I thought you did too."

"You know that I do."

"Then why do you not want it to have one of the best teachers out there?"

Beau's frown deepened. "That's not what this is."

Ellie crossed her arms and nodded. "You think that Autre isn't good enough for her."

"Autre is...Autre," Beau said, dragging his spoon through his gumbo. "She already knows it. It's got limitations. Becca deserves to have new adventures, a wide-open world, all the opportunities."

"You're afraid she's going to leave and the closer you get to her, the more that's going to hurt. So you're pushing her away. You're trying to make her leaving happen sooner versus later."

He sighed. She was right, of course. "That's part of it, yeah."

Ellie just stood studying him for several long moments. Then she said, "She could leave you while stayin' right here, you know."

Beau blew out a breath and lifted his eyes. "So this isn't gonna be a pep talk then?" he asked dryly.

"This is gonna be a talk," she said, moving to lean in on the bar. "If you get some pep out of it, great. But the main thing you need to get is the truth."

He pushed his bowl back. Ellie gave these talks on a regular basis. He'd seen them happen. And he'd seen the results. He knew this might hurt a little, but he was ready. "Okay, let's hear it."

"Adventures don't always involve travel," Ellie said. "Adventures are about discovering new things and having those things change your mind and heart. And, thank the good Lord, they can happen on your own front porch. Or while sitting on a bar stool. Or while sitting in a classroom. In fact, if they don't happen while sittin' in a classroom, you're not payin' attention."

"And Becca's going to give a lot of people great adventures that way," Beau agreed.

"She'll be takin' plenty too," Ellie said. "Every time you interact with another human in a meaningful way, you discover something, and you change a little bit. And it doesn't matter if the town it happens in is big or small, if the people around you are idiots or geniuses, if the building you're in has a million-dollar budget or barely keeps the lights on. It's about two people seeing each other, learning from each other, and being different afterward."

Beau pulled in a breath. "I'm not saying that Becca couldn't do great things here. Of course she could."

"And the kids in that school go home and influence their families who are a part of this town. They grow up and become the adults in this town. They take care of the other people in this town. I want those kids to be taken care of, to learn as much as they can, to be taken on the right adventures," Ellie said.

"Things are just so hard with her dad and some of these parents. Some of the people here don't want 'adventures'."

Ellie scoffed. "That's the thing about life—it gives you adventures whether you want them or not. It's how prepared you are for them and what you do with them that matters. Regardless of their parents, those kids deserve to have Becca's help getting them ready."

"But—"

"This town is not perfect," Ellie went on as if he hadn't started to speak. "I've never believed that it is. But if all the good people who want to solve the problems leave, the problems will never get solved. We need people who have the passion and the knowledge to make things happen. Becca wants Autre to be better. She's got the love and passion for it, but you're happy to let her take that up to Houma."

Okay, now Ellie sounded accusatory.

"Things are hard for her here," Beau said. But he knew that his voice had lost some heat. "She can still help kids be amazing and make the world a better place from Houma."

"So she and her dad are gonna butt heads sometimes. So what?"

"I want her to love her work. I want it to be the job she's always dreamed it would be. She shouldn't have to go to work every day and be tense and stressed out, should she?"

"I come to work and am tense and stressed out a lot of days and all I'm doing is serving beer and grits. She's teaching. She's shaping lives, she's expanding minds, she's teaching little people about the *world*. That's an important job, and if it matters to her—which I know it does—then doing it well will cause some stressful days. And that's what she needs good friends and a loving family for. She won't have that in Houma."

"Her dad is part of the problem here. I think it's really uncomfortable for him to be his daughter's boss."

Ellie scoffed. "Her dad is a man with some authority. People in positions of power need to be uncomfortable."

"You think Jonathan should be uncomfortable?" Beau knew that Ellie liked Jonathan a lot.

"Of course. People who are in charge of things, especially when they're in charge of other people, need to be questioned and they need to have answers to those questions. When they get too comfortable, when they get complacent, that means things aren't changing and they're not being challenged."

Beau knew he could argue that Becca's friends and family would still be her friends and family and would be there for her even if she was in Houma, but this was Ellie Landry. He sincerely doubted she'd ever had an argument that she hadn't won.

And that was probably because she was always right.

Stubborn too, for sure. But also right.

"You really think that she should stay here, and deal with all of that. And not be happy?" he tried one more time because, well, he was stubborn as hell too.

"She won't be happy? Just because something's hard doesn't mean that it's not wonderful. When we have to fight for things, we figure out what's important to us. Being challenged can be amazing."

"Yeah?"

Ellie rolled her eyes at him. Big and dramatically. "You don't like when a big order comes in where someone's asking you to do something new and beyond anything you've done in the past?"

See? She was always right.

"Emmaline Morris is a lot," Beau pointed out. "And she's young. And she's not going anywhere."

Ellie smiled. "So Becca will just have to be a lot more. With the Landrys on her side, that will *not* be a problem."

Beau just blew out a breath. He had no argument for that.

Ellie shook her head. "Leo knows Emmaline's grandpa Joe."

Beau nodded. "I know Joe too."

"Of course. But Leo and Joe served in the Navy together. And they've fished together a hundred times. And they've gotten drunk together. And they've fought. They've each given each other at least one black eye over the years."

Beau lifted a brow. "Sounds like most of the guys—and a few of the girls—who've spent seventy-some years together around here."

Ellie smiled. "Exactly. Just like I've known Emmaline's mama since she was a little bratty thing running around this town and teasin' Callie."

Callie was Ellie's daughter. The only girl of her and Leo's five kids.

"Emmaline's mom teased Callie?"

"Oh, yeah. We went 'round and 'round with her and her mom." Ellie made a disgusted noise. "I really don't like Allison. Never have."

Beau couldn't help but shake his head. There was a lot of history here.

"Now Allison's sister, Emmaline's Aunt Angela? Sweetest thing," Ellie said. "She was the one who finally told Callie she needed to punch Allison in the face. So Callie did. And everything was good after that."

"That's...a great story. I guess?" Beau said. "But I'm not following your point."

"'Cuz I'm not done makin' it," Ellie told him. "Hold on. Callie and Angela are still friends. Callie and Allison not so much. But, because of Angela, Allison gave Callie a job a few years ago. And about fifteen years back, there was a big shipping company that wanted to come to town and build a warehouse on that land up north and tear out a bunch of trees and tear down some old houses. Emmaline's grandpa was on the city council and was all for it. He said it would bring jobs and the company was going to pay the city big bucks for that land. But most of the town was against it. Didn't want to lose that land, knew the company had a bad reputation for how they treat their workers. Half the council wasn't listening though. So Leo took Joe out fishin' and they talked about it and when they came back, Joe was a no. The plan was defeated by one vote."

"So we need Leo to talk to Emmaline to keep her away from Becca? Or does he need to talk to Joe? Or should Leo talk to Jonathan about not being so hard on Becca?" Beau knew Ellie heard the sarcasm in his tone.

"We could try that," Ellie said. "Or *you* could talk to someone about what we can do for the art program that has no money or support."

"Ellie," Beau sighed. "I don't have anything to do with the school."

"Sure you do."

"I mean, I graduated from there. And played some pretty great football. But I don't think that counts."

"Beau, you're a part of this town. You're from here. You've been working your ass off to build your business. You've been a part of your mom's business since it started. You have roots and history here. You're a respected and trusted part of this community. That's powerful. You have a say in what happens here. This school and those kids matter to all of us. We don't have to work at the school to get involved."

"I..." He swallowed hard. "Who will listen to me?"

Ellie's expression softened. "Everyone." She reached over and squeezed his forearm. "You really don't realize that? You don't understand that all the hard work you've been putting in has been noticed? Everyone is so impressed with your business, Beau. The hard work and how seriously you take putting out amazing products. And everyone knows that you've always been there for your mom and...everyone really."

Beau felt his chest tighten. That meant so much to him.

"Home isn't just the address on the front of your house. It's a part of who you are. A place that's what it is because you were there."

Beau felt all of his emotions lodge in his throat. He simply nodded.

"What happens when you're in a roomful of candles and you start blowing them out?" Ellie asked.

"The room gets darker."

Ellie nodded. "But as long as there's one candle burning, there's still light."

"Right."

"You have to quit blowing candles out. If we want Autre to be as bright as it can be, we need to keep all of our candles here."

That hit him directly in the gut. "So you don't think it's selfish of me to ask her to stay?"

"As a life-long citizen of Autre, Louisiana, I think it's selfish as hell of you to ask her to leave," Ellie said. "It might make *you* feel good. It might make you feel all high and mighty and like you're making some huge sacrifice by letting her go. But we need that girl here. And as someone who loves her quite a lot, I want her to stay here *with you*, because that's how she'll be happiest."

Beau swallowed hard. "You sure about that?"

Ellie crossed her arms. "When has Becca Bollier ever been anything less than completely honest with you, Beau?"

His chest tightened. "Never. That's always been our thing."

Ellie nodded. "Exactly. You've always been fully honest with each other no matter what. When she says she loves you, she means it."

Ellie was, of course, completely right. The one thing he could always count on was Becca being totally honest with him.

That was why, when she'd gone along with him to annul

their marriage, and then had not spoken to him on the plane at all on the way home, it had torn him up even more than finding out that they were married.

He'd been shocked. Then angry. She'd known how he felt about all of it, and she'd still said the vows. He didn't remember it, but he was certain that the Elvis impersonator—he knew it was an Elvis impersonator only because he had actually located the marriage certificate and the photos—had certainly asked *do you take this man to be your lawfully wedded husband to have and to hold* etc., etc.

And she'd said *I do.*

But he'd said *I do* in return.

And they'd never lied to one another.

Drunk or not, he couldn't imagine ever saying those words to anyone else.

So yes, he definitely believed she loved him.

And that she wanted to spend her life with him.

He was the one insisting that they wait. He was the one insisting that she didn't want to stay in Autre.

No, she didn't know for sure that she wanted to.

But hell, no one knew what tomorrow would bring.

He was part of this community, though. He wasn't a kid anymore. He was a man and a business owner. That meant he could be a part of shaping the tomorrow around here.

He needed to get involved.

He reached into his back pocket and withdrew his wallet.

Ellie shook her head and held up a hand. "The beer and gumbo are on the house."

"Thanks. I appreciate it." He started to tuck his wallet back into his pocket.

"But the advice will be five bucks."

He grinned and laid a twenty on the counter. "Worth every penny."

THE MONTHLY SCHOOL board meeting was tonight.

And word had gotten out about the lack of funds for the musical. And *why* there was a lack of funds.

The room was packed. Absolutely packed. A huge section of the room was filled with Landrys, including Ellie and Leo, which made Becca's heart swell. She really loved that family. But there were plenty of other people in attendance too. On both sides. Those who were here to demand answers about the reallocation of funds from one program to another and those who were here to defend the decision—mostly the parents and grandparents of football players, as well as some alumni of the program who still lived and worked in Autre.

Savannah, Daniel, and Sam were sitting toward the back of the room as well, and as Becca took her seat next to Fletcher she realized that she really did have a lot of friends. Good friends. People she would always be able to depend on.

She took a deep breath and found her dad, sitting up at the front with the superintendent and the school board members. Her mom was sitting with the Landrys. Crystal and Heather were there as well.

There were only two people missing. Toby. And Beau.

She had no idea where Toby was. She didn't know if he was just running late or if he was so upset by everything that he'd decided to sit this one out.

Where's Toby? she texted Sam from her seat.

A moment later she got a reply. *Don't worry. It will all be fine.*

That was a weird response. But whatever. If Sam wasn't worried, she wasn't going to worry.

But Beau not being here hurt.

He was probably working. He didn't keep set hours. He

worked as projects came in, until they were finished. Or until something else needed his attention.

And this meeting didn't really have anything to do with him.

She swallowed hard as her throat tightened.

It didn't. He didn't have kids in the school here. He wasn't a teacher here. This meeting was really about getting answers and letting the board know that people were unhappy. She knew that there would be no solutions to come out of the meeting. Her dad had told her as much at home. There just was no money in the budget. The musical was screwed.

The board went through their agenda as usual until they got to new business and had to finally recognize the people in the room who had requested a chance to speak.

And there were a lot of them.

The back and forth went on for over an hour.

"Thank you all for coming and expressing your feelings," Mark Jasper, the board president, and longtime resident of Autre, finally said. "We will take all of that into consideration and—"

"What are you going to *do* about it?" someone shouted.

Mark sighed. Obviously, addressing shouted questions wasn't how he wanted to conduct the meeting, and up until now, everyone had been good about only speaking when it was their turn and coming to the microphone and respecting the three-minute speaking rule—for the most part—but he probably also knew that if he didn't acknowledge all the questions now, he'd just be fielding them at the grocery store and gas station and everywhere in between.

"We will review the budget," Mark said. "As well as the proposal from Mrs. Waterson regarding how much would be needed for the musical. But as has been discussed, to be fiscally responsible—"

"Fuck that!" someone else shouted. "That new scoreboard and the fancy PA system weren't fiscally responsible!"

"We should build the stage *on* the football field," someone called. "We can use the new bleachers for seating and that new PA system!"

"No way! That would damage the new turf!" one of the football field proponents yelled.

"Oh, how sad for your pretty grass that's more important than our kids!" another voice called.

"Our team could be state champs!" one of the fathers of a player shouted. "You should all be proud of that!"

"I'm proud that I've never once watched this team play!" a voice toward the back yelled.

"Okay!" Mark banged his gavel. "People, we need to settle down!"

"Football is *not* more important than everything else!"

"All the kids deserve equal opportunities!"

"This is bullshit!"

The door at the back of the room suddenly swung open, banging against the wall, making everyone jump and turn to look.

Beau Hebert stood in the doorway looking a little confused.

But Toby pushed past him with a big smile, striding forward. Beau followed.

Becca sat up straighter, her heart thundering.

Beau immediately located her, his eyes locking on hers as he shoved a hand through his hair. He took a deep breath, blew it out, and then looked over at his mother.

She pointed to where the podium stood at the front of the room facing the dais where the board sat.

"Toby? Beau?" Mark asked as they came to a stop in front of the podium. "Is everything all right?"

"Yeah." Then Beau shook his head. "No, not really. I need to say something."

"I don't think you're on the list of speakers tonight."

"I'm not. I guess I don't know how this works."

Mark nodded. "Evidently. You need to tell us ahead of time that you have something you'd like to say. You, on the other hand," he said to Toby, "should know how this works."

"We lost track of time," Toby said with a nod.

"Well, fuck." Beau grimaced. "Oops. Sorry. This is a little last-minute." He turned to face the very full room. "But it shouldn't be." He looked back at the board members. He tucked his hands in his back pocket. "It just took me a bit to figure out what to say. Or rather, how to say it. That I needed to come *here* to say it. Sorry to interrupt."

Jacob Morris, Emmaline's husband, leaned to speak into his microphone. "I'm sorry. We're to the end of the public statement period."

"Well, good. Then I'm not cutting anybody else off," Beau said.

Jacob frowned. "There's a proper way we do these things."

Beau nodded. "Yeah, I'm sure. Just like there's a proper way to treat people. People who've given money to the school. People who do things that we judge and think are less important than the things *we* like and value. People who are professional teachers who are giving their hearts and souls to educate the kids here. But since we've kind of blown 'proper' out of the water with all of this, I'm just gonna say what I came here to say."

"Mr. Landry," Jacob started firmly.

"*Jake*," Beau said just as firmly. "Give me a break. You're not using that name as a sign of respect or because we don't know each other, and I'm sure as hell not gonna call you Mr. Morris, for those same reasons, so let's just be what we are..." He looked around the room, his eyes landing on Becca and staying there.

She realized she was barely breathing, and she felt like she'd downed an energy drink and was now trying to sit still. She was jumpy and tingly and wanted to *do* something. Though she had no idea what.

"We're friends. We're a community. We've all chosen to live here," he said. Then he pulled his hands from his pockets and finally tore his eyes from Becca's to look around the room. "I've lived in this town my whole life. I've built my business here. I went to school here. Hell, someday maybe *I'll* be on the school board. I definitely intend to live and die here. So I feel like if I have something to say, I should say it." He paused and shrugged. "I suppose we could all go down to Ellie's and hash this out, but we're all already here, so we might as well do it now, right?"

Several people around the room nodded.

"We'll keep talkin' about this no matter where we are," someone said.

"Exactly," Beau agreed. "And we should, right? The things that affect one part of this town affect all of us really. In one way or another. Even if it's down the road."

Mark huffed out a breath. "Well, it's not like Autre's ever been all that formal. Even in these meetings."

"I protest," Emmaline said, rising from her seat in the front row.

"Wow, I'm shocked," Savannah said from the back row.

"Yeah, what *aren't* you pissed about tonight, Emmaline?" someone else called out.

Becca couldn't tell who, but the amazing thing was...it didn't matter.

"The way I see it, we're almost to the end of the meeting, so how about anybody who doesn't want to hear what Beau has to say can leave?" Leo said, standing up from his seat in the fourth row. "Everyone else can stay. And we can figure this out together." He gave Beau a grin. "I definitely want to hear this."

"Great idea!" someone shouted.

"Yeah, let's do that," someone else agreed.

There were lots of nods and murmured agreements.

Becca didn't know what to think. Or say. Or do. She just stared at Beau.

He looked completely...confident. Determined. Like he had a plan.

He might have walked in here not realizing how school board meetings worked, but he looked like he absolutely knew what he was about to say and do and had no reservations about any of it.

"Well, that's fine," Beau said with a nod. He turned and addressed the group of students who were standing at the very back of the room. "But I hope y'all will stay. I've got something to say that I think you'll like."

Toby stood beside him, looking almost...proud?

Becca wasn't sure what that was about, but it seemed clear that Toby and Beau had been conspiring and she really loved that. Whatever the result.

The kids all shifted their feet and looked intrigued and nervous at the same time. But one of them nodded. "Yeah, we'll stay."

"Okay, then. How about we wrap up the school board meeting and just make this a town meeting," Beau said. He glanced at his cousin Kennedy, who happened to be Autre's current Mayor.

"Unofficial," she said. "A *gathering* of the town is fine. But we have a process too. Agenda, rules, that kind of thing." She gave Beau a grin. "I'm happy to put you on our next agenda though."

"Not sure that will be necessary," Beau said. "Bein' a good neighbor and supporting the people in this community shouldn't have to require a bunch of formality like that, should it?"

He looked around. No one disagreed with him.

"I move that we table the remainder of tonight's agenda to the next meeting," Holly Robbins, one of the board members, said. "Nothing on the rest of the agenda needs to be addressed tonight."

Mark nodded. "All in favor."

Everyone voted yes, except for Jacob Morris, and the motion passed.

"I move to adjourn," Holly said.

Again everyone voted yes, but Jacob.

"Meeting adjourned," Mark said, banging the gavel. "Town meeting in five minutes—"

"*Unofficial* town meeting!" Kennedy called out.

Mark grinned. "Unofficial town meeting. Anyone not interested can now leave."

No one got up.

Everyone pivoted to look at Emmaline.

She crossed her arms and sat back in her chair. "I'm not going anywhere."

Beau was still standing at the podium. He nodded. "Good. Because honestly, I really want you to hear this." He looked around the rest of the room. "I'm glad you're all staying. I want you *all* to hear this."

"Might as well jump in," Mark said. "No one's even taking a bathroom break."

Beau pulled in a long breath. Then he looked at Becca. She gave him a smile and a nod of encouragement. He wasn't a public speaker. He was a guy who showed his strength by *being there*. By showing up. By doing the work. By supporting people with his two hands, and his strong back, and his tools and truck. He'd never been the center of attention, in any kind of spotlight, until this town had started matchmaking him and Becca.

They'd put the two of them up on stage—literally. They'd made them a group project for weeks. And now...he was standing at a podium without a script and without it being a part of someone else's plan.

This was all Beau.

Well, and maybe some Toby.

The butterflies in her stomach were swooping in double-time.

"Okay listen, I know this is about the football field versus the arts program," Beau started. "Specifically, the musical not having enough money. And I think that's bullshit. I think what the board did was wrong, and I think there needs to be better policy about how the *community* is informed about meeting agenda items so we can all weigh in."

Toby held up a piece of paper. "So I've drafted a proposed new policy." He looked up at the board. "I reviewed the rules about how new policies are introduced. I'd like this to go on the agenda for the next meeting." He crossed to Mark and handed the paper over. "This should give the town plenty of notice about what is on each meeting agenda so that we can show up and give input and hear the board's discussion."

Jake Morris's face was flushed, and Emmaline managed to look even more pissed off somehow.

Beau nodded. "I know it doesn't seem like something a guy like me would care about. I was a football player here. A good one. I had scholarship offers from three colleges. But because of Mr. Taggart, I discovered that I was good at, and loved, something else. Something artistic. Yes, I got some shit for it. Yes, I've questioned if it was the right decision to give up football and stay here to make furniture instead. But that art showed me that there was more to me than just football. That I could actually *make* something that would last. That people would keep and cherish. I'm not saying football can't be important in its own way, but for me, the woodworking, the art, was what *I* needed. And a teacher saw that." Beau put his hand on his heart and turned toward Becca's side of the room. "So, thank you, Mr. Taggart. I don't think I've ever said that. And I should have."

Becca knew Reggie Taggart was sitting toward the back of the cluster of teachers. She felt her eyes stinging. Nothing mattered more to a teacher than seeing a student be successful and happy. She knew Beau had just given Mr. Taggart a huge gift.

Beau cleared his throat and looked up at the school board, but she suspected that he was focusing on her father. "And thank you to the school here for having that program for a kid like me."

He looked at her again and Becca blinked back her tears as she gave him another nod.

"A lot of us have deep roots here," Beau went on. "But what are roots? Roots are what anchor you in place, sure, but they're what allow you to *grow*. The deeper and thicker the roots, the taller the tree can get and the healthier and stronger it is. When I was thinking about making furniture for a *living*, starting a business from scratch, taking that risk, there wasn't anywhere else I even considered doing it. Even if I got a little shit about being an artist"—He gave a grin to some of his cousins and friends and past football buddies in attendance— "I knew I'd be supported here."

He paused and took a deep breath and Becca found herself breathing deeply too.

Wow. She was so...in love. Impressed and proud and

touched that he was here and putting himself out there like this, of course. But she'd never been more in love with him than she was right now. He was not soft and open like this often and that made it even more impactful when he was.

"I am a part of this community," Beau said. "I always have been. From Little League and town clean up days to helping build my mom's business, then my own, to starring in the most recent community theater production here."

There was soft laughter from the crowd.

Beau grinned for a moment, but then his expression sobered. "There have been times when I've wondered if staying was the right decision. If giving up other things to work my ass off to build my business and keep my life here was worth it. But now, I know it was. For moments like this. Not because of the money I make or the furniture itself, but because I'm a part of this community and I can stand up and say...I'm in a position to fix something that's not right. And yeah, to look some of you in the eye and say, 'you were wrong'." He turned toward the kids at the back of the room. "So, I'm donating all of the supplies for the set for the upcoming musical. Anything you need."

The kids all straightened, their eyes widening.

"And you can build the sets in my shop. Full use of any tools you need. And I'll help. I know that some friends and family of mine"—He grinned at Mitch and Zeke—"are also willing to help. We'll do it after school hours if necessary but..." He looked over at Toby.

Toby held up more papers.

"Toby and I worked on another proposal tonight before comin' over here."

Toby again approached the dais with paperwork. "Because these hours at Beau's shop will be teaching the kids hands-on techniques, including carpentry, painting, welding, and possibly some electrical work, I propose that those hours be approved for school credit and the kids be allowed to go to the shop during class hours."

"We can put that on the next school board agenda," Beau said. "But I—"

"Actually, I think we can talk about that tonight," Becca's dad interjected.

Becca felt her mouth drop open.

Beau paused. "Yeah?"

Jonathan looked at the people seated next to him. "What do you think, Mark? An emergency meeting of the board tonight so we can get the arts program what it needs? In light of all the public commentary tonight?"

Mark smiled. "I think that can be arranged."

The rest of the board smiled and nodded as well. With one exception, of course.

"Well, damn," Beau said. "Okay. Thanks." Beau turned and looked directly at Becca again.

For some reason, this time her heart thumped even harder, and her breath caught in her throat.

"Becca...stay. Stay here and help me make Autre the town we want it to be. Instead of leaving because it's not what it should be, stay here and help me fix it when it needs to be fixed and make what's good even better."

Becca knew her eyes were wide. Her mouth was open, and her heart was pounding.

"I know I said I wanted you to go. To Houma or somewhere even bigger. Somewhere that was easier or had more resources or whatever, but...this is our town. No one will love it, and support it, and challenge it more than we will. We won't settle for it being less than it can be. For us, and our family and friends. For our kids. And grandkids."

Her eyes couldn't get any rounder, but her heart could

pound even harder it seemed. She almost couldn't hear him over the thumping in her chest.

"Bec?" Beau repeated.

She felt Fletcher elbow her in the side. "Becca, he's talking to you."

Finally, she opened her mouth. Nothing came out.

Beau crossed to her. The people in the chairs between them scooted out of the way, the sound of metal on tile filling the room. He knelt in front of her.

"Becca, I need you to stay here. I was wrong. If you leave, you take all of your talents and your love and your passion away from Autre. And we need all of that right here. Please. Stay. *I* need all of that right here."

"Is that a proposal?" She heard someone yell from the back of the room.

It was Savannah.

Beau's mouth curled up in a grin. "It *is* a proposal. Rebecca Jean Bollier, will you stay here and date me? For a little while? And then marry me?"

Again, Fletcher elbowed her. Suddenly Toby appeared over Beau's shoulder.

"For God's sake, girl, say yes."

Finally, she sniffed and threw herself at Beau. He gathered her in, crushing her to his chest as he rose to his feet.

"I'm going to assume that's a yes, to all of that," Beau said against the top of her head.

"It's a yes. But only to dating for a few months. *Not* two years."

She pulled back and he sealed his mouth over hers, kissing her deeply.

The whole room erupted into applause, laughter, and cheers.

Well, probably not the whole room. Becca very much doubted that Emmaline and Jacob were cheering.

After nearly a minute, Becca pulled back. She beamed up at him.

It seemed everyone was out of their seats and there were multiple conversations going on now.

"Becca?"

She turned to see her dad had made his way down from the dais. He was now frowning at her.

Oh, no.

She swiped a hand over her cheeks. "Thanks for agreeing to the late board meeting tonight."

"Yes. That's fine, of course. But I want to know what this is about you leaving?" Jonathan asked.

"Oh." She looked at Beau. He still had his arm around her waist, but he said nothing.

"Is it true? You're thinking about leaving?" her dad asked.

She took a deep breath and nodded. "Yes. Houma offered me a teaching position. Kindergarten. Starting after Christmas. I'd be replacing a teacher, but it would be permanent."

Her father looked sincerely shocked. "Becca, I..."

"It would make things easier here. For us."

His frown deepened. "But..." He shook his head. "Don't go. Stay. Please."

Her eyes widened. "What?"

"I don't want you to go. Beau's absolutely right that Autre needs you."

"But...we're arguing. Things are tense between us. You don't..." She stopped but then realized there was no reason not to finish that sentence. "You don't listen to me."

Jonathan seemed legitimately confused. "Of course I listen to you."

"You hear me," she conceded. "But you don't *listen*. My opinion doesn't matter. You can't play favorites."

"Of course I can't play favorites." Her dad moved in closer.

"Right. So you can't take my opinions into consideration."

"That is *not* what I meant by that, Rebecca," he said firmly. "I never gave you special attention or consideration because I never wanted *you* to think that anything you got—good grades, praise from teachers, accolades—were ever for any reason other than because you earned them. I needed you to know that you were amazing all on your own."

Becca stared at him. "But...with all of this...the arts program...I didn't change your mind about any of it."

"I didn't need my mind changed. I always agreed with you and everyone who thought it was bullshit that they reallocated that money."

Becca's eyes widened. Her father almost never swore.

"But you let them do it."

"I didn't have a say in it," he said, a little exasperated. "That's what you and Toby and Beau and others are figuring out. The school is a part of the community. Yes, the administration oversees the operations, but the community has a lot of say. As they should."

"I thought..." Her mind was spinning. "You were so upset with me."

"I got upset and we argued because I hate the idea of letting you down or making you think that I'm not doing my job well." He paused, then added. "And in *that* way you are different from the other teachers. I can handle it when they get upset with me. It's a typical employee-boss thing. I expect it. But with you...it does matter more. And I get more emotional. And in trying to keep it professional, I obviously did a bad job of communicating."

"Oh." Becca took a breath as that all sunk in. "I guess I was maybe a little unrealistic in my expectations too. And that comes from you being my dad," she realized as she said it out loud. "With another boss, I might not care as much, but I want *you* to be perfect and be able to fix everything for me." She gave him a little smile. "I guess we might need to work on that."

He nodded. "We will. And it might never be easy. You will always be my daughter, not just another teacher."

Her heart squeezed. "I'm glad. I never want to be just another teacher to you."

"I know you're being pressured by the other teachers. You're going to need to set up some boundaries," her dad said.

She nodded. "Yeah. I know. I'm learning."

"We're all learning. All the time," Jonathan said with a soft smile. "For instance, Toby realized that a policy change would allow more of the community to get involved in board discussions. That was smart," Jonathan said. "I can't override the board. But if the community gets more involved, the board members—who are elected by the town—will listen to that. That's how it should be. The school *should* matter to the community, and I'd love to see more involvement. As long as the teachers are fully respected and supported and their voices are heard too."

"You can make sure that happens," Becca said with a smile.

But Jonathan shook his head. "*You* can make sure that happens. You and Toby and Fletcher and everyone else. This is your job, but it's also your community. The people here know you and trust you. Just like Beau said. When you're a part of the community, you can make others understand things in a way strangers can't. It's complicated and gets a little messy, but some of the best things in life are like that."

He looked at Beau when he said that.

Beau nodded. "And I just want to say that I get that you

and Becca might set up some rules, like no talking about school at dinner."

Jonathan lifted a shoulder. "Maybe."

"But *I* will be talking to you about the school whenever I feel the need," Beau said. "Even if it's a family dinner. I mean, it will be my kids' school." He paused. "Your grandkids' school."

Becca felt her heart flip over in her chest and her gaze flew to her father's face. He looked flummoxed for just a second, then a grin spread over his face. He reached out and clapped Beau on the shoulder.

"If you're *not* an overly involved dad for my grandkids, we'll have words," Jonathan told him.

Beau smiled and nodded. "No problem."

Becca blew out a breath. So that was a weird way for Beau to ask Jonathan for permission to propose but that was essentially what he'd just done, it seemed.

"Becca," her father said, turning back to her.

"Yeah?"

He put his hands on her shoulders and met her gaze directly. "I love you. I'm so damned proud of you. Please stay and teach here in Autre."

Her chest tightened suddenly, and it took a second before she could take a deep breath. Her vision was blurry with tears as she nodded. "I love you too. And yes, okay. Yes, I want to stay."

He pulled her into a big hug. "Good. That's really good."

"Hey! So...who won the trophy?" Someone—it sounded like Savannah again—yelled over the din.

Jonathan let Becca go and Beau immediately tucked her against his side with a kiss on the top of her head. She snuggled against him, happiness filling her up.

Everyone quieted and looked around.

"Well, I did, obviously," Ellie said.

Beau looked over at her. Then he nodded. "Yeah. I guess so."

"Oh, *come on*," Owen groused.

Ellie looked at him. "As if there was ever any doubt I was going to win."

"Oh, I had doubts," Owen told his grandmother.

"There was no way I was going to allow a reserved table in my restaurant. And no way I was gonna let somebody have something on my menu named after them."

Everyone laughed again and conversations started around them.

Becca looked up at Beau. "Did she help get you here tonight?"

"She did. A little."

That felt right. And Becca was sure the alligator trophy was going to look amazing sitting on a shelf behind the bar. She'd bet Ellie already had a space cleared for it.

"Do you think she said whatever she said to you just so she'd win?" Becca asked.

"Do I think Ellie is capable of that?" Beau asked. "Yes. Would I be mad if that was the case here?" He paused, then brushed a strand of hair back from her face, tucking it behind her ear. "No. Because this...you in my arms, in Autre, making our life here together, *is* right, Bec."

Her heart melted like a chocolate kiss on the dash of his truck in the middle of a Louisiana July day. She nodded. "Yeah."

"*But*," he said, his thumb stroking over her cheek. "No, I don't think that's why she said what she did."

"She did it because she wants us together?"

"And because she was sick of having a broken-hearted blue-collar dumbass sittin' at her bar."

Becca laughed. "I think there have been more than one of those over the years."

"Yeah, maybe she just needed to make room for the next one," he said with a smile. "Or maybe she just can't help bein' wise and insightful and awesome."

"It's all of those things."

They both turned to find Ellie had come up beside them.

They laughed. "Of course it is," Becca said.

"And I also did it because this town deserved to see that proposal, just like they deserve to see your wedding." Ellie smiled at them both with genuine affection. "*Your* town deserves to see that."

Becca felt a wave of emotion go through her, but she wasn't aware that a tear had fallen until Beau lifted his hand and wiped it from her cheek. "Hey, Bec?"

"Yeah?" she asked, looking up at him.

"I love you more than I'll ever be able to tell you. But I intend to show you for the rest of my life."

Another tear slid down her cheek as she smiled. He wiped that one away too.

"I love you too. So much. Thank you for..." She sighed. "Everything."

He wiped yet another tear. "Welcome home."

"Oh my God." She quit trying not to cry and just let them fall, burrowing into his chest for a big hug.

Wow. She was home. For real.

For better or worse.

To stay.

Always.

epilogue

BECCA TURNED in front of the mirror checking out the back of the costume she had on.

This one was really good.

Beau was going to like this one a lot.

"Bec?"

Her heart tripped as she heard him come through the front door and call up the stairs.

She grinned. "Up here!"

His footsteps thundered up the stairs and she could picture him taking them two at a time.

They were going to a Halloween party tonight at Ellie's bar and he was here to pick her up. It wasn't actually Halloween. Everyone needed to be home on *the* night to hand out candy to trick-or-treaters. So the party at Ellie's was tonight. The twenty-seventh. Coincidentally, the two-year anniversary of the day she'd first asked Beau for opinions on Halloween costumes and started a hell of a domino effect. Not that anyone but she and Beau would realize that. If he even remembered.

"Are you ready—" He broke off as he came through the doorway to her bedroom, and he pulled up short. "Holy shit."

That was actually exactly the reaction she'd been going for. She grinned. "I need your opinion on which costume I should wear."

He swallowed hard as his eyes tracked over her. Three times.

"Beau?"

"Yeah?" His eyes were lingering on her breasts.

She propped a hand on her hip. "You didn't give me this much attention the last time I asked for your opinion about a costume."

He finally dragged his gaze back to her face. Then he took a huge step forward. "I had to try like hell not to drool all over the floor or let you see my massive hard-on when you were dressed like that little devil. And hell—" He gave her a grin. "That toolbelt? I kind of want you to get one of those again and wear it—and *only* that—while I fuck you sometime."

Her eyes wIdened, but then she grinned. "I could *so* do that."

His gaze was hot. "Yeah. Do that."

"Making a note."

"The devil too."

She nodded with a smirk. "Got it." Role-playing. Well, okay then.

She grinned up at him. "You were such a grump then. You seemed pissed the entire time."

"I was. Pissed that I was just then realizing how much I wanted you. Pissed that you were trying to get someone else's attention. Pissed that some other guy was going to get to run his hands all over this body."

"No one did, though."

"Fucking idiots. Thank God."

His hands settled on her waist. The cheerleading costume was made up of a very short skirt and a fitted top that dipped low between her breasts. The two pieces pulled apart and his palms met bare skin, causing goosebumps to break out and her to suck in a quick breath.

"But now you're all mine," he said, his voice low. "And I can give you *lots* of attention."

"Yeah?" she asked.

He gave her that sexy, half-grin. "Oh, darlin', this is a dream come true."

"You like this one too, then?"

He smoothed his hand down the skirt, over the curve of her ass, then up underneath the edge of it. His fingers teased the edge of the panties. "So much. You're keeping this one too." His fingers brushed against her center and she immediately felt her body getting wet. "But there's no way in hell you're wearing this to the bar tonight."

"Beau," she said, her voice a bit breathless. "I need to get ready."

"You feel ready to me," he said, lowering his head and brushing his lips against hers as his finger moved forward.

She grasped his arms to hold herself up and leaned into him. "Beau." But it wasn't really a protest.

"You look hot as fuck," he told her. "If you go dressed like this, we won't be staying long." His finger circled her clit. Then, without withdrawing his hand, he lifted his head and looked down at her. "And these fucking pigtails?" he asked, wrapping one around his other hand. "Really, Bec? You know what I'll be thinking about all night."

Holding onto them when she went to her knees...

She pulled in a breath. "We probably have some time. We could—"

He dragged his hand out of her panties with that. "We

don't, though," he said, shaking his head. "So I guess you'll have to go as a sweet kindergarten teacher."

A 'sweet' kindergarten teacher who was going to the party with wet panties and visions of later in her ex-football player's bedroom in a cheerleading costume that was—if she knew him, and she definitely did—going to be staying *on* while he did very dirty things to her.

"I do have another option."

"Bec," he said, his voice low and growly. "*Nothing* short and sexy. This is all *mine*. And, I don't have time to properly *appreciate* you in anything else."

She gave him a sly smile. "Just one more."

"Bec..."

But she slipped around him and into the bathroom, shutting the door and locking it just to be sure he didn't come in to stop her. Giggling to herself, she quickly pulled on the brightly colored pants, the loose shirt, and the wig.

"You ready?" she called as she unlocked the door.

"No," he replied, sounding a lot more like the grumpy Beau from the first year they'd done this.

She stepped back into the bedroom. "How about this?" She spread her arms wide.

Beau's eyes went wide as he took her in.

She laughed. "You told me last time that if I had a clown suit with baggy pants that's what I should go for."

He shook his head and ran a hand through his hair.

Becca frowned. "What's wrong?"

"I still want to fuck you. Even in that. And it's messing with me."

She snorted in surprise. "Really?"

"Need me to prove it?"

"Maybe."

He took a step forward. She put up a hand, laughing. "Never mind. This is a fetish I do *not* want to open up."

He nodded. "Same."

She laughed again. "Okay, this one is definitely comfortable. So clown pants it is. Let me put on some make-up and I'm ready."

"Actually..."

She lifted a brow.

"I've been thinking about this and...what would you say to a couple's costume?"

"You'd be willing to do that?" Beau Hebert was so not the Halloween costume type. "I mean, we could probably dress you up as a clown too." She'd bet some people would pay big money to see Beau dressed up as a clown in fact.

"I have another idea. In fact, I've already got the costumes."

Becca felt her mouth drop open. "Seriously?"

He looked very pleased with himself. "Yours is in your mom's bedroom."

"Yes. Whatever it is. If you came up with it and are willing to do it. I'm in."

He laughed. "You sure?"

"I love that you want to dress up. Yeah, for sure."

"Okay, you go in and get dressed. I'll get mine on in here."

She *ran* to her mother's room. She loved that Beau was into this. He could be so sweet. She loved the cinnamon roll underneath all the gruffness. She knew that his softness was all for her, and though he told her how much he loved her all the time now, these things *showed* her.

She stopped in the middle of her mother's room and turned a full three-sixty. She didn't see anything. Then she crossed to her mother's closet and pulled the door open. The white dress was hanging front and center. She immediately started laughing. "This is hilarious," she called to him.

It was a wedding dress.

And after everything that Autre had put them through, matchmaking, setting them up, pushing them together, it would be funnier than hell to walk into the Halloween party as a bride and groom. Especially after everything that had happened in Vegas.

"You think so?" he called from down the hall.

"Absolutely. This is the best." She shed the clown outfit and shimmied into the white silk and lace dress that fit her perfectly.

It was absolutely gorgeous. She'd always pictured herself in a fairly traditional gown with a fitted bodice and full skirt with a long train, but she hadn't thought of the specifics.

Now that she was wearing *this* gown though, she knew this was it. The silk skirt draped beautifully, falling from her hips to the floor, the perfect length. On one side, it had a long slit that made her feel sexy, even as the lacey overlay that continued to the train was pretty and sweet. The bodice was sleeveless but modest in the front, with no daring shows of cleavage. But Beau would love the back. It plunged low and left lots of bare skin for him to stroke as they danced. She couldn't wait for him to see it.

Costume or not, the dress made her feel beautiful and sexy and she knew she'd be smiling all night. She wondered if she could just wear it again when she was a bride for real.

She floated back down the hall, feeling like a princess, and stepped into her bedroom.

Beau was in a tux. And he took her breath away. He always did, but wow, he looked amazing.

"Whoa," was her only reaction.

He gave her a grin as he ran a hand over one lapel. "Yeah?"

"That is awesome," she told him. She turned, presenting her back. "Zip me up." She could have easily reached the zipper that only came to the curve of her lower back, but she wanted him to help her.

"God, you look gorgeous," he told her gruffly, as his fingers predictably skimmed up her spine after the zipper was done. "I knew you would. I was picturing you in the dress after I picked it up. But damn."

"Thank you."

"So you really like this idea?" he asked.

She smoothed the front of the dress, looking down at it. "I love it. This is really fun."

"I'm glad."

She turned to face him. "Let me just put my hair up and some makeup on." She stopped as she realized he was staring at her. The look on his face was a mix of love and something she couldn't quite place. "What?" she asked.

He lifted a hand and cupped her face. "I can't wait to do this for real, you know."

She pressed her cheek into his palm. "Yeah, well, you're the one saying we need to wait. You know where I stand on this."

Emotions flickered through his eyes. "Maybe you can get me drunk tonight and convince me to elope."

She pulled back, shaking her head and laughing. "Oh no, I did that once before. This ball is firmly in your court, Mr. Hebert."

"I have to be the instigator this time, huh?" he asked.

"You know I will say yes whenever you ask. But I get that you want to wait. So whenever you think we're ready, just say the word."

"Maybe I'll get you drunk and convince you to elope tonight."

She lifted a shoulder. "You won't have to get me drunk."

He shook his head. "You'd really be into that?"

"I mean...I do think that we should do it here, with everyone, the whole big to-do. The town would love to be a part of it. So I don't think eloping is the right thing. But if you said, "'Bec, let's do it. Right now. Tonight'", there's no way I'd say no."

He leaned in and kissed her. It was hot and sweet and full of love and need. "I'll remember you said that."

She put her hand against his cheek. "Good."

Becca did her hair in a quick twist, then applied light makeup. The thing about going as a bride, she didn't need to do anything elaborate in either of those categories. When she stepped out of the bathroom, Beau was holding a pair of white heels and a bouquet of flowers.

"You thought of everything."

"I had a little help from Savannah."

"That makes sense," Becca said. She looked down at the dress again. "This isn't just a costume. This is actually a wedding dress. She must have gotten it at a secondhand shop or something."

Beau nodded. "I put her in charge. With a few suggestions."

Her heart warmed. He'd even had suggestions about the dress. God, she loved him.

He offered her his arm. "You ready?"

Becca linked her arm with his. "Absolutely. Let's go party."

When they pulled up in front of Ellie's, Becca's eyes went wide. "This place is packed. I mean, I figured they threw a pretty good Halloween party here, but wow."

Beau nodded. "You know Autre doesn't like anything better than a reason to all get together and get rowdy."

"I can't wait to see what everyone's wearing," Becca said.

Beau got out and rounded the truck, opening her door and then swinging her to the ground.

She laughed. "I feel like a princess."

He leaned in and kissed her forehead. "Good. I plan to make you feel that way every day for the rest of your life."

"Wow. That was a great line."

He shook his head. "Not a line. I want you forever, you know that, right?"

She looked up at him, surprised by the seriousness in his tone and his expression. "I do know that."

"We've always been totally honest with one another, right?" he asked.

"We have. It's my favorite thing about us."

"I love you, Becca. I want to be with you forever."

"I love you too. And I want to be with you forever."

"Starting tonight," Beau said.

She nodded. "From here on."

He took her hand, lacing their fingers together, and lifted her hand to his lips. Then they started for the door.

Beau pulled it open, allowing Becca to step inside ahead of him. It looked like they were some of the last to arrive. The room was packed.

And it looked like everyone was dressed in costumes that looked like they were going to a wedding.

It was the strangest Halloween party she'd ever been to.

The next moment she realized she wasn't at a Halloween party.

She was at a wedding.

Her wedding.

She gasped. Then her eyes filled with tears.

She turned to Beau.

He just smiled and nodded.

"Tonight?" she asked.

"I don't need to wait," he said. "I was stupid to think that I could. But I realize I don't need to. I'm sure. About you. About us."

"Me too," she told him as the realization sunk in, and happiness bubbled up.

"So will you marry me? Tonight? Right now?"

"Hell yeah."

They turned and faced the room full of friends, family, and community.

"Okay, Autre," Beau said. "This is what you've been waiting for. Let's have a wedding!"

The room erupted with applause and cheers and they were quickly surrounded by their friends and family and ushered to the front of the room, where an archway had been set up and covered with autumn flowers.

Savannah, Toby, and Daniel were dressed up and standing on her side of the aisle as attendants. Mitch, Zeke, and Zander stood on Beau's side.

Their parents sat in the front row on one side together, smiling and teary-eyed.

Ellie and Leo were in the front row on the side opposite their parents.

And sure enough, Ellie Landry was clutching a gold alligator trophy in her lap as she watched Beau and Becca say their wedding vows. With a very smug smile on her face.

Thank you so much for reading Always Bayou! I hope you loved Beau and Becca's story!

And I hope you loved this little introduction to my bayou world and the fictional town of Autre, Louisiana and the Landry family!

There is *so* much more from this town and family!

And the best place to start is in the **Boys of the Bayou series!**

My Best Friend's Mardi Gras Wedding (Josh & Tori)
Sweet Home Louisiana (Owen & Maddie)
Beauty and the Bayou (Sawyer & Juliet)
Crazy Rich Cajuns (Bennett & Kennedy)
Must Love Alligators (Chase & Bailey)
Four Weddings and a Swamp Boat Tour (Mitch & Paige)

∿

Find all of my books at
ErinNicholas.com
including a printable book list!

ൡ
And join in on all the FAN FUN!

Join my **email list!**
bit.ly/Keep-In-Touch-Erin
(be sure you get those dashes and capital letters in there!)

And be the first to hear about my news, sales, freebies, behind-the-scenes, and more!

Or for even more fun, join my **Super Fan page** on Facebook and chat with me and other super fans every day! Just search Facebook for Erin Nicholas Super Fans!

more from erin's bayou world!

Want more from my bayou world? I've got so much more sexy fun for you!

Boys of the Bayou
My Best Friend's Mardi Gras Wedding (Josh & Tori)
Sweet Home Louisiana (Owen & Maddie)
Beauty and the Bayou (Sawyer & Juliet)
Crazy Rich Cajuns (Bennett & Kennedy)
Must Love Alligators (Chase & Bailey)
Four Weddings and a Swamp Boat Tour (Mitch & Paige)

*

Boys of the Bayou Gone Wild
Otterly Irresistible (Charlie & Griffin)
Heavy Petting (Fletcher & Jordan)
Flipping Love You (Zeke & Jill)
Sealed With a Kiss (Donovan & Naomi)
Say It Like You Mane It (Zander & Caroline)
Head Over Hooves (Drew & Rory)

Kiss My Giraffe (Knox & Fiona)

*

Badges of the Bayou
Gotta Be Bayou (Spencer & Max)
Bayou With Benefits (Michael & Ami)
Rocked Bayou (Colin & Hayden)

*

Bad Boys of the Bayou
The Best Bad Boy (Jase & Priscilla)
Bad Medicine (Nick & Brooke)
Bad Influence (Marc & Sabrina)
Bad Taste In Men (Luke & Bailey)
Not Such a Bad Guy (Reagan & Christopher)
Return of the Bad Boy (Jackson & Annabelle)
Bad Behavior (Carter & Lacey)
Got It Bad (Nolan & Randi)

*

Boys of the Big Easy
Easy Going prequel novella (Gabe & Addison)
Going Down Easy (Gabe & Addison)
Taking It Easy (Logan & Dana)
Eggnog Makes Her Easy (Matt & Lindsey)
Nice and Easy (Caleb & Lexi)
Getting Off Easy (James & Harper)

about erin nicholas

Erin Nicholas is the New York Times and USA Today bestselling
author of over thirty sexy contemporary romances. Her stories
have been described as toe-curling, enchanting, steamy and
fun. She loves to write about reluctant heroes, imperfect
heroines and happily ever afters. She lives in the Midwest with
her husband who only wants to read the sex scenes in her
books, her kids who will never read the sex scenes in her
books, and family and friends who say they're shocked by the
sex scenes in her books (yeah, right!).
Find her here:
www.ErinNicholas.com

Printed in the USA
CPSIA information can be obtained
at www.ICGtesting.com
LVHW091329021123
762340LV00004B/157